The dragon came in sight, plodding along the trail and swinging its head from side to side. Having just shed its skin, the dragon gleamed in a reticular pattern of green and black, as if it had been freshly painted. Its great, golden, split-pupiled eyes were now keen.

The horses screamed, causing the dragon to look up and speed its approach.

"Ready?" said Eudoric, setting the device in its rest.

"Aye, sir. Here goeth!" Without awaiting further command, Jillo applied the torch to the touchhole.

With a great boom and a cloud of smoke, the device discharged, rocking Eudoric back a pace. When the smoke cleared, the dragon was still rushing upon them, unharmed.

"Thou idiot!" screamed Eudoric. "I told thee not to give fire until I commanded! Thou hast made me miss it clean!"

"I'm s-sorry, sir. I was palsied with fear. What shall we do now?"

"Run, fool!"

—from **"Two Yards of Dragon" by
L. Sprague de Camp**

Magic Tales Anthology Series from Ace Books

UNICORNS! edited by Jack Dann and Gardner Dozois
MAGICATS! edited by Jack Dann and Gardner Dozois
FAERY! edited by Terri Windling
BESTIARY! edited by Jack Dann and Gardner Dozois
MERMAIDS! edited by Jack Dann and Gardner Dozois
SORCERERS! edited by Jack Dann and Gardner Dozois
DEMONS! edited by Jack Dann and Gardner Dozois
DOGTALES! edited by Jack Dann and Gardner Dozois
SEASERPENTS! edited by Jack Dann and Gardner Dozois
DINOSAURS! edited by Jack Dann and Gardner Dozois
LITTLE PEOPLE! edited by Jack Dann and Gardner Dozois
MAGICATS II edited by Jack Dann and Gardner Dozois
UNICORNS II edited by Jack Dann and Gardner Dozois
DRAGONS! edited by Jack Dann and Gardner Dozois

DRAGONS!

EDITED BY
JACK DANN & GARDNER DOZOIS

ACE BOOKS, NEW YORK

If you purchased this book without a cover, you should be aware that this book is stolen property. It was reported as "unsold and destroyed" to the publisher, and neither the author nor the publisher has received any payment for this "stripped book."

This book is an Ace original edition,
and has never been previously published.

DRAGONS!

An Ace Book/published by arrangement with
the editors

PRINTING HISTORY
Ace edition/August 1993

All rights reserved.
Copyright © 1993 by Jack Dann and Gardner Dozois.
Cover art by Bob Eggleton.
This book may not be reproduced in whole or in part,
by mimeograph or any other means, without permission.
For information address: The Berkley Publishing Group,
200 Madison Avenue, New York, NY 10016.

ISBN: 0-441-16631-8

Ace Books are published by The Berkley Publishing Group,
200 Madison Avenue, New York, NY 10016.
The name "ACE" and the "A" logo
are trademarks belonging to Charter Communications, Inc.

PRINTED IN THE UNITED STATES OF AMERICA

10 9 8 7 6 5 4 3 2 1

Acknowledgment is made for permission to reprint the following stories:

"Draco, Draco" by Tanith Lee, copyright © 1985 by Tanith Lee, was first published in *Beyond Lands of Never* (Unicorn); reprinted by permission of the author.

"Two Yards of Dragon" by L. Sprague de Camp, copyright © 1976 by Lin Carter, was first published in *Flashing Swords No. 3* (Doubleday); reprinted by permission of the author.

"Mrs. Byres and the Dragon" by Keith Roberts, copyright © 1990 by Davis Publications, Inc., was first published in *Isaac Asimov's Science Fiction Magazine*, August 1990; reprinted by permission of the author.

"A Handful of Hatchlings" by Mark C. Sumner, copyright © 1993 by Dell Magazines, was first published in *Asimov's Science Fiction*, February 1993; reprinted by permission of the author.

"Covenant with a Dragon" by Susan Casper, copyright © 1987 by Jeanne Van Buren Dann and Jack Dann, was first published in *In the Field of Fire* (Tor); reprinted by permission of the author.

"Paper Dragons" by James P. Blaylock, copyright © 1985 by James P. Blaylock, was first published in *Imaginary Lands* (Ace); reprinted by permission of the author.

"Up the Wall" by Esther M. Friesner, copyright © 1990 by Davis Publications, Inc., was first published in *Isaac Asimov's Science Fiction Magazine*, April 1990; reprinted by permission of the author.

"Lan Lung" by M. Lucie Chin, copyright © 1980 by Simulations Publications, Inc., was first published in *Ares*, March 1980; reprinted by permission of the author.

"Climacteric" by Avram Davidson, copyright © 1960 by Mercury Press, Inc., was first published in *The Magazine of Fantasy and Science Fiction*, August 1960; reprinted by permission of the author and the author's agent, Richard D. Grant.

"The Man Who Painted the Dragon Griaule" by Lucius Shepard, copyright © 1984 by Mercury Press, Inc., was first published in *The Magazine of Fantasy and Science Fiction*, December 1984; reprinted by permission of the author.

For

John Kessel and James Patrick Kelly

—firebreathing BOFFOS!

ACKNOWLEDGMENTS

The editors would like to thank the following people for their help and support:

Susan Casper, who helped with much of the word-crunching, and who lent us the use of her computer; Jeanne Van Buren Dann; Merrilee Heifetz; Janet Kagan; Ricky Kagan; Michael Swanwick; Peter Heck; Mark C. Sumner; M. Lucie Chin; Sheila Williams; Ian Randall Strock; Scott L. Towner; Trina King; Ellen Datlow; and special thanks to our own editors, Susan Allison and Ginjer Buchanan.

Contents

Preface — xiii

DRACO, DRACO
Tanith Lee — 1

TWO YARDS OF DRAGON
L. Sprague de Camp — 25

MRS. BYRES AND THE DRAGON
Keith Roberts — 55

A HANDFUL OF HATCHLINGS
Mark C. Sumner — 78

COVENANT WITH A DRAGON
Susan Casper — 92

PAPER DRAGONS
James P. Blaylock — 114

UP THE WALL
Esther M. Friesner — 134

LAN LUNG
M. Lucie Chin — 162

CLIMACTERIC
Avram Davidson — 186

THE MAN WHO PAINTED THE DRAGON GRIAULE
Lucius Shepard — 188

Further Reading — 221

Preface

Dragons are by far the most potent and widespread of all mythological beasts, and dragons or dragonlike creatures appear in just about every mythology in the world. So omnipresent is the image of the dragon, and so powerful the emotions that it evokes, that Carl Sagan, among others, has suggested that dragons are actually a racial memory of dinosaurs, left over from the days when our remote ancestors were tiny tree-dwelling insectivores who cowered in shivering terror whenever one of the immense flesh-eaters like Tyrannosaurus Rex came crashing through the forest. Whatever the truth of that, it's certainly true that dragons are one of the few mythological creatures that it's almost pointless to bother describing. As Avram Davidson puts it, "Although the wombat is real and the dragon is not, nobody knows what a wombat looks like, and everybody knows what a dragon looks like."

There *are* variations, of course—sometimes the dragon is wingless and rather like a gigantic worm; sometimes like a huge snake; most often like an immense, winged lizard. Sometimes it breathes fire, sometimes not. But, for the most part, the rule holds. With very few exceptions, almost everyone *does* know what a dragon looks like, which is why it is one of the master-symbols of fantasy. (Or perhaps it's the other way around.)

Although the Eastern dragon (and particularly the Chinese dragon) is usually depicted as a wise and benevolent creature, a divine being associated with the bringing of the life-giving rains, what we have been describing here primarily fits the Western dragon . . . and, not surprisingly, it is the Western dragon, the terrible fire-breathing dragon of folklore and fairy tales, that has been the dominant image of the dragon in Western literature and art, and which is the kind of dragon we'll encounter most frequently in the stories that follow (although we've thrown in a few Eastern dragons too, along the way, just for spice).

In addition to its well-known fondness for snacking on princesses, the Western dragon is a covetous beast, and can often be found guarding the immense treasures of gold and jewels that it's ravaged from human realms. Although sometimes portrayed as merely a huge mindless beast, the dragon is just as often depicted as having the gift of speech: in this guise, it is frequently a sorcerer, an active magic-user itself, as well as being just a magical *creature*. In fact, some say that Dragon Magic is the strongest and most ancient magic of all. . . .

The strength of that magic, and the sheer power to enchant and fascinate that the dragon still possesses, even in our busy modern world, is amply demonstrated in the pages that follow.

So open those pages, and be seized by Dragon Magic. You may never be able to snap the spell again!

DRAGONS!

Draco, Draco
by
Tanith Lee

Here, in keeping with long tradition, we get to watch a battle between a hero and a ferocious dragon of the genuine old-fashioned maiden-eating variety—but keep your eyes open, for in the compelling, tricky, and bitterly ironic story that follows, nothing is quite *what it seems. . . .*

Tanith Lee is one of the best-known and most prolific of modern fantasists, with over forty books to her credit, including (among many others) The Birth Grave, Drinking Sapphire Wine, Don't Bite the Sun, Night's Master, The Storm Lord, Sung in Shadow, Volkhavaar, Anackire, Night Sorceries, *and the collections* Tamastara, The Gorgon, *and* Dreams of Dark and Light. *Her short story "Elle Est Trois (La Mort)" won a World Fantasy Award in 1984 and her brilliant collection of retold folk tales,* Red As Blood, *was also a finalist that year, in the Best Collection category. Her most recent books are the novel* The Blood of Roses *and the collection* The Forests of the Night.

* * *

You'll have heard stories, sometimes, of men who have fought and slain dragons. These are all lies. There's no swordsman living ever killed a dragon, though a few swordsmen dead that tried.

On the other hand, I once travelled in company with a fellow who got the name of "dragon-slayer."

A riddle? No. I'll tell you.

I was coming from the North back into the South, to civilisation as you may say, when I saw him, sitting by the roadside. My first feeling was envy, I admit. He was smart and very clean for someone in the wilds, and he had the South all over him, towns and baths and money. He was crazy, too, because there was gold on his wrists and in one ear. But he had a sharp grey sword, an army sword, so maybe he could defend himself. He was also younger than me, and a great deal prettier, but the last isn't too difficult. I wondered what he'd do when he looked up from his daydream and saw me, tough, dark and sour as a twist of old rope, clopping down on him on my swarthy little horse, ugly as sin, that I love like a daughter.

Then he did look up and I discovered.

"Greetings, stranger. Nice day, isn't it?"

He stayed relaxed as he said it, and somehow you knew from that he really could look after himself. It wasn't he thought I was harmless, just that he thought he could handle me if I tried something. Then again, I had my box of stuff alongside. Most people can tell my trade from that, and the aroma of drugs and herbs. My father was with the Romans, in fact he was probably the last Roman of all, one foot on the ship to go home, the rest of him with my mother up against the barnyard wall. She said he was a camp physician and maybe that was so. Some idea of doctoring grew up with me, though nothing great or grand. An itinerant apothecary is welcome almost anywhere, and can even turn bandits civil. It's not a wonderful life, but it's the only one I know.

I gave the young soldier-dandy that it was a nice day. I added he'd possibly like it better if he hadn't lost his horse.

"Yes, a pity about that. You could always sell me yours."

"Not your style."

He looked at her. I could see he agreed. There was also a momentary idea that he might kill me and take her, so I said, "And she's well known as mine. It would get you a bad name. I've friends round about."

He grinned, good-naturedly. His teeth were good, too. What with that, and the hair like barley, and the rest of it—well, he was the kind usually gets what he wants. I was curious as to which army he had hung about with to gain the sword. But since the Eagles flew, there are kingdoms everywhere, chiefs, war-leaders, Roman knights, and every tide brings an invasion up some beach. Under it all, too, you can feel the earth, the actual ground, which had been measured and ruled with fine roads, the land which had been subdued but never tamed, beginning to quicken. Like the shadows that come with the blowing out of a lamp. Ancient things, which are in my blood somewhere, so I recognise them.

But he was like a new coin that hadn't got dirty yet, nor learned much, though you could see your face in its shine, and cut yourself on its edge.

His name was Caiy. Presently we came to an arrangement and he mounted up behind me on Negra. They spoke a smatter of Latin where I was born, and I called her that before I knew her, for her darkness. I couldn't call her for her hideousness, which is her only other visible attribute.

The fact is, I wasn't primed to the country round that way at all. I'd had word, a day or two prior, that there were Saxons in the area I'd been heading for. And so I switched paths and was soon lost. When I came on Caiy, I'd been pleased with the road, which was Roman, hoping it would go somewhere useful. But, about ten miles after Caiy joined me, the road petered out in a forest. My passenger was lost, too. He was going South, no surprise there, but last night his horse had broken loose and bolted, leaving him stranded. It sounded unlikely, but I wasn't inclined to debate on it. It seemed to me someone might have stolen the horse, and Caiy didn't care to confess.

There was no way round the forest, so we went in and the road died. Being summer, the wolves would be scarce and the bears off in the hills. Nevertheless, the trees had a feel I didn't take to, sombre and still, with the sound of little streams running through like metal chains, and birds that didn't sing but made purrings and clinkings. Negra never baulked or complained—if I'd waited to call her, I could have done it for her courage and warm-heartedness—but she couldn't come to terms with the forest, either.

"It smells," said Caiy, who'd been kind enough not to comment on mine, "as if it's rotting. Or fermenting."

I grunted. Of course it did, it was, the fool. But the smell told you other things. The centuries, for one. Here were the shadows that had come back when Rome blew out her lamp and sailed away, and left us in the dark.

Then Caiy, the idiot, began to sing to show up the birds who wouldn't. A nice voice, clear and bright. I didn't tell him to leave off. The shadows already knew we were there.

When night came down, the black forest closed like a cellar door.

We made a fire and shared my supper. He'd lost his rations with his mare.

"Shouldn't you tether that—your horse," suggested Caiy, trying not to insult her since he could see we were partial to each other. "My mare was tied, but something scared her and she broke the tether and ran. I wonder what it was," he mused, staring in the fire.

About three hours later, we found out.

I was asleep, and dreaming of one of my wives, up in the far North, and she was nagging at me, trying to start a brawl, which she always did for she was taller than me, and liked me to hit her once in a while so she could feel fragile, feminine and mastered. Just as she emptied the beer jar over my head, I heard a sound up in the sky like a storm that was not a storm. And I knew I wasn't dreaming any more.

The sound went over, three or four great claps, and the tops of the forest reeling, and left shuddering. There was a sort of quiver in the air, as if sediment were stirred up in it. There was even an extra smell, dank, yet tingling. When the noise was only a memory, and the bristling hairs began to subside along my body, I opened my eyes.

Negra was flattened to the ground, her own eyes rolling, but she was silent. Caiy was on his feet, gawping up at the tree-tops and the strands of starless sky. Then he glared at me.

"What in the name of the Bull was that?"

I noted vaguely that the oath showed he had Mithraic allegiances, which generally meant Roman. Then I sat up, rubbed my arms and neck to get human, and went to console Negra. Unlike his silly cavalry mare she hadn't bolted.

"It can't," he said, "have been a bird. Though I'd have sworn something flew over."

"No, it wasn't a bird."

"But it had wings. Or—no, it couldn't have had wings the size of that."

"Yes it could. They don't carry it far, is all."

"Apothecary, stop being so damned provoking. If you know, out with it! Though I don't see how you can know. And don't tell me it's some bloody woods demon I won't believe in."

"Nothing like that," I said. "It's real enough. Natural, in its own way. Not," I amended, "that I ever came across one before, but I've met some who did."

Caiy was going mad, like a child working up to a tantrum. "*Well?*"

I suppose he had charmed and irritated me enough I wanted to retaliate, because I just quoted some bastard non-sensical jabber-Latin chant at him:

Bis terribilis—
Bis appellare—
Draco! Draco!

At least, it made him sit down.

"What?" he eventually said.

At my age I should be over such smugness. I said, "It was a dragon."

Caiy laughed. But he had glimpsed it, and knew better than I did that I was right.

Nothing else happened that night. In the morning we started off again and there was a rough track, and then the forest began to thin out. After a while we emerged on the crown of a moor. The land dropped down to a valley, and on the other side there were sunny smoky hills and a long streamered sky. There was something else, too.

Naturally, Caiy said it first, as if everything new always surprised him, as if we hadn't each of us, in some way, been waiting for it, or something like it.

"This place stinks."

"Hn."

"Don't just grunt at me, you blasted quack doctor. It does, doesn't it. Why?"

"Why do you think?"

He brooded, pale gold and citified, behind me. Negra tried to paw the ground, and then made herself desist.

Neither of us brave humans had said any more about what had interrupted sleep in the forest, but when I'd told him no dragon could fly far on its wings, for from all I'd ever heard they were too large and only some freakish lightness in their bones enabled them to get air-borne at all, I suppose we had both taken it to heart. Now here were the valley and the hills, and here was this reek lying over everything, strange, foul, alien, comparable to nothing, really. Dragon smell.

I considered. No doubt, the dragon went on an aeriel patrol most nights, circling as wide as it could, to see what might be there for it. There were other things I'd learnt. These beasts hunt nocturnally, like cats. At the same time, a dragon is more like a crow in its habits. It will attack and kill, but normally it eats carrion, dead things, or dying and immobilised. It's light, as I said, it has to be to take the skies, but the lack of weight is compensated by the armour, the teeth and talons. Then again, I'd heard of dragons that breathed fire. I've never been quite convinced there. It seems more likely to me such monsters only live in volcanic caves, the mountain itself belching flame and the dragon taking credit for it. Maybe not. But certainly, this dragon was no fire-breather. The ground would have been scorched for miles; I've listened to stories where that happened. There were no marks of fire. Just the insidious pervasive stench that I knew, by the time we'd gone down into the valley, would be so familiar, so soaked into us, we would hardly notice it any more, or the scent of anything else.

I awarded all this information to my passenger. There followed a long verbal delay. I thought he might just be flabbergasted at getting so much chat from me, but then he said, very hushed, "You truly believe all this, don't you?"

I didn't bother with the obvious, just clucked to Negra, trying to make her turn back the way we'd come. But she was unsure and for once uncooperative, and suddenly his strong hand, the nails groomed even now, came down on my arm.

"Wait, Apothecary. If it *is* true—"

"Yes, yes," I said. I sighed. "You want to go and challenge it, and become a hero." He held himself like marble, as if I were speaking of some girl he thought he loved. I didn't see why I should waste experience and wisdom on him, but then. "No man ever killed a dragon. They're plated, all over, even the underbelly. Arrows and spears just bounce off—even a pilum. Swords clang and snap in half. Yes, yes," I reiterated, "you've heard of men who slashed the tongue, or stabbed into an eye. Let me tell you, if they managed to reach that high and actually did it, then they just made the brute angry. Think of the size and shape of a dragon's head, the way the pictures show it. It's one hell of a push from the eye into the brain. And you know, there's one theory the eyelid is armoured, too, and can come down faster that *that*."

"Apothecary," he said. He sounded dangerous. I just knew what he must look like. Handsome, noble and insane.

"Then I won't keep you," I said. "Get down and go on and the best of luck."

I don't know why I bothered. I should have tipped him off and ridden for it, though I wasn't sure Negra could manage to react sufficiently fast, she was that edgy. Anyway, I didn't, and sure enough next moment his sword was at the side of my throat, and so sharp it had drawn blood.

"You're the clever one," he said, "the know-all. And you do seem to know more than I do, about this. So you're my guide, and your scruff-bag of a horse, if it even deserves the name, is my transport. Giddy-up, the pair of you."

That was that. I never argue with a drawn sword. The dragon would be lying up by day, digesting and dozing, and by night I could hole up someplace myself. Tomorrow Caiy would be dead and I could leave. And I would, of course, have seen a dragon for myself.

After an hour and a half's steady riding—better once I'd persuaded him to switch from the sword to poking a dagger against my ribs, less tiring for us both—we came around a stand of woods, and there was a village. It was the savage Northern kind, thatch and wattle and turf banks, but big for all that, a good mile of it, not all walled. There were walls this end, however, and men on the gate, peering at us.

Caiy was aggrieved because he was going to have to ride up to them pillion, but he knew better now than to try managing Negra alone. He maybe didn't want to pretend she was his horse in any case.

As we pottered up the pebbled track to the gate, he sprang off and strode forward, arriving before me, and began to speak.

When I got closer I heard him announcing, in his dramatic, beautiful voice,

"—And if it's a fact, I swear by the Victory of the Light that I will meet the thing and kill it."

They were muttering. The dragon smell, even though we were used to it, sodden with it, seemed more acid here. Poor Negra had been voiding herself from sheer terror all up the path. With fortune on her side, there would be somewhere below ground, some cave or dug out place, where they'd be putting their animals out of the dragon's way, and she could shelter with the others.

Obviously, the dragon hadn't always been active in this region. They'd scarcely have built their village if it had. No, it would have been like the tales. Dragons live for centuries. They can sleep for centuries, too. Unsuspecting, man moves in, begins to till and build and wax prosperous. Then the dormant dragon wakes under the hill. They're like the volcanoes I spoke of, in that. Which is perhaps, more than habitat, why so many of the legends say they breathe fire when they wake.

The interesting thing was, even clouded by the dragon stink, initially, the village didn't seem keen to admit anything.

Caiy, having made up his mind to accept the dragon—and afraid of being wrong—started to rant. The men at the gate were frightened and turning nasty. Leading Negra now, I approached, tapped my chest of potions and said:

"Or, if you don't want your dragon slain, I can cure some of your other troubles. I've got medicines for almost everything. Boils, warts. Ear pains. Tooth pains. Sick eyes. Womens' afflictions. I have here—"

"Shut up, you toad-turd," said Caiy.

One of the guards suddenly laughed. The tension sagged.

Ten minutes after, we had been let in the gate and were trudging through the cow-dung and wild flowers—neither of which were to be smelled through the other smell—to the head-man's hall.

It was around two hours after that when we found out why the appearance of a rescuing champion-knight had given them the jitters.

It seemed they had gone back to the ancient way, propitiation, the scape-goat. For three years, they had been making an offering to the dragon, in spring, and at midsummer, when it was likely to be most frisky.

Anyone who knew dragons from a book would tell them this wasn't the way. But they knew their dragon from myth. Every time they made sacrifice, they imagined the thing could understand and appreciate what they'd done for it, and would therefore be more amenable.

In reality, of course, the dragon had never attacked the village. It had thieved cattle off the pasture by night, elderly or sick cows at that, and lambs that were too little and weak to run. It would have taken people, too, but only those who were disabled and alone. I said, a dragon is lazy and prefers carrion, or what's defenceless. Despite being big, they aren't so big they'd go after a whole tribe of men. And though even forty men together undoubtedly couldn't wound a dragon, they could exhaust it, if they kept up a rough-house. Eventually it would keel over and they could brain it. You seldom hear of forty men going off in a band to take a dragon, however. Dragons are still ravelled up with night fears and spiritual mysteries, and latterly with an Eastern superstition of a mighty demon who can assume the form of a dragon which is invincible and—naturally— breathes sheer flame. So, this village, like many another, would put out its sacrifice, one girl tied to a post, and leave her there, and the dragon would have her. Why not? She was helpless, fainting with horror—and young and tender into the bargain. Perfect. You never could convince them that, instead of appeasing the monster, the sacrifice encourages it to stay. Look at it from the dragon's point of view. Not only are there dead sheep and stray cripples to devour, but once in a while a nice juicy damsel on a stick. Dragons don't think like a man, but they do have memories.

When Caiy realized what they were about to do, tonight, as it turned out, he went red then white, exactly as they do in a bardic lay. Not anger, mind you. He didn't comprehend any more than they did. It was merely the awfulness of it.

He stood up and chose a stance, quite unconsciously impressive, and assured us he'd save her. He swore to it in front of us all, the chieftain, his men, me. And he swore it by the Sun, so I knew he meant business.

They were scared, but now also childishly hopeful. It was part of their mythology again. All mythology seems to take this tack somewhere, the dark against the light, the Final Battle. It's rot, but there.

Following a bit of drinking to seal the oath, they cheered up and the chief ordered a feast. Then they took Caiy to see the chosen sacrifice.

Her name was Niemeh, or something along those lines.

She was sitting in a little lamplit cell off the hall. She wasn't fettered, but a warrior stood guard beyond the screen, and there was no window. She had nothing to do except weave flowers together, and she was doing that, making garlands for her death procession in the evening.

When Caiy saw her, his colour drained away again.

He stood and stared at her, while somebody explained he was her champion.

Though he got on my nerves, I didn't blame him so much this time. She was about the most beautiful thing I ever hope to see. Young, obviously, and slim, but with a woman's shape, if you have my meaning, and long hair more fair even than Caiy's, and green eyes like sea pools and a face like one of the white flowers in her hands, and a sweet mouth.

I looked at her as she listened gravely to all they said. I remembered how in the legends it's always the loveliest and the most gentle gets picked for the dragon's dinner. You perceive the sense in the gentle part. A girl with a temper might start a ruckus.

When Caiy had been introduced and once more sworn by the sun to slay the dragon and so on, she thanked him. If things had been different, she would have blushed and trembled, excited by Caiy's attention. But she was past all that. You could see, if you looked, she didn't believe anyone could save her. But though she must have been half dead already of despair and fright, she still made space to be courteous.

Then she glanced over Caiy's head straight at me, and she smiled so I wouldn't feel left out.

"And who is this man?" she asked.

They all looked startled, having forgotten me. Then someone who had warts recalled I'd said I could fix him something for warts, and told her I was the apothecary.

A funny little shiver went through her then.

She was so young and so pretty. If I'd been Caiy I'd have stopped spouting rubbish about the dragon. I'd have found some way to lay out the whole village, and grabbed her, and gone. But that would have been a stupid thing to do too. I've enough of the old blood to know about such matters. She was the sacrifice and she was resigned to it; more, she didn't dream she could be anything else. I've come across rumours, here and there, of girls, men too, chosen to die, who escaped. But the fate stays on them. Hide them securely miles off, across water, beyond tall hills, still they feel the geas weigh like lead upon their souls. They kill themselves in the end, or go mad. And this girl, this Niemeh, you could see it in her. No, I would never have abducted her. It would have been no use. She was convinced she must die, as if she'd seen it written in light on a stone, and maybe she had.

She returned to her garlands, and Caiy, tense as a bowstring, led us back to the hall.

Meat was roasting and more drink came out and more talk came out. You can kill anything as often as you like, that way.

It wasn't a bad feast, as such up-country things go. But all through the shouts and toasts and guzzlings, I kept thinking of her in her cell behind the screen, hearing the clamour and aware of this evening's sunset, and how it would be to die . . . as she would have to. I didn't begin to grasp how she could bear it.

By late afternoon they were mostly sleeping it off, only Caiy had had the sense to go and sweat the drink out with soldiers' exercises in the yard, before a group of sozzled admirers of all sexes.

When someone touched my shoulder, I thought it was warty after his cure, but no. It was the guard from the girl's cell, who said very low, "She says she wants to speak to you. Will you come, now?"

I got up and went with him. I had a spinning minute, wondering if perhaps she didn't believe she must die after all, and would appeal to me to save her. But in my heart of hearts I guessed it wasn't that.

There was another man blocking the entrance, but they let me go in alone, and there Niemeh sat, making garlands yet, under her lamp.

But she looked up at me, and her hands fell like two more white flowers on the flowers in her lap. "I need some medicine, you see," she said. "But I can't pay you. I don't have anything. Although my uncle—"

"No charge," I said hurriedly.

She smiled. "It's for tonight."

"Oh," I said.

"I'm not brave," she said, "but it's worse than just being afraid. I know I shall die. That it's needful. But part of me wants to live so much—my reason tells me one thing but my body won't listen. I'm frightened I shall panic, struggle and scream and weep—I don't want that. It isn't right. I have to consent, or the sacrifice isn't any use. Do you know about that?"

"Oh, yes," I said.

"I thought so. I thought you did. Then. . . . Can you give me something, a medicine or herb—so I shan't feel anything? I don't mean the pain. That doesn't matter. The

gods can't blame me if I cry out then, they wouldn't expect
me to be beyond pain. But only to make me not care, not
want to live so very much."

"An easy death."

"Yes." She smiled again. She seemed serene and beautiful. "Oh, yes."

I looked at the floor.

"The soldier. Maybe he'll kill it," I said.

She didn't say anything.

When I glanced up, her face wasn't serene any more. It
was brimful of terror. Caiy would have been properly
insulted.

"Is it you can't give me anything? Don't you have
anything? I was sure you did. That you were sent here to me
to—to help, so I shouldn't have to go through it all
alone—"

"There," I said, "it's all right. I do have something. Just
the thing. I keep it for women in labour when the child's
slow and hurting them. It works a treat. They go sort of
misty and far off, as if they were nearly asleep. It'll dull
pain, too. Even—any kind of pain."

"Yes," she whispered, "I should like that." And then
she caught my hand and kissed it. "I knew you would," she
said, as if I'd promised her the best and loveliest thing in all
the earth. Another man, it would have broken him in front
of her. But I'm harder than most.

When she let me, I retrieved my hand, nodded reassuringly, and went out. The chieftain was awake and genial
enough, so I had a word with him. I told him what the girl
had asked. "In the East," I said, "it's the usual thing, give
them something to help them through. They call it Nektar,
the drink of the gods. She's consented," I said, "but she's
very young and scared, delicately-bred too. You can't
grudge her this." He acquiesced immediately, as glad as she
was, as I'd hoped. It's a grim affair, I should imagine, when
the girl shrieks for pity all the way up to the hills. I hadn't
thought there'd be any problem. On the other hand, I hadn't
wanted to be caught slipping her potions behind anyone's
back.

I mixed the drug in the cell where she could watch. She was interested in everything I did, the way the condemned are nearly always interested in every last detail, even how a cobweb hangs.

I made her promise to drink it all, but none of it until they came to bring her out. "It may not last otherwise. You don't want it to wear off before—too early."

"No," she said. "I'll do exactly what you say."

When I was going out again, she said, "If I can ask them for anything for you, the gods, when I meet them. . . ."

It was in my mind to say: Ask them to go stick—but I didn't. She was trying to keep intact her trust in recompence, immortality. I said, "Just ask them to look after you."

She had such a sweet, sweet mouth. She was made to love and to be loved, to have children and sing songs and die when she was old, peacefully, in her sleep.

And there would be others like her. The dragon would be given those, too. Eventually, it wouldn't just be maidens, either. The taboo states it had to be a virgin so as to safeguard any unborn life. Since a virgin can't be with child—there's one religion says different, I forget which—they stipulate virgins. But in the end any youthful woman, who can reasonably be reckoned as not with child, will do. And then they go on to the boys. Which is the most ancient sacrifice there is.

I passed a very young girl in the hall, trotting round with the beer-dipper. She was comely and innocent, and I recollected I'd seen her earlier and asked myself, Are you the next? And who'll be next after you?

Niemeh was the fifth. But, I said, dragons live a long while. And the sacrifices always get to be more frequent. Now it was twice a year. In the first year it had been once. In a couple more years it would happen at every season, with maybe three victims in the summer when the creature was most active.

And in ten more years it would be every month, and they'd have learned to raid other villages to get girls and young men to give it, and there would be a lot of bones

about, besides, fellows like Caiy, dragon-slayers dragon
slain.

I went after the girl with the beer-dipper and drained it.
But drink never did comfort me much.

And presently, it would be time to form the procession
and start for the hills.

It was the last gleaming golden hour of day when we set off.

The valley was fertile and sheltered. The westering light
caught and flashed in the trees and out of the streams.
Already there was a sort of path stamped smooth and kept
clear of undergrowth. It would have been a pleasant
journey, if they'd been going anywhere else.

There was sunlight warm on the sides of the hills, too.
The sky was almost cloudless, transparent. If it hadn't been
for the tainted air, you would never have thought anything
was wrong. But the track wound up the first slope and
around, and up again, and there, about a hundred yards off,
was the flank of a bigger hill that went down into shadow at
its bottom, and never took the sun. That underside was bare
of grass, and eaten out in caves, one cave larger than the rest
and very black, with a strange black stillness, as if light and
weather and time itself stopped just inside. Looking at that,
you'd know at once, even with sun on your face and the
whole lucid sky above.

They'd brought her all this way in a Roman litter which
somehow had become the property of the village. It had lost
its roof and its curtains, just a kind of cradle on poles, but
Niemeh had sat in it on their shoulders, motionless, and
dumb. I had only stolen one look at her, to be sure, but her
face had turned mercifully blank and her eyes were opaque.
What I'd given her started its work swiftly. She was beyond
us all now. I was only anxious everything else would occur
before her condition changed.

Her bearers set the litter down and lifted her out. They'd
have to support her, but they would know about that, girls
with legs gone to water, even passed out altogether. And I
suppose the ones who fought and screamed would be forced
to sup strong ale, or else concussed with a blow.

Everyone walked a little more, until we reached a natural palisade of rock. This spot provided concealment, while overlooking the cave and the ground immediately below it. There was a stagnant dark pond caught in the gravel there, but on our side, facing the cave, a patch of clean turf with a post sticking up, about the height of a tall man.

The two warriors supporting Niemeh went on with her towards the post. The rest of us stayed behind the rocks, except for Caiy.

We were all garlanded with flowers. Even I had had to be, and I hadn't made a fuss. What odds? But Caiy wasn't garlanded. He was the one part of the ritual which, though arcanely acceptable, was still profane. And that was why, even though they would let him attack the dragon, they had nevertheless brought the girl to appease it.

There was some kind of shackle at the post. It wouldn't be iron, because anything fey has an allergy to stable metals, even so midnight a thing as a dragon. Bronze, probably. They locked one part around her waist and another round her throat. Only the teeth and claws could get her out of her bonds now, piece by piece.

She sagged forward in the toils. She seemed unconscious at last, and I wanted her to be.

The two men hurried back, up the slope and into the rock cover with the rest of us. Sometimes the tales have the people rush away when they've put out their sacrifice, but usually the people stay, to witness. It's quite safe. The dragon won't go after them with something tasty chained up right under its nose.

Caiy didn't remain beside the post. He moved down towards the edge of the polluted pond. His sword was drawn. He was quite ready. Though the sun couldn't get into the hollow to fire his hair or the metal blade, he cut a grand figure, heroically braced there between the maiden and Death.

At the end, the day spilled swiftly. Suddenly all the shoulders of the hills grew dim, and the sky became the colour of lavender, and then a sort of mauve amber, and the stars broke through.

There was no warning.

I was looking at the pond, where the dragon would come to drink, judging the amount of muck there seemed to be in it. And suddenly there was a reflection in the pond, from above. It wasn't definite, and it was upside down, but even so my heart plummeted through my guts.

There was a feeling behind the rock, the type you get, they tell me, in the battle lines, when the enemy appears. And mixed with this, something of another feeling, more maybe like the inside of some god's house when they call on him, and he seems to come.

I forced myself to look then, at the cave mouth. This, after all, was the evening I would see a real dragon, something to relate to others, as others had related such things to me.

It crept out of the cave, inch by inch, nearly down on its belly, cat-like.

The sky wasn't dark yet, a Northern dusk seems often endless. I could see well, and better and better as the shadow of the cave fell away and the dragon advanced into the paler shadow by the pond.

At first, it seemed unaware of anything but itself and the twilight. It flexed and stretched itself. There was something uncanny, even in such simple movements, something evil. And timeless.

The Romans know an animal they call Elephantus, and I mind an ancient clerk in one of the towns describing this beast to me, fairly accurately, for he'd seen one once. The dragon wasn't as large as elephantus, I should say. Actually not that much higher than a fair-sized cavalry gelding, if rather longer. But it was sinuous, more sinuous than any snake. The way it crept and stretched and flexed, and curled and slewed its head, its skeleton seemed fluid.

There are plenty of mosaics, paintings. It was like that, the way men have shown them from the beginning. Slender, tapering to the elongated head, which is like a horse's, too, and not like, and to the tail, though it didn't have that spade-shaped sting they put on them sometimes, like a scorpion's. There were spines, along the tail and the back-ridge, and the neck and head. The ears were set back, like a dog's. Its legs were short, but that didn't make it seem ungainly. The ghastly fluidity was always there, not grace, but something so like grace it was nearly unbearable.

It looked almost the colour the sky was now, slatey, bluish-grey, like metal but dull; the great overlapping plates of its scales had no burnish. Its eyes were black and you didn't see them, and then they took some light from somewhere, and they flared like two flat coins, cat's eyes, with nothing—no brain, no soul—behind them.

It had been going to drink, but had scented something more interesting than dirty water, which was the girl.

The dragon stood there, static as a rock, staring at her over the pond. Then gradually its two wings, that had been folded back like fans along its sides, opened and spread.

They were huge, those wings, much bigger than the rest of it. You could see how it might be able to fly with them. Unlike the body, there were no scales, only skin, membrane, with ribs of external bone. Bat's wings, near enough. It seemed feasible a sword could go through them, damage them, but that would only maim, and all too likely they were tougher than they seemed.

Then I left off considering. With its wings spread like that, unused—like a crow—it began to sidle around the water, the blind coins of eyes searing on the post and the sacrifice.

Somebody shouted. My innards sprang over. Then I realized it was Caiy. The dragon had nearly missed him, so intent it was on the feast, so he had had to call it.

Bis terribilis—Bis appellare—Draco! Draco!

I'd never quite understood that antic chant, and the Latin was execrable. But I think it really means to know a dragon exists is bad enough, to call its name and summon it—call twice, twice terrible—is the notion of a maniac.

The dragon wheeled. It—*flowed*. Its elongated horse's-head-which-wasn't was before him, and Caiy's sharp sword slashed up and down and bit against the jaw. It happened, what they say—sparks shot glittering in the air. Then the head spit, not from any wound, just the chasm of the mouth. It made a sound at him, not a hissing, a sort of *hroosh*. Its breath would be poisonous, almost as bad as fire. I saw Caiy stagger at it, and then one of the long feet on the short legs went out through the gathering dark. The blow looked slow and harmless. It threw Caiy thirty feet, right across the pond. He fell at the entrance to the cave, and lay quiet. The sword was still in his hand. His grip must have clamped down on it involuntarily. He'd likely bitten his tongue as well, in the same way.

The dragon looked after him, you could see it pondering whether to go across again and dine. But it was more attracted by the other morsel it had smelled first. It knew from its scent this was the softer, more digestible flesh. And so it ignored Caiy, leaving him for later, and eddied on towards the post, lowering its head as it came, the light leaving its eyes.

I looked. The night was truly blooming now, but I could see, and the darkness didn't shut my ears; there were sounds, too. You weren't there, and I'm not about to try to make you see and hear what I did. Niemeh didn't cry out. She was senseless by then, I'm sure of it. She didn't feel or know any of what it did to her. Afterwards, when I went down with the others, there wasn't much left. It even carried some of her bones into the cave with it, to chew. Her garland was lying on the ground since the dragon had no interest in garnish. The pale flowers were no longer pale.

She had consented, and she hadn't had to endure it. I've seen things as bad that had been done by men, and for men there's no excuse. And yet, I never hated a man as I hated the dragon, a loathing, deadly, sickening hate.

The moon was rising when it finished. It went again to the pond, and drank deeply. Then it moved up the gravel back towards the cave. It paused beside Caiy, sniffed him, but there was no hurry. Having fed so well, it was sluggish. It stepped into the pitch-black hole of the cave, and drew itself from sight, inch by inch, as it had come out, and was gone.

Presently Caiy pulled himself off the ground, first to his hands and knees, then on to his feet.

We, the watchers, were amazed. We'd thought him dead, his back broken, but he had only been stunned, as he told us afterwards. Not even stunned enough not to have come to, dazed and unable to rise, before the dragon quite finished its feeding. He was closer than any of us. He said it maddened him—as if he hadn't been mad already—and so, winded and part stupefied as he was, he got up and dragged himself into the dragon's cave after it. And this time he meant to kill it for sure, no matter what it did to him.

Nobody had spoken a word, up on our rocky place, and no one spoke now. We were in a kind of communion, a trance. We leaned forward and gazed at the black gape in the hill where they had both gone.

Maybe a minute later, the noises began. They were quite extraordinary, as if the inside of the hill itself were gurning and snarling. But it was the dragon, of course. Like the stink of it, those sounds it made were untranslatable. I could say it looked this way comparable to an elephantus, or that way to a cat, a horse, a bat. But the cries and roars—no. They were like nothing else I've heard in the world, or been told of. There were, however, other noises, as of some great heap of things disturbed. And stones rattling, rolling.

The villagers began to get excited or hysterical. Nothing like this had happened before. Sacrifice is usually predictable.

They stood, and started to shout, or groan and invoke supernatural protection. And then a silence came from inside the hill, and silence returned to the villagers.

I don't remember how long it went on. It seemed like months.

Then suddenly something moved in the cave mouth.

There were yells of fear. Some of them took to their heels, but came back shortly when they realized the others were rooted to the spot, pointing and exclaiming, not in anguish but awe. That was because it was Caiy, and not the dragon, that had emerged from the hill.

He walked like a man who has been too long without food and water, head bowed, shoulders drooping, legs barely able to hold him up. He floundered through the edges of the pond and the sword trailed from his hand in the water. Then he tottered over the slope and was right before us. He somehow raised his head then, and got out the sentence no one had ever truly reckoned to hear.

"It's—dead," said Caiy, and slumped unconscious in the moonlight.

They used the litter to get him to the village, as Niemeh didn't need it any more.

We hung around the village for nearly ten days. Caiy was his merry self by the third, and since there had been no sign of the dragon, by day or night, a party of them went up to the hills, and, kindling torches at noon, slunk into the cave to be sure.

It was dead all right. The stench alone would have verified that, a different perfume than before, and all congealed there, around the cave. In the valley, even on the second morning, the live dragon smell was almost gone. You could make out goats and hay and meade and unwashed flesh and twenty varieties of flowers.

I myself didn't go in the cave. I went only as far as the post. I understood it was safe, but I just wanted to be there once more, where the few bones that were Niemeh had fallen through the shackles to the earth. And I can't say why, for you can explain nothing to bones.

There was rejoicing and feasting. The whole valley was full of it. Men came from isolated holdings, cots and huts, and a rough looking lot they were. They wanted to glimpse Caiy the dragon-slayer, to touch him for luck and lick the finger. He laughed. He hadn't been badly hurt, and but for bruises was as right as rain, up in the hay-loft half the time with willing girls, who would afterwards boast their brats were sons of the hero. Or else he was blind drunk in the chieftain's hall.

In the end, I collected Negra, fed her apples and told her she was the best horse in the land, which she knows is a lie and not what I say the rest of the time. I had sound directions now, and was planning to ride off quietly and let Caiy go on as he desired, but I was only a quarter of a mile from the village when I heard the splayed tocking of horse's hooves. Up he galloped beside me on a decent enough horse, the queen of the chief's stable, no doubt, and grinning, with two beer skins.

I accepted one, and we continued, side by side.

"I take it you're sweet on the delights of my company," I said at last, an hour after, when the forest was in view over the moor.

"What else, Apothecary? Even my insatiable lust to steal your gorgeous horse has been removed. I now have one of my very own, if not a third as beautiful." Negra cast him a sidelong look as if she would like to bite him. But he paid no attention. We trotted on for another mile or so before he added, "and there's something I want to ask you, too."

I was wary, and waited to find out what came next.

Finally, he said, "you must know a thing or two in your trade about how bodies fit together. That dragon, now. You seemed to know all about dragons."

I grunted. Caiy didn't cavil at the grunt. He began idly to describe how he'd gone into the cave, a tale he had flaunted a mere three hundred times in the chieftain's hall. But I didn't cavil either, I listened carefully.

The cave entry-way was low and vile, and soon it opened into a cavern. There was elf-light, more than enough to see by, and water running here and there along the walls and over the stony floor.

There in the cavern's centre, glowing now like filthy silver, lay the dragon, on a pile of junk such as dragons always accumulate. They're like crows and magpies in that, also, shiny things intrigue them and they take them to their lairs to paw possessively and to lie on. The rumours of hoards must come from this, but usually the collection is worthless, snapped knives, impure glass that had sparkled under the moon, rusting armlets from some victim, and all of it soiled by the devil's droppings, and muddled up with split bones.

When he saw it like this, I'd bet the hero's reckless heart failed him. But he would have done his best, to stab the dragon in the eye, the root of the tongue, the vent under the tail, as it clawed him in bits.

"But you see," Caiy now said to me, "I didn't have to."

This, of course, he hadn't said in the hall. No. He had told the village the normal things, the lucky lunge and the brain pierced, and the death-throes, which we'd all heard plainly enough. If anyone noticed his sword had no blood on it, well, it had trailed in the pond, had it not?

"You see," Caiy went on, "it was lying there comatose one minute, and then it began to writhe about, and to go into a kind of spasm. Something got dislodged off the hoard-pile—a piece of cracked-up armour, I think, gilded—and knocked me silly again. And when I came round, the dragon was all sprawled about, and dead as yesterday's roast mutton."

"Hn," I said. "*Hn*n."

"The point being," said Caiy, watching the forest and not me, "I must have done something to it with the first blow, outside. Dislocated some bone or other. You told me their bones have no marrow. So to do that might be conceivable. A fortunate stroke. But it took a while for the damage to kill it."

"Hn*n*."

"Because," said Caiy, softly, "you do believe I killed it, don't you?"

"In the legends," I said, "they always do."

"But you said before that in reality, a man can't kill a dragon."

"One did," I said.

"Something I managed outside then. Brittle bones. That first blow to its skull."

"Very likely."

Another silence. Then he said:

"Do you have any gods, Apothecary?"

"Maybe."

"Will you swear me an oath by them, and then call me 'dragon-slayer'? Put it another way. You've been a help. I don't like to turn on my friends. Unless I have to."

His hand was nowhere near that honed sword of his, but the sword was in his eyes and his quiet, oh-so-easy voice. He had his reputation to consider, did Caiy. But I've no reputation at all. So I swore my oath and I called him dragon-slayer, and when our roads parted my hide was intact. He went off to glory somewhere I'd never want to go.

Well, I've seen a dragon, and I do have gods. But I told them, when I swore that oath, I'd almost certainly break it, and my gods are accustomed to me. They don't expect honour and chivalry. And there you are.

Caiy never killed the dragon. It was Niemeh, poor lovely loving gentle Niemeh who killed it. In my line of work, you learn about your simples. Which cure, which bring sleep, which bring the long sleep without awakening. There are some miseries in this blessed world can only end in death, and the quicker death the better. I told you I was a hard man. I couldn't save her, I gave you reasons why. But there were all those others who would have followed her. Other Niemeh's. Other Caiy's, for that matter. I gave her enough in the cup to put out the life of fifty strong men. It didn't pain her, and she didn't show she was dead before she had to be. The dragon devoured her, and with her the drug I'd dosed her with. And so Caiy earned the name of dragon-slayer.

And it wasn't a riddle.

And no, I haven't considered making a profession of it. Once is enough with any twice-terrible thing. Heroes and knights need their impossible challenges. I'm not meant for any bard's romantic song, a look will tell you that. You won't ever find me in the Northern hills calling "Draco! Draco!"

Two Yards of Dragon
by
L. Sprague de Camp

L. Sprague de Camp is a seminal figure, one whose career spans almost the entire development of modern fantasy and SF. For the fantasy magazine Unknown *in the late 1930s, he helped create a whole new modern style of fantasy writing—funny, whimsical, and irreverent—of which he is still the most prominent practitioner. His most famous books include* Lest Darkness Fall, The Complete Enchanter *(with Fletcher Pratt), and* Rogue Queen. *His short fiction has been collected in* A Gun for Dinosaur, The Purple Pterodactyls, *and* The Best of L. Sprague de Camp, *among many other collections. His most recent book, written in collaboration with his wife, writer Catherine Crook de Camp, is* The Pixilated Peeress.

In the sly and funny tale that follows, he suggests that when you go a-hunting, you'd better be prepared to find *what you're looking for. . . .*

* * *

Eudoric Dambertson, Esquire, rode home from his courting of Lusina, daughter of the enchanter Baldonius, with a face as long as an olifant's nose. Eudoric's sire, Sir Dambert, said:

"Well, how fared thy suit, boy? Ill, eh?"

"I—" began Eudoric.

"I told you 'twas an asinine notion, eh? Was I not right? When Baron Emmerhard has more daughters than he can count, any one of which would fetch a pretty parcel of land with her, eh? Well, why answerest not?"

"I—" said Eudoric.

"Come on, lad, speak up!"

"How can he, when ye talk all the time?" said Eudoric's mother, the Lady Aniset.

"Oh," said Sir Dambert. "Your pardon, son. Moreover

and furthermore, as I've told you, an ye were Emmerhard's son-in-law, he'd use his influence to get you your spurs. Here ye be, a strapping youth of three-and-twenty, not yet knighted. 'Tis a disgrace to our lineage.''

"There are no wars toward, to afford opportunity for deeds of knightly dought," said Eudoric.

"Aye, 'tis true. Certes, we all hail the blessings of peace, which the wise governance of our sovran emperor hath given us for lo these thirteen years. Howsomever, to perform a knightly deed, our young men must needs waylay banditti, disperse rioters, and do suchlike fribbling feats."

As Sir Dambert paused, Eudoric interjected, "Sir, that problem now seems on its way to solution."

"How meanest thou?"

"If you'll but hear me, Father! Doctor Baldonius has set me a task, ere he'll bestow Lusina on me, which should fit me for knighthood in any jurisdiction."

"And that is?"

"He's fain to have two square yards of dragon hide. Says he needs 'em for his magical mummeries."

"But there have been no dragons in these parts for a century or more!"

"True; but, quoth Baldonius, the monstrous reptiles still abound far to eastward, in the lands of Pathenia and Pantorozia. Forsooth, he's given me a letter of introduction to his colleague, Doctor Raspiudus, in Pathenia."

"What?" cried the Lady Aniset. "Thou, to set forth on some year-long journey to parts unknown, where, 'tis said, men hop on a single leg or have faces in their bellies? I'll not have it! Besides, Baldonius may be privy wizard to Baron Emmerhard, but 'tis not to be denied that he is of no gentle blood."

"Well," said Eudoric, "so who was gentle when the Divine Pair created the world?"

"Our forebears were, I'm sure, whate'er were the case with those of the learned Doctor Baldonius. You young people are always full of idealistic notions. Belike thou'lt fall into heretical delusions, for I hear that the Easterlings have not the true religion. They falsely believe that God is one, instead of two as we truly understand."

"Let's not wander into the mazes of theology," said Sir Dambert, his chin in his fist. "To be sure, the paynim Southrons believe that God is three, an even more pernicious notion than that of the Easterlings."

"An I meet God in my travels, I'll ask him the truth o't," said Eudoric.

"Be not sacrilegious, thou impertinent whelp! Still and all and notwithstanding, Doctor Baldonius were a man of influence to have in the family, be his origin never so humble. Methinks I could prevail upon him to utter spells to cause my crops, my neat, and my villeins to thrive, whilst casting poxes and murrains on my enemies. Like that caitiff Rainmar, eh? What of the bad seasons we've had? The God and Goddess know we need all the supernatural help we can get to keep us from penury. Else we may some fine day awaken to find that we've lost the holding to some greasy tradesman with a purchased title, with pen for lance and tally sheet for shield."

"Then I have your leave, sire?" cried Eudoric, a broad grin splitting his square, bronzed young face.

The Lady Aniset still objected, and the argument raged for another hour. Eudoric pointed out that it was not as if he were an only child, having two younger brothers and a sister. In the end, Sir Dambert and his lady agreed to Eudoric's quest, provided he return in time to help with the harvest, and take a manservant of their choice.

"Whom have you in mind?" asked Eudoric.

"I fancy Jillo the trainer," said Sir Dambert.

Eudoric groaned. "That old mossback, ever canting and haranguing me on the duties and dignities of my station?"

"He's but a decade older than ye," said Sir Dambert. "Moreover and furthermore, ye'll need an older man, with a sense of order and propriety, to keep you on the path of a gentleman. Class loyalty above all, my boy! Young men are wont to swallow every new idea that flits past, like a frog snapping at flies. Betimes they find they've engulfed a wasp, to their scathe and dolor."

"He's an awkward wight, Father, and not overbrained."

"Aye, but he's honest and true, no small virtues in our degenerate days. In my sire's time there was none of this newfangled saying the courteous 'ye' and 'you' even to mere churls and scullions. 'Twas always 'thou' and 'thee.'"

"How you do go on, Dambert dear," said the Lady Aniset.

"Aye, I ramble. 'Tis the penalty of age. At least, Eudoric, the faithful Jillo knows horses and will keep your beasts in prime fettle." Sir Dambert smiled. "Moreover and furthermore, if I know Jillo Godmarson, he'll be glad to get away from his nagging wife for a spell."

So Eudoric and Jillo set forth to eastward, from the knight's holding of Arduen, in the barony of Zurgau, in the county of Treveria, in the kingdom of Locania, in the New Napolitanian Empire. Eudoric—of medium height, powerful build, dark, with square-jawed but otherwise undistinguished features—rode his palfrey and led his mighty destrier Morgrim. The lank, lean Jillo bestrode another palfrey and led a sumpter mule. Morgrim was piled with Eudoric's panoply of plate, carefully nested into a compact bundle and lashed down under a canvas cover. The mule bore the rest of their supplies.

For a fortnight they wended uneventfully through the duchies and counties of the Empire. When they reached lands where they could no longer understand the local dialects, they made shift with Helladic, the tongue of the Old Napolitanian Empire, which lettered men spoke everywhere.

They stopped at inns where inns were to be had. For the first fortnight, Eudoric was too preoccupied with dreams of his beloved Lusina to notice the tavern wenches. After that, his urges began to fever him, and he bedded one in Zerbstat, to their mutual satisfaction. Therefore, however, he forbore, not as a matter of sexual morals but as a matter of thrift.

When benighted on the road, they slept under the

stars—or, as befell them on the marches of Avaria, under a rain-dripping canopy of clouds. As they bedded down in the wet, Eudoric asked his companion:

"Jillo, why did you not remind me to bring a tent?"

Jillo sneezed. "Why, sir, come rain, come snow, I never thought that so sturdy a springald as ye be would ever need one. The heroes in the romances never travel with tents."

"To the nethermost hell with heroes of the romances! They go clattering around on their destriers for a thousand cantos. Weather is ever fine. Food, shelter, and a change of clothing appear, as by magic, whenever desired. Their armor never rusts. They suffer no tisics and fluxes. They pick up no fleas or lice at the inns. They're never swindled by merchants, for none does aught so vulgar as buying and selling."

"If ye'll pardon me, sir," said Jillo, "that were no knightly way to speak. It becomes not your station."

"Well, to the nethermost hells with my station, too! Wherever these paladins go, they find damsels in distress to rescue, or have other agreeable, thrilling, and sanitary adventures. What adventures have we had? The time we fled from robbers in the Turonian Forest. The time we fished you out of the Albis half drowned. The time we ran out of food in the Asciburgi Mountains and had to plod fodderless over those hair-raising peaks for three days on empty stomachs."

"The Divine Pair do but seek to try the mettle of a valorous aspirant knight, sir. Ye should welcome these petty adversities as a chance to prove your manhood."

Eudoric made a rude noise with his mouth. "That for my manhood! Right now, I'd fainer have a stout roof overhead, a warm fire before me, and a hot repast in my belly. An ever I go on such a silly jaunt again, I'll find one of those versemongers—like that troubadour, Landwin of Kromnitch, that visited us yesteryear—and drag him along, to show him how little real adventures are like those of the romances. And if he fall into the Albis, he may drown, for all of me. Were it not for my darling Lusina—"

Eudoric lapsed into gloomy silence, punctuated by sneezes.

They plodded on until they came to the village of Liptai, on the border of Pathenia. After the border guards had questioned and passed them, they walked their animals down the deep mud of the main street. Most of the slatternly houses were of logs or of crudely hewn planks, innocent of paint.

"Heaven above!" said Jillo. "Look at that, sir!"

"That" was a gigantic snail shell, converted into a small house.

"Knew you not of the giant snails of Pathenia?" asked Eudoric. "I've read of them in Doctor Baldonius' encyclopedia. When full grown, they—or rather their shells—are ofttimes used for dwellings in this land."

Jillo shook his head. "'Twere better had ye spent more of your time on your knightly exercises and less on reading. Your sire hath never learnt his letters, yet he doth his duties well enow."

"Times change, Jillo. I may not clang rhymes so featly as Doctor Baldonius, or that ass Landwin of Kromnitch; but in these days a stroke of the pen were oft more fell than the slash of a sword. Here's a hostelry that looks not too slummocky. Do you dismount and inquire within as to their tallage."

"Why, sir?"

"Because I am fain to know, ere we put our necks in the noose! Go ahead. An I go in, they'll double the scot at sight of me."

When Jillo came out and quoted prices, Eudoric said, "Too dear. We'll try the other."

"But, Master! Mean ye to put us in some flea-bitten hovel, like that which we suffered in Bitava?"

"Aye. Didst not prate to me on the virtues of petty adversity in strengthening one's knightly mettle?"

"'Tis not that, sir."

"What, then?"

"Why, when better quarters are to be had, to make do

with the worse were an insult to your rank and station. No gentleman—"

"Ah, here we are!" said Eudoric. "Suitably squalid, too! You see, good Jillo, I did but yestere'en count our money, and lo! more than half is gone, and our journey not yet half completed."

"But, noble Master, no man of knightly mettle would so debase himself as to tally his silver, like some baseborn commercial—"

"Then I must needs lack true knightly mettle. Here we be!"

For a dozen leagues beyond Liptai rose the great, dense Motolian Forest. Beyond the forest lay the provincial capital of Velitchovo. Beyond Velitchovo, the forest thinned out *gradatim* to the great grassy plains of Pathenia. Beyond Pathenia, Eudoric had been told, stretched the boundless deserts of Pantorozia, over which a man might ride for months without seeing a city.

Yes, the innkeeper told him, there were plenty of dragons in the Motolian Forest. "But fear them not," said Kasmar in broken Helladic. "From being hunted, they have become wary and even timid. An ye stick to the road and move yarely, they'll pester you not unless ye surprise or corner one."

"Have any dragons been devouring maidens fair lately?" asked Eudoric.

Kasmar laughed. "Nay, good Master. What were maidens fair doing, traipsing round the woods to stir up the beasties? Leave them be, I say, and they'll do the same by you."

A cautious instinct warned Eudoric not to speak of his quest. After he and Jillo had rested and had renewed their equipment, they set out, two days later, into the Motolian Forest. They rode for a league along the Velitchovo road. Then Eudoric, accoutered in full plate and riding Morgrim, led his companion off the road into the woods to southward. They threaded their way among the trees, ducking branches, in a wide sweep around. Steering by the sun, Eudoric brought them back to the road near Liptai.

The next day they did the same, except that their circuit was to the north of the highway.

After three more days of this exploration, Jillo became restless. "Good Master, what do we, circling round and about so bootlessly? The dragons dwell farther east, away from the haunts of men, they say."

"Having once been lost in the woods," said Eudoric, "I would not repeat the experience. Therefore do we scout our field of action, like a general scouting a future battlefield."

"'Tis an arid business," said Jillo with a shrug. "But then, ye were always one to see further into a millstone than most."

At last, having thoroughly committed the byways of the nearer forest to memory, Eudoric led Jillo farther east. After casting about, they came at last upon the unmistakable tracks of a dragon. The animal had beaten a path through the brush, along which they could ride almost as well as on the road. When they had followed this track for above an hour, Eudoric became aware of a strong, musky stench.

"My lance, Jillo!" said Eudoric, trying to keep his voice from rising with nervousness.

The next bend in the path brought them into full view of the dragon, a thirty-footer facing them on the trail.

"Ha!" said Eudoric. "Meseems 'tis a mere cockadrill, albeit longer of neck and of limb than those that dwell in the rivers of Agisymba—if the pictures in Doctor Baldonius' books lie not. Have at thee, vile worm!"

Eudoric counched his lance and put spurs to Morgrim. The destrier bounded forward.

The dragon raised its head and peered this way and that, as if it could not see well. As the hoofbeats drew nearer, the dragon opened its jaws and uttered a loud, hoarse, groaning bellow.

At that, Morgrim checked his rush with stiffened forelegs, spun ponderously on his haunches, and veered off the trail into the woods. Jillo's palfrey bolted likewise, but in another direction. The dragon set out after Eudoric at a shambling trot.

Eudoric had not gone fifty yards when Morgrim passed close aboard a massive old oak, a thick limb of which jutted into their path. The horse ducked beneath the bough. The branch caught Eudoric across the breastplate, flipped him backwards over the high cantle of his saddle, and swept him to earth with a great clatter.

Half stunned, he saw the dragon trot closer and closer—and then lumber past him, almost within arm's length, and disappear on the trail of the fleeing horse. The next that Eudoric knew, Jillo was bending over him, crying:

"Alas, my poor heroic Master! Be any bones broke, sir?"

"All of them, methinks," groaned Eudoric. "What's befallen Morgrim?"

"That I know not. And look at this dreadful dent in your beauteous cuirass!"

"Help me out of the thing. The dent pokes most sorely into my ribs. The misadventures I suffer for my dear Lusina!"

"We must get your breastplate to a smith to have it hammered out and filed smooth again."

"Fiends take the smiths! They'd charge half the cost of a new one. I'll fix it myself, if I can find a flat rock to set it on and a big stone wherewith to pound it."

"Well, sir," said Jillo, "ye were always a good man of your hands. But the mar will show, and that were not suitable for one of your quality."

"Thou mayst take my quality and stuff it!" cried Eudoric. "Canst speak of nought else? Help me up, pray." He got slowly to his feet, wincing, and limped a few steps.

"At least," he said, "nought seems fractured. But I misdoubt I can walk back to Liptai."

"Oh, sir, that were not to be thought of! Me allow you to wend afoot whilst I ride? Fiends take the thought!" Jillo unhitched the palfrey from the tree to which he had tethered it and led it to Eudoric.

"I accept your courtesy, good Jillo, only because I must. To plod the distance afoot were but a condign punishment for so bungling my charge. Give me a boost, will you?" Eudoric grunted as Jillo helped him into the saddle.

"Tell me, sir," said Jillo, "why did the beast ramp on past you without stopping to devour you as ye lay helpless? Was't that Morgrim promised a more bounteous repast? Or that the monster feared that your plate would give him a disorder of the bowels?"

"Meseems 'twas neither. Marked you how gray and milky appeared its eyes? According to Doctor Baldonius' book, dragons shed their skins from time to time, like serpents. This one neared the time of its skin change, wherefore the skin over its eyeballs had become thickened and opaque, like glass of poor quality. Therefore it could not plainly discern objects lying still, and pursued only those that moved."

They got back to Liptai after dark. Both were barely able to stagger, Eudoric from his sprains and bruises and Jillo footsore from the unaccustomed three-league hike.

Two days later, when they had recovered, they set out on the two palfreys to hunt for Morgrim. "For," Eudoric said, "that nag is worth more in solid money than all the rest of my possessions together."

Eudoric rode unarmored save for a shirt of light mesh mail, since the palfrey could not carry the extra weight of the plate all day at a brisk pace. He bore his lance and sword, however, in case they should again encounter a dragon.

They found the site of the previous encounter, but no sign either of the dragon or of the destrier. Eudoric and Jillo tracked the horse by its prints in the soft mold for a few bowshots, but then the slot faded out on harder ground.

"Still, I misdoubt Morgrim fell victim to the beast," said Eudoric. "He could show clean heels to many a steed of lighter build, and from its looks the dragon was no courser."

After hours of fruitless searching, whistling, and calling, they returned to Liptai. For a small fee, Eudoric was allowed to post a notice in Helladic on the town notice board, offering a reward for the return of his horse.

No word, however, came of the sighting of Morgrim. For all that Eudoric could tell, the destrier might have run clear to Velitchovo.

"You are free with advice, good Jillo," said Eudoric. "Well, rede me this riddle. We've established that our steeds will bolt from the sight and smell of dragon, for which I blame them little. Had we all the time in the world, we could doubtless train them to face the monsters, beginning with a stuffed dragon, and then, perchance, one in a cage in some monarch's menagerie. But our lucre dwindles like the snow in spring. What's to do?"

"Well, if the nags won't stand, needs we must face the worms on foot," said Jillo.

"That seems to me to throw away our lives to no good purpose, for these vasty lizards can outrun and outturn us and are well harnessed to boot. Barring the luckiest of lucky thrusts with the spear—as, say, into the eye or down the gullet—that fellow we erst encountered could make one mouthful of my lance and another of me."

"Your knightly courage were sufficient defense, sir. The Divine Pair would surely grant victory to the right."

"From all I've read of battles and feuds," said Eudoric, "methinks the Holy Couple's attention oft strays elsewhither when they should be deciding the outcome of some mundane fray."

"That is the trouble with reading; it undermines one's faith in the True Religion. But ye could be at least as well armored as the dragon, in your panoply of plate."

"Aye, but then poor Daisy could not bear so much weight to the site—or, at least, bear it thither and have breath left for a charge. We must be as chary of our beasts' welfare as of our own, for without them 'tis a long walk back to Treveria. Nor do I deem that we should like to pass our lives in Liptai."

"Then, sir, we could pack the armor on the mule, for you to don in dragon country."

"I like it not," said Eudoric. "Afoot, weighted down by

that lobster's habit, I could move no more spryly than a tortoise. 'Twere small comfort to know that if the dragon ate me, he'd suffer indigestion afterward."

Jillo sighed. "Not the knightly attitude, sir, if ye'll pardon my saying so."

"Say what you please, but I'll follow the course of what meseems were common sense. What we need is a brace of those heavy steel crossbows for sieges. At close range, they'll punch a hole in a breastplate as 'twere a sheet of papyrus."

"They take too long to crank up," said Jillo. "By the time ye've readied your second shot, the battle's over."

"Oh, it would behoove us to shoot straight the first time; but better one shot that pierces the monster's scales than a score that bounce off. Howsomever, we have these fell little hand catapults not, and they don't make them in this barbarous land."

A few days later, while Eudoric still fretted over the lack of means to his goal, he heard a sudden sound like a single thunderclap from close at hand. Hastening out from Kasmar's Inn, Eudoric and Jillo found a crowd of Pathenians around the border guard's barracks.

In the drill yard, the guard was drawn up to watch a man demonstrate a weapon. Eudoric, whose few words of Pathenian were not up to conversation, asked among the crowd for somebody who could speak Helladic. When he found one, he learned that the demonstrator was a Pantorozian. The man was a stocky, snub-nosed fellow in a bulbous fur hat, a jacket of coarse undyed wool, and baggy trousers tucked into soft boots.

"He says the device was invented by the Sericans," said the villager. "They live half a world away, across the Pantorozian deserts. He puts some powder into that thing, touches a flame to it, and *boom!* it spits a leaden ball through the target as neatly as you please."

The Pantorozian demonstrated again, pouring black powder from the small end of a horn down his brass barrel. He placed a wad of rag over the mouth of the tube, then a leaden ball, and pushed both ball and wad down the tube with a rod. He poured a pinch of powder into a hole on the upper side of the tube near its rear, closed end.

Then he set a forked rest in the ground before him, rested the barrel in the fork, and took a small torch that a guardsman handed him. He pressed the wooden stock of the device against his shoulder, sighted along the tube, and with his free hand touched the torch to the touchhole. Ffft, *bang!* A cloud of smoke, and another hole appeared in the target.

The Pantorozian spoke with the captain of the guard, but they were too far for Eudoric to hear, even if he could have understood their Pathenian. After a while, the Pantorozian picked up his tube and rest, slung his bag of powder over his shoulder, and walked with downcast air to a cart hitched to a shade tree.

Eudoric approached the man, who was climbing into his car. "God den, fair sir!" began Eudoric, but the Pantorozian spread his hands with a smile of incomprehension.

"Kasmar!" cried Eudoric, sighting the innkeeper in the crowd. "Will you have the goodness to interpret for me and this fellow?"

"He says," said Kasmar, "that he started out with a wainload of these devices and has sold all but one. He hoped to dispose of his last one in Liptai, but our gallant Captain Boriswaf will have nought to do with it."

"Why?" asked Eudoric. "Meseems 'twere a fell weapon in practiced hands."

"That is the trouble, quoth Master Vlek. Boriswaf says that should so fiendish a weapon come into use, 'twill utterly extinguish the noble art of war, for all men will down weapons and refuse to fight rather than face so devilish a device. Then what should he, a lifelong soldier, do for his bread? Beg?"

"Ask Master Vlek where he thinks to pass the night."

"I have already persuaded him to lodge with us, Master Eudoric."

"Good, for I would fain have further converse with him."

Over dinner, Eudoric sounded out the Pantorozian on the

price he asked for his advice. Acting as translator, Kasmar said, "If ye strike a bargain on this, I should get ten per centum as a broker's commission, for ye were helpless without me."

Eudoric got the gun, with thirty pounds of powder and a bag of leaden balls and wadding, for less than half of what Vlek had asked of Captain Boriswaf. As Vlek explained, he had not done badly on this peddling trip and was eager to get home to his wives and children.

"Only remember," he said through Kasmar, "overcharge it not, lest it blow apart and take your head off. Press the stock firmly against your shoulder, lest it knock you on your arse like a mule's kick. And keep fire away from the spare powder, lest it explode all at once and blast you to gobbets."

Later, Eudoric told Jillo, "That deal all but wiped out our funds."

"After the tradesmanlike way ye chaffered that barbarian down?"

"Aye. The scheme had better work, or we shall find ourselves choosing betwixt starving and seeking employment as collectors of offal or diggers of ditches. Assuming, that is, that in this reeky place they even bother to collect offal."

"Master Eudoric!" said Jillo. "Ye would not really lower yourself to accept menial wage labor?"

"Sooner than starve, aye. As Helvolius the philosopher said, no rider wears sharper spurs than Necessity."

"But if 'twere known at home, they'd hack off your gilded spurs, break your sword over your head, and degrade you to base varlet!"

"Well, till now I've had no knightly spurs to hack off, but only the plain silvered ones of an esquire. For the rest, I count on you to see that they don't find out. Now go to sleep and cease your grumbling."

The next day found Eudoric and Jillo deep into the Motolian Forest. At the noonday halt, Jillo kindled a fire. Eudoric made a small torch of a stick whose end was wound with a rag soaked in bacon fat. Then he loaded the device as he had been shown how to do and fired three balls at a mark on a tree. The third time, he hit the mark squarely, although the noise caused the palfreys frantically to tug and rear.

They remounted and went on to where they had met the dragon. Jillo rekindled the torch, and they cast up and down the beast's trail. For two hours they saw no wildlife save a fleeing sow with a farrow of piglets and several huge snails with boulder-sized shells.

Then the horses became unruly. "Methinks they scent our quarry," said Eudoric.

When the riders themselves could detect the odor and the horses became almost unmanageable, Eudoric and Jillo dismounted.

"Tie the nags securely," said Eudoric. " 'Twould never do to slay our beast and then find that our horses had fled, leaving us to drag this land cockadrill home afoot."

As if in answer, a deep grunt came from ahead. While Jillo secured the horses, Eudoric laid out his new equipment and methodically loaded his piece.

"Here it comes," said Eudoric. "Stand by with that torch. Apply it not ere I give the word!"

The dragon came in sight, plodding along the trail and swinging its head from side to side. Having just shed its skin, the dragon gleamed in a reticular pattern of green and black, as if it had been freshly painted. Its great, golden, slit-pupiled eyes were now keen.

The horses screamed, causing the dragon to look up and speed its approach.

"Ready?" said Eudoric, setting the device in its rest.

"Aye, sir. Here goeth!" Without awaiting further command, Jillo applied the torch to the touchhole.

With a great boom and a cloud of smoke, the device discharged, rocking Eudoric back a pace. When the smoke cleared, the dragon was still rushing upon them, unharmed.

"Thou idiot!" screamed Eudoric. "I told thee not to give fire until I commanded! Thou hast made me miss it clean!"

"I'm s-sorry, sir. I was palsied with fear. What shall we do now?"

"Run, fool!" Dropping the device, Eudoric turned and fled.

Jillo also ran. Eudoric tripped over a root and fell sprawling. Jillo stopped to guard his fallen master and turned to face the dragon. As Eudoric scrambled up, Jillo hurled the torch at the dragon's open maw.

The throw fell just short of its target. It happened, however, that the dragon was just passing over the bag of black powder in its charge. The whirling torch, descending in its flight beneath the monster's head, struck this sack.

BOOM!

When the dragon hunters returned, they found the dragon writhing in its death throes. Its whole underside had been blown open, and blood and guts spilled out.

"Well!" said Eudoric, drawing a long breath. "That is enough knightly adventure to last me for many a year. Fall to; we must flay the creature. Belike we can sell that part of the hide that we take not home ourselves."

"How do ye propose to get it back to Liptai? Its hide alone must weigh in the hundreds."

"We shall hitch the dragon's tail to our two nags and lead them, dragging it behind. 'Twill be a weary swink, but we must needs recover as much as we can to recoup our losses."

An hour later, blood-spattered from head to foot, they were still struggling with the vast hide. Then, a man in forester's garb, with a large gilt medallion on his breast, rode up and dismounted. He was a big, rugged-looking man with a rat-trap mouth.

"Who slew this beast, good my sirs?" he inquired.

Jillo spoke: "My noble master, the squire Eudoric Dambertson here. He is the hero who hath brought this accursed beast to book."

"Be that sooth?" said the man to Eudoric.

"Well, ah," said Eudoric, "I must not claim much credit for the deed."

"But ye were the slayer, yea? Then, sir, ye are under arrest."

"What? But wherefore?"

"Ye shall see." From his garments, the stranger produced a length of cord with knots at intervals. With this he measured the dragon from nose to tail. Then the man stood up again.

"To answer your question, on three grounds: *imprimis*, for slaying a dragon out of lawful season; *secundus*, for slaying a dragon below the minimum size permitted; and *tertius*, for slaying a female dragon, which is protected the year round."

"You say this is a female?"

"Aye, 'tis as plain as the nose on your face."

"How does one tell with dragons?"

"Know, knave, that the male hath small horns behind the eyes, the which this specimen patently lacks."

"Who are you, anyway?" demanded Eudoric.

"Senior game warden Voytsik of Prath, at your service. My credentials." The man fingered his medallion. "Now, show me your licenses, pray!"

"Licenses?" said Eudoric blankly.

"Hunting licenses, oaf!"

"None told us that such were required, sir," said Jillo.

"Ignorance of the law is no pretext; ye should have asked. That makes four counts of illegality."

Eudoric said, "But why—why in the name of the God and Goddess—"

"Pray, swear not by your false, heretical deities."

"Well, why should you Pathenians wish to preserve these monstrous reptiles?"

"*Imprimis*, because their hides and other parts have commercial value, which would perish were the whole race extirpated. *Secundus*, because they help to maintain the balance of nature by devouring the giant snails, which otherwise would issue forth nightly from the forest in such numbers as to strip bare our crops, orchards, and gardens and reduce our folk to hunger. And *tertius*, because they add a picturesque element to the landscape, thus luring foreigners to visit our land and spend their gold therein. Doth that explanation satisfy you?"

Eudoric had a fleeting thought of assaulting the stranger

and either killing him or rendering him helpless while Eudoric and Jillo salvaged their prize. Even as he thought, three more tough-looking fellows, clad like Voytsik and armed with crossbows, rode out of the trees and formed up behind their leader.

"Now come along, ye two," said Voytsik.

"Whither?" asked Eudoric.

"Back to Liptai. On the morrow, we take the stage to Velitchovo, where your case will be tried."

"Your pardon, sir; we take the what?"

"The stagecoach."

"What's that, good my sir?"

"By the only God, ye must come from a barbarous land indeed! Ye shall see. Now come along, lest we be benighted in the woods."

The stagecoach made a regular round trip between Liptai and Velitchovo thrice a sennight. Jillo made the journey sunk in gloom, Eudoric kept busy viewing the passing countryside and, when opportunity offered, asking the driver about his occupation: pay, hours, fares, the cost of the vehicle, and so forth. By the time the prisoners reached their destination, both stank mightily because they had had no chance to wash the dragon's blood from their blood-soaked garments.

As they neared the capital, the driver whipped up his team to a gallop. They rattled along the road beside the muddy river Pshora until the river made a bend. Then they thundered across the planks of a bridge.

Velitchovo was a real city, with a roughly paved main street and an onion-domed, brightly colored cathedral of the One God. In a massively timbered municipal palace, a bewhiskered magistrate asked, "Which of you two aliens truly slew the beast?"

"The younger, hight Eudoric," said Voytsik.

"Nay, Your Honor, 'twas I!" said Jillo.

"That is not what he said when we came upon them red-handed from their crime," said Voytsik. "This lean fellow plainly averred that his companion had done the deed, and the other denied it not."

"I can explain that," said Jillo. "I am the servant of the most worshipful squire Eudoric Damberston of Arduen. We set forth to slay the creature, thinking this a noble and heroic deed that should redound to our glory on earth and our credit in Heaven. Whereas we both had a part in the act, the fatal stroke was delivered by your humble servant here. Howsomever, wishing like a good servant for all the glory to go to my master, I gave him the full credit, not knowing that this credit should be counted as blame."

"What say ye to that, Master Eudoric?" asked the judge.

"Jillo's account is essentially true," said Eudoric. "I must, however, confess that my failure to slay the beast was due to mischance and not want of intent."

"Methinks they utter a pack of lies to confuse the court," said Voytsik. "I have told Your Honor of the circumstances of their arrest, whence ye may judge how matters stand."

The judge put his fingertips together. "Master Eudoric," he said, "ye may plead innocent, or as incurring sole guilt, or as guilty in company with your servant. I do not think that you can escape some guilt, since Master Jillo, being your servant, acted under your orders. Ye be therefore responsible for his acts and at the very least a fautor of dragocide."

"What happens if I plead innocent?" said Eudoric.

"Why, in that case, an ye can find an attorney, ye shall be tried in due process. Bail can plainly not be allowed to foreign travelers, who can so easily slip through the law's fingers."

"In other words, I needs must stay in jail until my case comes up. How long will that take?"

"Since our calendar be crowded, 'twill be at least a year and a half. Whereas, an ye plead guilty, all is settled in a trice."

"Then I plead sole guilt," said Eudoric.

"But, dear Master—" wailed Jillo.

"Hold thy tongue, Jillo. I know what I do."

The judge chuckled. "An old head on your shoulders, I perceive. Well, Master Eudoric, I find you guilty on all four counts and amerce you the wonted fine, which is one hundred marks on each count."

"Four hundred marks!" exclaimed Eudoric. "Our total combined wealth at this moment amounts to fourteen marks and thirty-seven pence, plus some items of property left with Master Kasmar in Liptai."

"So, ye'll have to serve out the corresponding prison term, which comes to one mark a day—unless ye can find someone to pay the balance of the fine for you. Take him away, jailer."

"But, Your Honor!" cried Jillo, "what shall I do without my noble master? When shall I see him again?"

"Ye may visit him any day during the regular visiting hours. It were well if ye brought him somewhat to eat, for our prison fare is not of the daintiest."

At the first visiting hour, when Jillo pleaded to be allowed to share Eudoric's sentence, Eudoric said, "Be not a bigger fool than thou canst help! I took sole blame so that ye should be free to run mine errands; whereas had I shared my guilt with you, we had both been mewed up here. Here, take this letter to Doctor Raspiudus; seek him out and acquaint him with our plight. If he be in sooth a true friend of our own Doctor Baldonius, belike he'll come to our rescue."

Doctor Raspiudus was short and fat, with a bushy white beard to his waist. "Ah, dear old Baldonius!" he cried in good Helladic. "I mind me of when we were lads together at the Arcane College of Saalingen University! Doth he still string verses together?"

"Aye, that he does," said Eudoric.

"Now, young man, I daresay that your chiefest desire is to get out of this foul hole, is't not?"

"That, *and* to recover our three remaining animals and other possessions left behind in Liptai, *and* to depart with the two square yards of dragon hide that I've promised to Doctor Baldonius, with enough money to see us home."

"Methinks all these matters were easily arranged, young sir. I need only your power of attorney to enable me to go to Liptai, recover the objects in question, and return hither to pay your fine and release you. Your firearm is, I fear, lost to you, having been confiscated by the law."

"'Twere of little use without a new supply of the magical powder," said Eudoric. "Your plan sounds splendid. But, sir, what do you get out of this?"

The enchanter rubbed his hands together. "Why, the pleasure of favoring an old friend—and also the chance to acquire a complete dragon hide for my own purposes. I know somewhat of Baldonius' experiments. An he can do thus and so with two yards of dragon, I can surely do more with a score."

"How will you obtain this dragon hide?"

"By now the foresters will have skinned the beast and salvaged the other parts of monetary worth, all of which will be put up at auction for the benefit of the kingdom. And I shall bid them in." Raspiudus chuckled. "When the other bidders know against whom they bid, I think not that they'll force the price up very far."

"Why can't you get me out of here now and then go to Liptai?"

Another chuckle. "My dear boy, first I must see that all is as ye say in Liptai. After all, I have only your word that ye be in sooth the Eudoric Dambertson of whom Baldonius writes. So bide ye in patience a few days more. I'll see that ye be sent better ailment than the slop they serve here. And now, pray, your authorization. Here are pen and ink."

To keep from starvation, Jillo got a job as a paver's helper and worked in hasty visits to the jail during his lunch hour. When a fortnight had passed without word from Doctor Raspiudus, Eudoric told Jillo to go to the wizard's home for an explanation.

"They turned me away at the door," reported Jillo. "They told me that the learned doctor had never heard of us."

As the import of this news sank in, Eudoric cursed and beat the wall in his rage. "That filthy, treacherous he-witch! He gets me to sign that power of attorney; then, when he has my property in his grubby paws, he conveniently forgets about us! By the God and Goddess, if ever I catch him—"

"Here, here, what's all this noise?" said the jailer. "Ye disturb the other prisoners."

When Jillo explained the cause of his master's outrage, the jailer laughed. "Why, everyone knows that Raspiudus is the worst skinflint and treacher in Velitchovo! Had ye asked me, I'd have warned you."

"Why has none of his victims slain him?" asked Eudoric.

"We are a law-abiding folk, sir. We do not permit private persons to indulge their feuds on their own, and we have some *most* ingenious penalties for homicide."

"Mean ye," said Jillo, "that amongst you Pathenians a gentleman may not avenge an insult by the gage of battle?"

"Of course not! We are not bloodthirsty barbarians."

"Ye mean there are no true gentlemen amongst you," sniffed Jillo.

"Then, Master Tiolkhof," said Eudoric, calming himself by force of will, "am I stuck here for a year and more?"

"Aye, but ye may get time off for good behavior at the end—three or four days, belike."

When the jailer had gone, Jillo said, "When ye get out, Master, ye must needs uphold our honor by challenging this runagate to the trial of battle, to the death."

Eudoric shook his head. "Heard you not what Tiolkhof said? They deem dueling barbarous and boil the duelists in oil, or something equally entertaining. Anyway, Raspiudus could beg off on grounds of age. We must, instead, use what wits the Holy Couple gave us. I wish now that I'd sent you back to Liptai to fetch our belongings and never meddled with this rolypoly sorcerer."

"True, but how could ye know, dear Master? I should probably have bungled the task in any case, what with my ignorance of the tongue and all."

After another fortnight, King Vladmor of Pathenia died. When his son Yogor ascended the throne, he declared a general amnesty for all crimes lesser than murder. Thus Eudoric found himself out in the street again, but without horse, armor, weapons, or money beyond a few marks.

"Jillo," he said that night in their mean little cubicle, "we must needs get into Raspiudus' house somehow. As we saw this afternoon, 'tis a big place with a stout, high wall around it.

"An ye could get a supply of that black powder, we could blast a breach in the wall."

"But we have no such stuff, nor means of getting it, unless we raid the royal armory, which I do not think we can do."

"Then how about climbing a tree near the wall and letting ourselves down by ropes inside the wall from a convenient branch?"

"A promising plan, *if* there were such an overhanging tree. But there isn't, as you saw as well as I when we scouted the place. Let me think. Raspiudus must have supplies borne into his stronghold from time to time. I misdoubt his wizardry is potent enough to conjure foodstuffs out of air."

"Mean ye that we should gain entrance as, say, a brace of chicken farmers with eggs to sell?"

"Just so. But nay, that won't do. Raspiudus is no fool. Knowing of this amnesty that enlarged me, he'll be on the watch for such a trick. At least, so should I be, in his room, and I credit him with no less wit than mine own . . . I have it! What visitor would logically be likely to call upon him now, whom he will not have seen for many a year and whom he would hasten to welcome?"

"That I know not, sir."

"Who would wonder what had become of us and, detecting our troubles in his magical scryglass, would follow upon our track by uncanny means?"

"Oh, ye mean Doctor Baldonius!"

"Aye. My whiskers have grown nigh as long as his since last I shaved. And we're much of a size."

"But I never heard that your old tutor could fly about on an enchanted broomstick, as some of the mightiest magicians are said to do."

"Belike he can't, but Doctor Raspiudus wouldn't know that."

"Mean ye," said Jillo, "that ye've a mind to play Doctor Baldonius? Or to have me play him? The latter would never do."

"I know it wouldn't, good my Jillo. You know not the learned patter proper to wizards and other philosophers."

"Won't Raspiudus know you, sir? As ye say he's a shrewd old villain."

"He's seen me but once, in that dark, dank cell, and that for a mere quarter hour. You he's never seen at all. Methinks I can disguise myself well enough to befool him—unless you have a better notion."

"Alack, I have none! Then what part shall I play?"

"I had thought of going in alone."

"Nay, sir, dismiss the thought! Me let my master risk his mortal body and immortal soul in a witch's lair without my being there to help him?"

"If you help me the way you did by touching off that firearm whilst our dragon was out of range—"

"Ah, but who threw the torch and saved us in the end? What disguise shall I wear?"

"Since Raspiudus knows you not, there's no need for any. You shall be Baldonius' servant, as you are mine."

"Ye forget, sir, that if Raspiudus knows me not, his gatekeepers might. Forsooth, they're likely to recall me because of the noisy protests I made when they barred me out."

"Hm. Well, you're too old for a page, too lank for a bodyguard, and too unlearned for a wizard's assistant. I have it! You shall go as my concubine!"

"Oh, Heaven above, sir, not that! I am a normal man! I should never live it down!"

To the massive gate before Raspiudus' house came Eudoric, with a patch over one eye, and his beard, uncut for a month, dyed white. A white wig cascaded down from under his hat. He presented a note, in a plausible imitation of Baldonius' hand, to the gatekeeper:

Doctor Baldonius of Treveria presents his compliments to his old friend and colleague Doctor Raspiudus of Velitchovo, and begs the favor of an audience to discuss the apparent disappearance of two young protégés of his.

A pace behind, stooping to disguise his stature, slouched a rouged and powdered Jillo in woman's dress. If Jillo was a homely man, he made a hideous woman, at least as far as his face could be seen under the headcloth. Nor was his beauty enhanced by the dress, which Eudoric had stitched together out of cheap cloth. The garment looked like what it was: the work of a rank amateur at dressmaking.

"My master begs you to enter," said the gatekeeper.

"Why, dear old Baldonius!" cried Raspiudus, rubbing his hands together. "Ye've not changed a mite since those glad, mad days at Saalingen! Do ye still string verses?"

"Ye've withstood the ravages of time well yourself, Raspiudus," said Eudoric, in an imitation of Baldonius' voice. "'As fly the years, the geese fly north in spring; Ah, would the years, like geese, return a-wing!'"

Raspiudus roared with laughter, patting his paunch. "The same old Baldonius! Made ye that one up?"

Eudoric made a deprecatory motion. "I am a mere poetaster; but had not the higher wisdom claimed my allegiance, I might have made my mark in poesy."

"What befell your poor eye?"

"My own carelessness in leaving a corner of a pentacle open. The demon got in a swipe of his claws ere I could banish him. But now, good Raspiudus, I have a matter to discuss whereof I told you in my note."

"Yea, yea, time enow for that. Be ye weary from the road? Need ye baths? Aliment? Drink?"

"Not yet, old friend. We have but now come from Velitchovo's best hostelry."

"Then let me show you my house and grounds. Your lady . . . ?"

"She'll stay with me. She speaks nought but Treverian and fears being separated from me among strangers. A mere swineherd's chick, but a faithful creature. At my age, that is of more moment than a pretty face."

Presently, Eudoric was looking at his and Jillo's palfreys and their sumpter mule in Raspiudus' stables. Eudoric made a few hesitant efforts, as if he were Baldonius seeking his young friends, to inquire after their disappearance. Each time Raspiudus smoothly turned the question aside, promising enlightenment later.

An hour later, Raspiudus was showing off his magical sanctum. With obvious interest, Eudoric examined a number of squares of dragon hide spread out on a workbench. He asked:

"Be this the integument of one of those Pathenian dragons, whereof I have heard?"

"Certes, good Baldonius. Are they extinct in your part of the world?"

"Aye. 'Twas for that reason that I sent my young friend and former pupil, of whom I'm waiting to tell you, eastward to fetch me some of this hide for use in my work. How does one cure this hide?"

"With salt, and—*unh!*"

Raspiudus collapsed, Eudoric having just struck him on the head with a short bludgeon that he whisked out of his voluminous sleeves.

"Bind and gag him and roll him behind the bench!" said Eudoric.

"Were it not better to cut his throat, sir?" said Jillo.

"Nay. The jailer told us that they have ingenious ways of punishing homicide, and I have no wish to prove them by experiment."

While Jillo bound the unconscious Raspiudus, Eudoric chose two pieces of dragon hide, each about a yard square. He rolled them together into a bundle and lashed them with a length of rope from inside his robe. As an afterthought, he helped himself to the contents of Raspiudus' purse. Then he hoisted the roll of hide to his shoulder and issued from the laboratory. He called to the nearest stableboy.

"Doctor Raspiudus," he said, "asks that ye saddle up those two nags." He pointed. "Good saddles, mind you! Are the animals well shod?"

"Hasten, sir," muttered Jillo. "Every instant we hang about here—"

"Hold thy peace! The appearance of haste were the surest way to arouse suspicion." Eudoric raised his voice. "Another heave on that girth, fellow! I am not minded to have my aged bones shattered by a tumble into the roadway."

Jillo whispered, "Can't we recover the mule and your armor, to boot?"

Eudoric shook his head. "Too risky," he murmured. "Be glad if we get away with whole skins."

When the horses had been saddled to his satisfaction, he said, "Lend me some of your strength in mounting, youngster." He groaned as he swung awkwardly into the saddle. "A murrain on thy master, to send us off on this footling errand—me that hasn't sat a horse in years! Now hand me that accursed roll of hide. I thank thee, youth; here's a little for thy trouble. Run ahead and tell the gatekeeper to have his portal wall opened. I fear that if this beast pulls up of a sudden, I shall go flying over its head!"

A few minutes later, when they had turned a corner and were out of sight of Raspiudus' house, Eudoric said, "Now trot!"

"If I could but get out of this damned gown," muttered Jillo. "I can't ride decently in it."

"Wait till we're out of the city gate."

When Jillo had shed the offending garment, Eudoric said, "Now ride, man, as never before in your life!"

They pounded off on the Liptai road. Looking back, Jillo gave a screech. "There's a thing flying after us! It looks like a giant bat!"

"One of Raspiudus' sendings," said Eudoric. "I knew he'd get loose. Use your spurs! Can we but gain the bridge . . ."

They fled at a mad gallop. The sending came closer and closer, until Eudoric thought he could feel the wind of its wings.

Then their hooves thundered across the bridge over the Pshora.

"Those things will not cross running water," said Eudoric, looking back. "Slow down, Jillo. These nags must bear us many leagues, and we must not founder them at the start."

". . . so here we are," Eudoric told Doctor Baldonius.

"Ye've seen your family, lad?"

"Certes. They thrive, praise to the Divine Pair. Where's Lusina?"

"Well—ah—ahem—the fact is, she is not here."

"Oh? Then where?"

"Ye put me to shame, Eudoric. I promised you her hand in return for the two yards of dragon hide. Well, ye've fetched me the hide, at no small effort and risk, but I cannot fulfill my side of the bargain."

"Wherefore?"

"Alas! My undutiful daughter ran off with a strolling player last summer, whilst ye were chasing dragons—or perchance 'twas the other way round. I'm right truly sorry . . ."

Eudoric frowned silently for an instant, then said, "Fret not, esteemed Doctor. I shall recover from the wound—provided, that is, that you salve it by making up my losses in more materialistic fashion."

Baldonius raised bushy gray brows. "So? Ye seem not so grief-stricken as I should have expected, to judge from the lover's sighs and tears wherewith ye parted from the jade last spring. Now ye'll accept money instead?"

"Aye, sir. I admit that my passion had somewhat cooled during our long separation. Was it likewise with her? What said she of me?"

"Aye, her sentiments did indeed change. She said you were too much an opportunist altogether to please her. I would not wound your feelings. . . ."

Eudoric waved a deprecatory hand. "Continue, pray. I have been somewhat toughened by my months in the rude, rough world, and I am interested."

"Well, I told her she was being foolish; that ye were a shrewd lad who, an ye survived the dragon hunt, would go far. But her words were: 'That is just the trouble, Father. He is too shrewd to be very lovable.'"

"Hmph," grunted Eudoric. "As one might say: I am a man of enterprise, thou art an opportunist, he is a conniving scoundrel. 'Tis all in the point of view. Well, if she prefers the fools of this world, I wish her joy of them. As a man of honor, I would have wedded Lusina had she wished. As things stand, trouble is saved all around."

"To you, belike, though I misdoubt my headstrong lass'll find the life of an actor's wife a bed of violets:

'Who'd wed on a whim is soon filled to the brim
Of worry and doubt, till he longs for an out.
So if ye would wive, beware of the gyve
Of an ill-chosen mate; 'tis a harrowing fate.'

But enough of that. What sum had ye in mind?"

"Enough to cover the cost of my good destrier Morgrim and my panoply of plate, together with lance and sword, plus a few other chattels and incidental expenses of travel. Fifteen hundred marks should cover the lot."

"Fif-teen *hundred!* Whew! I could ne'er afford—nor are these moldy patches of dragon hide worth a fraction of the sum."

Eudoric sighed and rose. "You know what you can afford, good my sage." He picked up the roll of dragon hide. "Your colleague Doctor Calporio, wizard to the Count of Treveria, expressed a keen interest in this material. In fact, he offered me more than I have asked of you, but I thought it only honorable to give you the first chance."

"What!" cried Baldonius. "That mountebank, charlatan, that faker? Misusing the hide and not deriving a tenth of the magical benefits from it that I should? Sit down, Eudoric; we will discuss these things."

An hour's haggling got Eudoric his fifteen hundred marks. Baldonius said, "Well, praise the Divine Couple that's over. And now, beloved pupil, what are your plans?"

"Would ye believe it, Doctor Baldonius," said Jillo, "that

my poor, deluded master is about to disgrace his lineage and betray his class by a base commercial enterprise?"

"Forsooth, Jillo? What's this?"

"He means my proposed coach line," said Eudoric.

"Good Heaven, what's that?"

"My plan to run a carriage on a weekly schedule from Zurgau to Kromnitch, taking all who can pay the fare, as they do in Pathenia. We can't let the heathen Easterlings get ahead of us."

"What an extraordinary idea! Need ye a partner?"

"Thanks, but nay. Baron Emmerhard has already thrown in with me. He's promised me my knighthood in exchange for the partnership."

"There is no nobility anymore," said Jillo.

Eudoric grinned. "Emmerhard said much the same sort of thing, but I convinced him that anything to do with horses is a proper pursuit for a gentleman. Jillo, you can spell me at driving the coach, which will make you a gentleman, too!"

Jillo sighed. "Alas! The true spirit of knighthood is dying in this degenerate age. Woe is me that I should live to see the end of chivalry! How much did ye think of paying me, sir?"

Mrs. Byres and the Dragon
by
Keith Roberts

One of the most powerful talents to enter the field in the last thirty years, Keith Roberts secured an important place in genre history in 1968 with the publication of his classic novel Pavane, *one of the best books of the '60s, and certainly one of the best alternate-history novels ever written, rivaled only by books such as L. Sprague de Camp's* Lest Darkness Fall, Ward Moore's *Bring the Jubilee*, and Philip K. Dick's *The Man in the High Castle. Trained as an illustrator—he did work extensively as an illustrator and cover artist in the British SF world of the '60s—Roberts made his first sale to* Science Fantasy *in 1964. Later, he would take over the editorship of* Science Fantasy, *by then called* SF Impulse, *as well as providing many of the magazine's striking covers. But his career as an editor was short-lived, and most of his subsequent impact on the field would be as a writer, including the production of some of the best short stories of the last two decades. Roberts's other books include the novels* The Chalk Giants, The Furies, The Inner Wheel, Molly Zero, Grainne, *and* The Boat of Fate, *one of the finest historical novels of the '70s. His short work can be found in the collections* Machines and Men, The Grain Kings, The Passing of the Dragons, Ladies from Hell, *and* The Lordly Ones. *His most recent books are the well-received novel* Kiteworld, *and a collection,* Winterwood and Other Hauntings. *Coming up is a new collection,* Kaeti on Tour.

Here he tells a bittersweet tale of mutual apprehension and discovery, all played out against the deceptively small and simple compress of an English country garden....

* * *

The garden was elongated and small, paved for much of its area. The irregular slabs were laid without benefit of cement; between them, rock plants had been encouraged to grow. Camomile, decorative thymes; and a shamrock-like affair with dark maroon leaves. In late summer its seed pods, like the small shell cases they resembled, became explosive; let the breeze but stir them and they jerked in unison, there was a sound like the tiny clatter of musketry as the barrage was discharged. It startled the Dragon once when he sniffed at it; he fled hissing, vanished beneath the garden shed. He turned in his own length, lay glaring with his lovely dark amber eyes; but he was not pursued. In time, his breathing became more regular.

At the sides of the garden, between the paving and the low walls that enclosed it, narrow beds had been invaded by the flat rosettes of the London Pride. In their season, the plants sent up a host of delicate flower stalks; the many tiny blooms made a mist of palest pink, interspersed by the blue of the forget-me-nots that still maintained a foothold. Mrs. Byres had been tempted to thin out the invasive saxifrage; in the end she had allowed it to remain. It belonged there; as indeed did the Dragon.

In the center of the place, a round, raised pond held koi; it was Mrs. Byres' pleasure of an evening to sit on the stone coping, drop crumbs of biscuit to the clumsy, gentle fish. The multicolored shoal moved slowly, rising faster to snap and gulp, then resuming its slow circling. The patterns it made were endlessly repeated, never twice the same. The air pump gurgled gently, drops pattered from the bowl of the tiny fountain; she would find her thoughts drifting far off, aimless as the fish, to distant folk and lands. Till the cooling air impinged on her awareness; she would pull at the cardigan round her shoulders, walk to the house and gently close the door.

The fish intrigued the Dragon, too. He would crouch, neck weaving and tail lashing, eyeing the parapet above him. Nerving himself for the spring and clatter with which he finally gained the vantage point. Once arrived he would stare intently, golden eyes flicking as he followed the movements in the water. Once, greatly daring, he reached to dabble with a claw, some vague thought of hunting maybe formed in his mind; but the biggest of the fish turned quickly. The great mouth globbed and plopped, sent him scurrying for his refuge once more. The hissing sounded from beneath the shed; wisps of vapor escaped from his nostrils. It was some time before he was calm again.

He was a small Dragon; perhaps some twenty inches from nose to tail. Though the flexibility of his neck was deceptive, as were the length and dexterity of his tongue. This he used to take the black and brown beetles that scurried from time to time across the flags. He would crunch them with quick movements of his jaws, spitting out the hard wing cases. These he brushed into the cracks between the paving slabs, anxious it seemed to leave no trace of his presence; though Mrs. Byres in fact knew the whereabouts of each tiny hoard. The beetles, with the pill bugs he nosed from beneath the rosettes of the London Pride, comprised his major diet. Plus earthworms when the need arose, though the latter he disliked; for their fustiness of flavor, their slow, shining movements, their faster looping when attacked and caught. He would snort with disgust, rubbing at his slender jaws and nose, spitting out the fragments of dirt and mold with which their intestines were crammed; he was much relieved when he found the first plate of cereal tucked beneath the shed. Though for some time he was afraid to approach the strange object. Instead, he eyed it from a distance. It lay directly in his path; the track worn by the passage of his body, the deeper hollow he had scooped out for himself and in which he slept. He approached finally, by cautious, six-inch rushes. His neck snaked, unsure; his nose moved from side to side, skimming the surface of the bowl, savoring the delicate, unknown odor. Finally his tongue flicked out to touch the milk; next instant he was drinking and snapping, unsure how best to cope with the strange food. He didn't stop till the offering was licked clean. He slept contented that night, and with a full belly; for the first time, it seemed, in his life.

Next day he found the tall door of the shed left open a little. Previously it had always been securely locked; though it is doubtful if his brain had registered the fact. He sniffed at the crack, cautious as ever, weaving his head, blinking his brilliant eyes. The darkness attracted with its promise of a lair, concealment; yet also he sensed danger. A trap maybe. He was a creature built largely of instincts; now they conflicted, hopelessly. He ran in small circles, claws tapping, growling a little; backed off, moved forward, backed away again. He sat on his haunches, propping himself on his tail like a small green and gold kangaroo. Finally, greatly daring, he extended a claw to the edge of the door. He pulled at it a little. A long creak from somewhere; he tensed, but nothing further happened. He jumped inside, spun round instantly to make sure his way of escape had remained clear. A further period of immobility; and he began to explore, timidly and with many backward glances. Nothing happened however; and soon he was trotting round busily, snuffling at the board floor of the place, snorting from time to time at the dust that entered his nostrils.

The shed was mostly empty. Some garden tools leaned against the wall; to one side was a small wooden bench. On it, inaccessible to him, stood paint tins and the like; a roll of plastic netting, stacks of old magazines, assorted seed trays and flower pots. The sprays and cans of weed-killer, usual appurtenances of suburban culture, were absent; but Mrs. Byres hadn't studied with the Theravadians for nothing.

At the rear of the place, immediately below the one small window, was a round, flat bag filled with some crunchy substance. He climbed onto it, was alarmed afresh by the unsure, yielding surface. He turned round several times; finally he settled, eyes fixed warily on the crack of light from the door. He crossed his forelegs, dropped his muzzle to them. Despite himself, he felt secure and comfortable. He started once or twice, at half-imagined sounds; finally his lids drooped. The orange glow faded, was eclipsed.

He was roused, finally, by the light that streamed in from the square of glass above him. The yellow patch angled across the boards; above it, specks of brilliance swirled and were lost. He was off the beansack in an instant, claws scrabbling; but the door was still ajar, showing its tall strip of sky. Just inside it stood the bowl, blue patterns round its edge. He stared, long neck snaking suspiciously. But nothing had been moved; the tools stood by the wall, there was the same scent of dry earth and dust. He hurried to the bowl. He buried his muzzle, drank thirstily; once more he didn't stop till the china gleamed.

He was late for his first patrol. Though it is doubtful if the notion would have held meaning for him. Rather, it was a habit formed; and in habit lies security. He nosed the door a fraction wider, pausing carefully; but the fountain still tinkled, the flags lay quiet in early sunlight. Beyond the garden the house rose tall, Edwardian and sturdy. Its rear walls had been rendered, though over the years the finish had begun to crack and peel. Mrs. Byres had ordered it renewed, in vivid white; the contrast with the terraces to either side was sharp. From the road beyond came the steady sound of traffic; but the noise was muted, barely impinging on the awareness of the Dragon.

His tongue flicked from his muzzle, tasting, it seemed, the morning air. He hurried forward, moving as ever in quick diagonal rushes. To one side, the wall was topped by trelliswork; climbing plants shielded the garden and pond from view. On the other, the barrier was lower; but the property had been vacant for some time now. The house stood quietly, moldering a little perhaps, garnering its hourly profit; the profit it attracted merely by existing, here so close to the city.

By the kitchen drain, a flash of movement caught the Dragon's eye. He snapped at it, but the insect had already scurried into a crack. He probed for it, snuffling; but the thing had gone. He turned back, searched the nearer of the borders. Its edge, where it joined the paving, was marked by tiles of dark, glistening blue, each set upright in the earth. The line of them was crooked; their tops were decorated with wavy indentations. He crunched a small snail that clung to one of them, and hurried on.

Behind the shed, past the rhubarb clump and the tiny vegetable patch, chestnut palings leaned uncertainly, rotted here and there and patched vividly with fungus. He eased through one of the gaps thus formed and stopped, claw raised. Close to the fence grew the remnants of an old gnarled hedge. Its roots twisted and writhed; sprays of small green leaves burst up, making an overarching canopy. Here the biggest worms of all came, sudden and unexpected, spurting from the carpet of damp humus; and here too he had once encountered a cat. The animal stared at first, as if unable to believe its eyes; then it approached stiff-legged, fur bristling. A threat rumbled deep in its throat; and the Dragon backed, his own tail lashing. A flurry of paws, brief scuffle of black and white; and the cat fled squalling, gained the roof of an outhouse with a single galvanic bound. It crouched there an hour or more, glaring; from time to time it scrubbed at its face with a paw. The fur of its jaw was singed, its whiskers shorter on that side and curling at the tips. Since when, at sight of a flicker of green and gold, it had turned away, staring into distance with the fixity only a discomforted cat can achieve. In the tomcat's world, Dragons had ceased to exist; they were figments, obviously, of another imagination.

The Dragon paused again beneath the hedge, glancing upward briefly; today though, nothing moved. A plane flew across the brilliant gap of sky, the sun glinting on its fuselage as it turned for the airport a few miles distant; but it was disregarded. The Dragon scuttled forward, pausing only to take a woodlouse that bumbled aimlessly over the fallen leaves.

Access to the rest of his domain was gained by a similar gap in the once-stout line of fencing. Here, the Dragon at once felt more secure. The grass in the untended garden had sprouted high; under cover of its drifts and clumps he was hidden from all but the most vigilant eyes. The bases of the old walls yielded a rich supply of livestock; above, buddleias drooped their white and purple cones of flowers. Butterflies came to them through the warm afternoons; he would watch their bright movements, hissing a little, making tiny, futile rushes. Sometimes, when the insects dropped down to the lank-stalked dandelions, he would snap at them. He never missed; but there was little substance to be had. He shredded the wings, irritably; his muzzle became marked by pastel tints, brightness added to his own bright scales. Later, tiring of the game, he would curl up in a beaten nest of grass to sleep. As he slept now.

Mrs. Byres was unsure just when she had become aware of the existence of the Dragon. At first he was a shadow; a hint, a vagueness, a twinkling in the dusk. It was only later, and by slow degrees, that he took on form and color. Though he was best perceived still from the corner of the eye; the glance that, in traveling away, reveals more than the full, ungracious stare. As the mind, lulled by the glidings of the koi, may itself glide off, to light on other things. She smiled at that and took herself upstairs, left him to his sunlit scutterings. She herself had seen much strangeness; seen, and finally accepted. She had seen fires blaze where no fires could be, fires that burned silver against the high snow; she had seen the *tulpa*, the creature of the mind, glide mysteriously through room after strange room. While the priests chanted, the mantras extended themselves; delicate lines of chalk and sand, growing by the hour, the week, in honor of a God who was, and yet was not. Set against that, a Dragon more or less was nothing extraordinary; not in the real scheme of things. He came from the Otherworld, where fact and fable blend; an alien place perhaps, to all right-thinking folk. He was one with the jaguars and pumas that frighten city dwellers, that flourish in the newspapers only to vanish away; the black dogs, born of thunderbolts, that terrorized the folk of former times. Their own fears, given form and substance, come to score displeasure on the stout oak doors of churches, leave the marks for all the world to see. Though there was no fear in the Dragon; not if he had truly sprung from her own mind.

She took down a book, old and bound in leather. She turned the pages gently, found the place she sought. *There is nothing strange,* she read, *in the fact that I may have created my own hallucination. The interesting point is that in these cases of materialization, others see the thought-forms that may have been created.*

Tibetans disagree in their explanations of such phenom-

ena; some think a material form is really brought into being, others consider the apparition as a mere case of suggestion, the creator's thought impressing others and causing them to see what he himself sees.

Mrs. Byres closed the book and set it aside. Madame David-Neel had understood a little; as much, perhaps, as any one person may. She laid her head back, against the dark plush of the chair. In time, the light from the tall windows before her became diffused. Her consciousness drifted away, among ten thousand Buddha-fields.

There had been much speculation, when she first arrived in the street; the tall, solitary woman, so soberly and plainly dressed, the mane of iron-grey hair always so neatly coiffured, held firmly by great combs. She was old, very old some said; but her great eyes were tilted still and clear, of a color not readily to be described, the skin smooth across her broad, high cheekbones. Wealthy she must be though. The neighbors decided it, watching the furniture carefully carried in; piece after piece, massive, unfashionable, and black. Wife of a planter, a Commissioner; or higher still said some, nodding sagely. Others voiced darker thoughts. England, they said, was for the English, Britannia for the Brits; black lands for the black folk, white lands for the whites. These though were the resentful ones; encountering her in the street, on her way down to the shops, they had found they could not readily meet her glance. Her face was gentle and calm; but she looked into you, through you, in a way that was disconcerting. They repeated their suspicions to their wives; slammed their front doors; settled, relieved, to their suppers and their telly.

Perhaps Mrs. Byres heard the rumors, perhaps not. Either way, it made little difference. She was not rich; a little saved, from a lifetime of quiet service, a pension from a Government that at the end had recognized her worth, but that was all. Bringing her belongings back, the belongings collected over so many years, had strained her slender resources; but that had been in accordance with the Sahib's wish. Unspoken perhaps, but nonetheless keenly felt. As for the rest; there had once been a time for anger but that was in the past, too distant almost for recall. Then, certainly, her eyes had flashed, the color risen to her cheeks; but it was all so long ago. She had seen too much of human frailty since; her own, and that of others.

She relaxed deeper into the chair, in the study she had made for herself and where, surrounded by familiar things, she still felt most at home. Here were the square dark cupboards with their ornate, once-gilded handles, the great sideboard, mirror-backed, standing on its many tiny legs; the bookcases with their black, carved tops, fashioned with such crude care. Brass trays shone softly from the walls; Hanuman, the monkey god, gestured above the hearth, trampling his tiny enemy. The sacred cobra spread his seven hoods; while in an alcove were the old coffee pots, with their bulbous bellies, their long, incised spouts. All but valueless, as she was well aware; but she wouldn't willingly have parted with them. They spoke of another life, another land, both gone now into the past. Somewhere though the blades of fans still whispered, their sound mixed with the rustling of garden trees; the sun burned through the slats of white-painted jalousies. Mrs. Byres smiled slightly to herself. When they placed the infant Buddha beneath the rose apple tree, its shadow became fixed; it was Earth, and the cosmos, that circled round it. Shadows, perhaps, became fixed in memory, too.

She shook her head, eyes closed. There had been good times, in those far-off days; when she was young, before she learned of pain. They glimmered in the mind, like the scoured wards of the hospitals to which she came, the uniforms of the young men who paid court, in their scarlet and blue and gold. Though it had been difficult, she supposed, to see things in their proper light; difficult at least for one so fresh from home, so eager. Her mother's whispered warnings, the insinuations, hints; sudden anger with which she clattered kitchen things, pounded at the bowl held in her lap. She who was normally so gentle. "Never smile for them," she said once, bitterly. "Never show your teeth. That way they can tell . . ." It had all seemed pointless, in the bright environment, in the bright new life, vague as nursery fears. Though children's fears were often sharp enough; the shadow-beasts had teeth and claws and eyes. They existed of course, and had their being; but their realm lay beyond the bedroom walls.

The flowers, calling cards, brought new responsibilities; impossible to refuse, gross, in that climate, to accede. She swung, helpless, between unreachable poles; lowered her eyes uncertainly, feeling herself besieged. It made her suitors the more ardent.

One young man had become special. She resisted; but despite herself the dreams had come. The voyage, over so much ocean; the house she would come to as a bride, the great house in a land she had never seen. She didn't blame him, hadn't blamed him then; but it had been hard. He should have been warned, by the averted eyes, the whisperings; by the raven-gloss of hair, the skin that tanned too readily, however she might seek to avoid the sun. She should have warned him; but her throat seemed blocked, the words refused to form. She twined her fingers in her lap; till the monstrous revelation came, the moment that could no longer be avoided. "Open your mouth," he said in disbelief. "*Open your mouth . . .*" Shocked, she obeyed; and the sounds of the little orchestra, the chatter of the diners, faded quite away. He took her jaw, turned her head as he might the head of a colt, before he started back. Her legs unfroze then so that she ran from the place, left her wrap, her purse, ran into the hot, stinging night. She wrenched the flowers from her dress, the bouquet that had turned all eyes; worn at the waist, like the romances she had read. But romance was over now. A pin tore her finger. The blood that ran was red enough, bright as a white girl's blood; the rest of her was chichi, and disgraced.

The Dragon had been dreaming. His legs twitched, his snufflings became more urgent; finally his eyes jerked open. They blazed momentarily with alarm; but the grass round him was undisturbed. The sun was lower now, the shadow of the fence creeping forward; and a breeze had risen, tempering the warmth of the day. He blinked, brushed briefly at his muzzle and scurried for the hedge. Just what the dream had been he could not recall; but there had been great shapes moving, noise and blood and fear. He made for the little shed, and the safety of his beansack.

Mrs. Byres straightened, rubbing her face a little ruefully. India, allegedly, was a land of ghosts; it seemed some had traveled with her, locked away behind the drawers and paneling, now to be released. She replaced the book on its shelf, walked through to her bedroom. She removed the inlaid combs, began, carefully, to brush out her hair.

She had not, of course, been able to remain in her employment; not after the shame she had brought. Thinking of that, her brow furrowed momentarily, her hands paused in their work. After the first anger, it had been the shame that was hardest to bear. Yet bear it she must, for she had transgressed. How, and in what manner, had been made hideously plain; and the tale had spread. The same thought was in all their minds, the same look in their eyes; Matron, the priest, her fellow workers on the wards, the casteless women who scrubbed and waxed the floors. She sat at her dressing table, then as now, touched the skin that had betrayed her while the great dark eyes watched back in misery; in the morning, she packed her things. But flee as she might, rise, as she strove to rise, in the esteem of others, the whispering pursued her. Despite her beauty, and beautiful she was alleged to be, she was a renegade, an outcast; a black girl who had tried to pass for white. Till finally she came to the high snows; and there at last, perhaps, was whiteness enough for all.

She brooded momentarily, eyes vague. That dream, too, was soon enough besmirched. They were harsh times, in the high hill stations; for the land itself was harsh. The land, and its people. The women came to her, trudging miles through snow, their bellies slit by jealousy, their entrails in their hands. She saved them, saved their babies; she became to them a god. But her own hands could never be clean again. The hills could never be clean; they were stained with more than sunset light. Until she watched the making of the mantras. She realized then that all was an illusion, that pain and suffering are fleeting as the pangs of joy. And there was peace at last.

Mrs. Byres rose, slipped a shawl round her shoulders. She walked down to the kitchen, began methodically preparing her evening meal. Later, the telephone rang. She eased the shawl back into place, went through to the hall. She stood a moment listening; then she smiled. "Of course, Sister," she said. "Yes, I'll come at once."

The Dragon was both puzzled and alarmed. His head rose, bobbed, ducked again till his long jaw all but touched the earth; his neck extended, telescoped with shock. He raised a claw uncertainly, set it back down; his body trembled, poised as if for flight. But it seemed he could not take his eyes from the scene in front of him.

There were strangers in the garden; the wild place that had once been part of his domain. The men advanced steadily; in their hands were strange devices that barked and screamed, jetted cones of bright blue smoke. Trees and bushes fell remorselessly; sunlight struck the walls beyond, at brash and unexpected angles.

The Dragon edged back, one foot at a time, toward the shelter of the hedge. The men were close to the fence now, his beautiful grass all but gone. A fire blazed brightly, fed by the dry swathes; later the smoke swirled low, adding its acridness to the fumes of petrol. Nictating membranes slid across the Dragon's eyes; he blinked, and his nerve broke abruptly. He scurried for home, quick as a flame himself, dived for his old lair beneath the garden shed.

The strangers seized the heaps of branches, breaking them roughly with their hands. They dragged them to the fire; and the flames licked up again. They blazed well into the night; when they finally died down, the Dragon once more ventured forth. He eased through the fence, approached the quivering bed of ash. Heat still radiated from it; the walls were lit by a dull and alien glow. He craned his neck, still only half believing. The garden had been reduced to a rectangle of earth and roots; an alien place, in which he could never feel secure again. He prospected sadly for a time; then he retired to his lair. He no longer felt safe, even on the beansack. He lay pressed to earth, watching the horizontal slit of lesser dark before him, his own eyes glowing a rich, reproachful amber. He wondered how his mistress, if indeed he thought of her as such, could have permitted such a thing; but Mrs. Byres, of course, had had no say in the matter. Vans had been arriving all day long at the house next door; in the small front garden, the blue and white board that had stood forlornly for so long had finally been removed.

He saw more strange things, in the days that followed.

The children the newcomers brought with them were unprepossessing. The girl, a pallid, dumpy creature, adopted the little attic bedroom for her own. She painted its walls blue, spent a week or more decorating them with hearts and rainbows. Mrs. Byres, divining the activity, smiled a little sadly to herself. The results, of course, would be gross. She wondered, not for the first time, at the lack of charity of the Christian god; to gracelessness he so often accords an equal lack of skill. At once, a certain Shade was in the room. Her husband, the Sahib. Strange how she still thought of him as that. It had always been a joke between them; or perhaps it had had its serious aspect. Perhaps the old ideas still lived in her, there was the notion of expiation. He smiled with equal sadness; and she bowed her head. Later, to ease her mind, she took up her sewing frame. On the linen grew broideries of other gods, dark dancing girls; finally, of Dragons. Their eyes were amber, their undersides ridged and pale; their bodies glittered with scales of green and gold. For a time she quite ignored the garden, and the pond. If she was disappointed at finding the shed deserted, she gave no sign of it; she had half expected it anyway. She still left the offerings of cereal; later she prepared her own meals, calmly. Each carrot scraped, each zucchini rinsed and halved, was itself an Act completed, needing no rationale.

Liam, the younger of the next door children, was coming six; though as yet he had spoken no words. In their place, he made certain sounds; his mother, a wispy, defeated-looking woman, knew the meaning of them all. The commonest, a throaty chuckle, meant that something was undergoing pain; though she had long since concluded it was best to turn a deaf ear. There was nothing wrong with the child, nothing that time wouldn't cure; and in any case the torture had its benefits. It stopped him squalling, got him out from underfoot. The screaming was too much for her, it was all too much; the house, the workmen, constant noise of hammering. One of the men brought a kitten for the boy; a tiny thing mewing and pot-bellied. Taken from the nest too young, if she was any judge; not that she cared overmuch for cats. Nasty dirty creatures, always underfoot like Liam. Nonetheless she did her best, only to be rewarded by messes. In the hall, under the sink, on the new-laid carpet. Her temper snapped at that; she added pepper to the filth, pushed the little creature's face into it to teach it better manners. Then Liam took it away, and she heard the chuckling start. Next morning it was dead; a damp rag of a thing, scarcely noticed till she all but stepped on it. Liam drowned it, in a hole he filled with water; he held its head down many times, for the pleasure of the bubbles, releasing it occasionally to allow it to cough and spit. But that was of equal unimportance; he was merely growing up a healthy, normal lad.

The Dragon watched the process, again with puzzlement. His raised claw quivered, his head weaved and bobbed; twice his tiny wings rose and rustled, as though he was indeed prepared to fly the scene. When it was over, and the small creature showed no more signs of life, the man-child lost interest. He stumped toward the house, forgetting his bucket and spade, bawling already for food.

The Dragon edged forward, across the dangerous open ground. He nuzzled the little animal; but its eyes were closed, the mud caked into its fur already beginning to stiffen into points. He stared up at the house. As ever, his expression was inscrutable; but it seemed that for a moment his eyes blazed with more than their customary fire.

In the house the woman lay back wearily, a glass in her hand. She drank from it deeply, felt the thirst that always seemed to be on her temporarily assuaged. As ever, she had tried to pace herself through the day. She had done well; supper was in the oven before she turned to the corner cupboard. There was ample need for caution. Only a moment ago, glancing into the garden, she was sure she had seen a flash of green and gold; as though some small, bright animal had scuttled beneath the hedge. She knew from experience what such visual portents meant. She had stiffened with alarm; but now, the gin fumes sliding into her brain, she was more relaxed.

At least Liam had drifted off to sleep; suddenly and unexpectedly, as was customary with him. He sprawled in the high chair they still used, remnants of food drying round his mouth. If only Mandy would stop making that goddam row though. The thudding from the record player drifted down the stairs, endless and repetitive; but her mother knew yelling would have no effect. She wouldn't even be heard. She lit a cigarette, glanced quickly at her wrist. Her husband would be home at six sharp; and supper had best be on the table, or he would know the reason why. There was time to finish the fag though.

Not that Tom hadn't been good to her, after his fashion; she had a lot really to be grateful for. He had his faults, but that was just his way. He took after his father; real chip off the old block, as he was found of proclaiming. And his Dad had been a wild one, in his younger days. She wished of course that she could talk to him about Liam; but the subject was a delicate one. Dangerous, if he was just back from the pub. He'd made his own way, like his father before him; these people in white coats, these doctors and psychiatrists, what did they know? Timeservers, the whole pack of them; ought to be given an honest job of work, find out what the world was really like. No son of his would ever need their help; if they knew what was good for them, they'd best keep out of his affairs.

The woman took another sip of gin. He'd had a lot to put up with; she always reminded herself of that. All those years slaving away; and him a full-fledged butcher, paid as a Meat Operative. The chance of promotion had been unexpected; but he'd grasped it with both hands, she was proud of him for that. He was a manager now; which was why they'd sunk every penny into buying the house. She'd been unsure. She hadn't argued though; Tom didn't pay for crossing, not when his mind was set. "Just think of it," he'd said. "Thirty bob an hour that's earning us, just by sitting there. Thirty-six quid a day. We can't lose . . ." And that had been the end of it.

She shivered slightly. The thought of white coats had conjured up an image of the *abattoir*; the slaughterhouse, as he preferred to call it. None of those fancy frog terms for him. The lines of men, alien in their protective clothing; hissing of the great hoses; and the flood of crimson, swirling toward the drains. She'd visited the place just once, at his insistence; but she'd refused to go again. Liam though had seemed excited; he'd cooed and chuckled, all the jolting journey home.

The noise from upstairs ceased abruptly. She looked up. Her daughter was standing pouting in the doorway. "I'm 'ungry," she said accusingly.

The woman stubbed her cigarette. "All right," she said tiredly. "All right, don't start. I'm comin' . . ."

The Dragon was in trouble; trouble of the worst possible sort.

It had all started innocently enough; innocently at least on his part. The folk next door had acquired, or had been given, a puppy; a four-month-old Alsatian, with paws like large soft sponges and a fine, glossy coat of tan and black. Liam's father, the squat, redfaced man the Dragon feared so much, had taken charge, hammering a great stake into the hard earth by the kitchen door. To it she was tethered, without benefit of kennel. Kennels cost hard-earned cash; besides, the dog was to grow up tough. Dogs should be tough and mean; and the process was to start at once. A plate of scraps was produced, and she was left alone. She keened for a while, interspersing the sounds with hopeful yaps; later it seemed she became resigned to her lot. She settled, nose on paws, watching the kitchen door a few feet away. Presently it opened, and a small boy appeared. He was chubby and fair-haired, and walked with a staggering, curiously uncertain gait. The pup's tail began to thump the ground; but he made no response. He stared down, expressionlessly; after a time he stumped away. When he returned, he was carrying a pointed stick. He gauged the distance, thrust it at the creature's face. She flinched, twisting her head, hampered by the shortness of the chain. The stick missed by inches. Liam thrust again, aiming for the eyes. He began to chuckle.

The Dragon had been attracted by the high-pitched sounds of misery. He left his foraging, eased his way under the hedge. He was unable for a time to locate the source of the distress; an old shed, built largely of tar paper, masked his view. The ugliest object in the garden, it was the one thing that had been suffered to remain. He was forced to advance farther than was advisable across the open ground. He gained, finally, the partial security of a stack of old crates; some of the rubbish the newcomers had brought with them. He was in time to see the puppy, tired of the lethal game, butt the small boy gently with her head. Liam sat down with a thump, and began to howl.

The house door popped open. In her hand, the thin woman clutched an old-fashioned carpet beater. She wielded it, tight-lipped; and the dog began to scream.

The Dragon was transfixed. There was a time, perhaps, when he was confused; but pain-signals are not to be mistaken. He blinked and hissed, scrabbling with his claws; but once again, his instincts were in conflict. A part of him wished perhaps to aid the sufferer; but his paramount need was to stay concealed, hidden from the eyes of all but Mrs. Byres. She, certainly, would never have allowed such a thing; but Mrs. Byres was not at home. The knowledge added to his helplessness; he danced on the spot, in an agony of indecision.

It seemed the beating went on for an age. When it was over, the pup retreated to the farthest extent of her chain and was sick. A final imprecation; and the house door closed with a bang. The Dragon ducked and gulped; and the light above him was occulted.

He glared up, blinking. He had stayed too long. Liam was

standing over him. His eyes were gleaming; and in his hand was the pointed stick.

The Dragon fled, flame-fast; down the path, into and through the hedge. He dived beneath the hut, scrabbled his way as far as possible into the dark. He hissed again and panted, claws gripping the earth; and in front of him the light was once more blocked. The boy still gripped the weapon; and his movements, now his interest was focused, had become more purposive. He lay down, puffing a little, began to work his way into the narrow gap. The stick wobbled, moving steadily closer.

The Dragon took a great breath, and another. He was trapped; it seemed his heart, in its pounding, might break clear of his body. The stick jabbed; and the fear that was in him exploded, in a great burst of light and heat. The light was dazzling almost, in the confined space.

Mrs. Byres was late back from the hospital. It had not been one of her normal days for visiting; but a lunchtime call had needed her attention and she had stayed on, moving quietly from ward to ward, helping calm and settle the new patients. She spoke to all in the language of their birth, or in a close approximation. The Hindi she had learned at her mother's knee, the Pushtoo she had acquired in circumstances frequently distressing and bizarre; but she had a working knowledge of many other dialects. She knew these people, understood their pride and fear; from small beginnings she had become a tower of strength to patients and staff alike. Though the notion would have been the last to enter her mind. The Surgeon-Registrar, himself a hardworked Anglo-Indian, realized her worth; and his word carried weight. He it was who had defended her, in no uncertain terms, when Admin queried her non-official presence; but of that she was equally unaware. The great place needed her, it needed many like her; but they were seldom to be found.

She rubbed her eyes tiredly, as the bus ground up the long hill toward her home. Today it seemed much power had flowed from her, so that she felt drained; though that of course was a mere effect of age. It had troubled the

Reverend Byres, the Sahib, increasingly as his ministry drew toward its close. Though of course he had never yielded to fatigue; if anything, he had driven himself the harder. She would chide him for it, gently; but his answer was always the same. He would take her hand and draw her to him, where he lay back in the long cane chair. "The Lord provides the work, Richenda," he would say, smiling. "It is up to us to provide the strength." And she would smile in turn, lay her hand softly on his forehead; while the fans swished, moths chirred in the endless, velvet night. The image had stayed with her, strongly; it was with her now. She did not resent it; rather she welcomed its recurrences. It was a comfort sent by that same Lord, whoever he might be.

The bus had reached her stop; she climbed down, waited her opportunity to cross the wide, endlessly busy road. She turned the corner, past the old cinema that was now a supermarket, headed toward her house.

She paused, frowning slightly. The normally quiet street was full of bustle. Neighbors gawped and clustered; lights of amber and blue flashed from the roofs of cars. The reflections dazzled; so that she raised an arm to shield her eyes, her purse, with the keys, still gripped in her other hand. There were policemen with radios and clipboards, others who wore vivid orange surcoats. The questions confused her momentarily. Yes, she was Mrs. Byres; yes, this was her home. In what way could she help?

A shouting began. Who though was this squat, redfaced man, waving his arms so furiously? She recognized her neighbor, vaguely; the husband of the family who had moved next door. Yet it was not her neighbor. Anger depersonalizes; she had seen such raging faces once before. They surrounded the car in which she sat, helpless; while fists beat at the roof and windows, the Sahib struggled vainly to start the engine. They had been his parishioners once, his friends perhaps; but they were his friends no longer. They had become possessed.

Mrs. Byres shook her head. Someone, it seemed, had been hurt. The child, the stolid, curiously silent boy.

Burned, by some chemical; some noxious substance hidden in her shed.

She stepped back, bemused; and the shouting was redoubled. There was the proof, if they needed it; the guilt was written on her face.

But she owned no chemicals, kept nothing there at all. Some garden tools, old newspapers perhaps; they were welcome to see for themselves.

The squalling had not finished. Nor would it, she realized. The man's rage was directed at the world; a cloak and justification for his own inadequacy. Liam, his son, had been seen crawling from her shed. Crawling and screaming, smoke coming from his very clothes. They might yet save his sight; but if she had seen his face. His poor, swollen face . . .

Mrs. Byres opened the front door quietly, moved forward with the others at her heels. She had seen disfigured faces times enough; most had belonged to corpses. One had been her husband.

The handlamps flashed suspiciously, in the little shed. The beams touched ceilings, walls and floor. The policemen prized the lids from paint cans, sniffed solemnly and agreed. There was nothing here.

Still the man had not done. The stuff was in the house. Or she had got wind of what had happened. Yes, that was it; she'd slipped back in the afternoon, disposed of the evidence. Her, the nigger, come to this respectable street, disrupting the lives of decent folk, poisoning their children. Yes, poisoning their children. He grabbed her arm, and shook.

The bullet shattered her wrist; the one shot fired by the mob as the car finally jolted away. There was no pain as such; she stared instead at the sudden red tunnel through her flesh. Then the spurting began; and she reached methodically to find the pressure points.

The ball had struck a double mark; the carpet was stained beneath the Sahib's seat, his fingers slippery where they gripped the wheel. She said, "You'd best drive to the hospital," but he had shaken his head. "I'm sorry, my dear," he said faintly. "I don't think I can make it." He had, of course; he always completed what he undertook. But it was not Byres Sahib they wheeled into Emergency; the spirit had already fled.

The rioting had spread by then. A lampshade swung and shattered; the orderly who dressed her arm crouched below the level of the windows. The wound healed; but her wrist had never recovered its strength. Now she gave a faint cry, at the sudden pain.

The Dragon heard the sound from where he waited, and his last doubts were resolved. His mistress was in danger; and he felt the strength rise in him. He was growing too, expanding by the second. He reared and bellowed, turned his blazing eyes on the tiny folk below him. His neck arched; flame roared from his jaws. It licked at the houses and the street, the people and the cars. It circled Mrs. Byres, protecting; the others were engulfed. They were dazzled by the glare, and were never subsequently able to explain what happened. "Some sort of thunderbolt it was," confided one young constable to his superior. "Hit the house, then sort of bounced off somehow. Must have done; stands to reason." The sergeant shook his head, riffled the papers in his hands and suggested he start again. Thunderbolts don't go down well, in police reports; the elastic variety least of all.

The erstwhile butcher alone saw what opposed them; so that he ran screaming, and was glad enough, later, of the white coats that surrounded him, the security they brought. He told the tale over and again; the great head swooping from the sky, the burning eyes, cat-slitted in their rage, the mouth that barraged fire. To see it was to see into Hell. The doctors wrote busily, stroking their neat-trimmed beards; then they drove home to their neat suburban villas, where their children placed their toys on labeled shelves. Logic was triumphant.

Hysteria readily becomes infectious. The panic spread outward from the focus at lightning speed. The street outside the house became filled with fleeing bodies, tumbling over each other in their haste to escape they knew not what. The airwaves became garbled. Pistols and riot guns were issued, police cars growled from their yards. The Dragon roared and bobbed, cloud-tall now and lighting up the sky. Hot winds tore at Mrs. Byres' clothes. She raised her arms; and his wings unfolded, with a crashing like the long sound of thunder. He soared, gleeful and avenging, into his new element.

The stories became wilder. Reports spread, of a beast that terrified the city; there were tales of fireballs, comets, alien invasions. Lightning flashed and flickered; strange plasmas boiled and spread. The most commonplace of objects, trees and housetops, garden sheds, were outlined with a fierce and spectral glare. In the confusion the Alsatian pup broke free and bolted, having in her mind the beginnings of a thought that subsequently proved true; that the world is a large place, and is not filled exclusively with folk who chain animals to stakes, beat them with wire frames. Nothing more was heard of the unfortunate Liam; while his mother ended her flight on the very edge of town. At which point it seemed best to keep on walking. She and her daughter settled finally in a rural slum, where at least the daily stress was less.

The Dragon writhed forlornly, immense now and himself as vaporous as clouds. The shots, the missiles, tore into him and through. The feeling was defocused; but there was none the less a sense of pain. He realized at that the nature of release, the plane to which he properly belonged. A last convulsion; and far off a woman screamed. A gout of something dark and sticky splashed her wrist; the strange rain pattered on the path around her. She stared; but even as she watched, the spots boiled away to nothing. She set off for home, puzzled at the hallucination; if hallucination it had been. She had read books on the subject; the strangest of phenomena can be explained. Freak winds snatch up red desert mud, whirl it with tornado force; insects in their mass emergences release a bloodlike fluid. Nonetheless she paused, a hand on her garden gate. The sky to the west was furnace red; across it, the last cloud streak of evening took the sinuous form of a Dragon.

• • •

The eastern sky was clear and green, the air cool after the disturbed night. Mrs. Byres moved quietly, from the house to the raised pool. She scotched on its edge; ploppings sounded as she scattered food from the round tin she carried. She adjusted the shawl across her shoulders, watched for a while; then she walked to the little shed. Its door was ajar; on the step she placed a china bowl, blue patterns round its edge. She paused a moment longer; then on a whim she plumped up the beanbag that lay at the rear of the little place. The Dragon would be tired, after his adventurings; he would need somewhere to rest.

Straightening, she half smiled. From the tail of her eye she had caught a flash of green and gold; as if some small animal indeed scuttered beneath the hedge. She didn't though stare after him or search; instead she walked to the house, and gently closed the kitchen door.

A Handful of Hatchlings
by
Mark C. Sumner

Here's a fast-paced and fascinating look at a world where dragons are not *the stuff of legends, where instead they are a problem that must be dealt with in the ordinary, everyday world—and dealt with damn* carefully *at that!*

New writer Mark C. Sumner has sold to Dragon Magazine *and to* Isaac Asimov's Science Fiction Magazine, *as well as to other magazines and anthologies. He was a first-place winner in the Writers of the Future contest, and has just sold his first young adult novel. He lives in Arnold, Missouri.*

* * *

The wyvern twisted its skinny neck and looked at me with dull yellow eyes. Then it tucked its snout back under a tattered wing and appeared to sleep.

A sign informed me that the animal was a Golden Spade-Tailed Wyvern, the gift of a Chinese emperor, and the oldest resident of the zoo. Another sign warned against throwing coins. The ancient wyvern was half-blind from the impact of errant pennies.

I rested my hands on the brass railing and squinted through the mesh of the cage at the withered sides of the emperor's gift. If the animal's hide had once matched the color of its name, it had since darkened until the whole of the beast was a flat, leathery black. The skin seemed dry and loosely draped over jutting bones. The long snout was wrinkled and incredibly ugly.

I turned away, walked past long rows of exotic lizards and snakes and pushed open the front door of the reptile house, relieved to be free of the thick gamy air. Across a broad walking path, the tall concrete aries of Dragon Mountain were dotted with visitors. At the grassy base of the artificial hill, children slid over verdigris-stained, life-sized bronzes of a dozen dragon species.

"Find any old friends running loose?" said a voice.

I turned and saw Janey coming toward me up the sloping path. "No," I said. "Looks like they've got all their beasties under lock and key."

She stopped in front of me. "That's good. They'd probably get upset if you started shooting their exhibits." In her colorful dress, and with her face carefully made up, she didn't look much like the Janey I'd fallen in love with. Not that she didn't look awfully good, great actually, just not like the blue-jeans-and-sweatshirt girl I knew. She stared at my face, frowned, and landed a gentle punch on my shoulder. "What's wrong?"

"Nothing," I said. "Just thinking that you look like you're ready to settle in to city life."

She laughed. "Come off it, cowboy. You're from L.A. I'm the one from Montana, remember?"

I tugged at my wide-brimmed hat, suddenly conscious that it was the only piece of headgear in sight that didn't bear the logo of a sports team.

"I've got someone here I want you to meet," said Janey.

That's when I noticed the kid standing behind her. He was a head taller than me, skinny, with the kind of flannel shirt and sleeveless vest that rich college kids wear when they want to look "woodsy."

He stepped forward and stuck out a long hand. "I'm Thom Marion. Thom with an 'h,'" he said. "I work with the Drake Rehabilitation Center. We help animals that have been shot, or hit by cars, or things like that."

"Doesn't that sound wonderful?" asked Janey as I shook his hand.

"Sure," I said, "very nice."

"Thom, this is my friend Bill Mackie."

He pulled his hand back sharply. "The one that used to shoot endangered species from an airplane?"

"Look," I said. "I only shot one endangered wyvern in my whole life. I paid a big fine, lost my license, and I'm sorry as heck. Okay?"

Janey stepped between us. "Thom was just telling me something interesting. Why don't you tell Bill about it?"

"We've got a problem," said Thom-with-an-'h'. "And we were hoping that, with Ms. Bochie's experience in working with large drakes, she might be able to help us."

I felt a sinking feeling in my stomach.

"There's this dragon," he said. "It's nesting on a building downtown."

"Take a look." Janey handed the binoculars to me.

I squinted, turning the knob until the monolithic side of the building jumped into clear view. At first I saw nothing but acres of tinted glass and panel after panel of imported Italian marble. Then I came to a ledge and saw the dark mass of material that was gathered there. "I see something that looks like a pile of wood. Is that it?"

"Yes," said Janey. "It's the nest of a large drake."

"Drake?" I said, lowering the binoculars. "You mean it is a dragon?"

"Or a really large wyvern." She shrugged. "Arboreal species of both families build similar nests. Has to be a wyvern. I guess, no dragons in the U.S. But I've never seen one build a nest like this."

"Oh, it's a dragon," said Thom. "I've seen it myself."

I handed the binoculars back to Janey. "Whatever it is, that nest looks big enough to raise a family of buffalo."

Janey spent a few seconds looking at the nest again, then gave the binoculars to Thom. "No sign of the nest maker at the moment. Okay, so you've got a large drake nesting in an urban area. It's unusual, but exactly what is the problem? Has the drake hurt anyone?"

"Naw," said Thom. "Nothing like that. The problem is with Americo Life Insurance, the building's owner. They're worried about damage to the building, tenants leaving, lawsuits, things like that. They've gone to the city and gotten a permit to trap or kill the dragon. They're going after it today."

"How long has the nest been there?" asked Janey.

"Over a month. Almost two."

Thom and Janey stared at each other with such force I had

to break in. "Would somebody mind telling me why that's important?"

"A big drake only nests for one reason," said Janey, "to lay eggs. And if the nest has been there for as long as Thom says, the eggs must be near to hatching."

"Great," I said. "Just what we need. A big lizard with a nest full of eggs."

"Those babies will need food within a few hours of hatching. If they take away the mother now, the babies will die." Janey turned to Thom. "Is your center equipped to care for drake infants?"

Thom nodded.

"Then let's go."

By the time we'd gone back to our hotel and changed clothes, swung by the Drake Rehabilitation Center for some equipment, and waded our way through the representatives of Americo Life, the sun had dipped below the lower buildings to the east and the sky was beginning to get dark. At last, accompanied by a security guard and an elevator full of gear, we were headed for the thirty-sixth floor.

It was a maintenance floor, with knots of industrial air conditioners, elevator motors, and power boxes spaced in a huge expanse of unfinished concrete. There were no windows, but the guard showed us an access panel that lead out to the ledge.

I grabbed the handle of the panel and started to run.

"Watch out for the pressure differential," said the security guard.

Immediately, the hatch was pulled out of my hand with enough force that it almost took me with it. I found myself with my legs still inside the building, my chest lying on the ledge and my head hanging in the void with a great view of the street five hundred feet below. Hands grabbed at my belt and hauled me back inside.

Janey held me by the shoulders and said something, but I couldn't hear it over the pounding of my heart. She helped me away from the opening, and I took a few minutes to catch my breath.

"Be careful, Bill," said Janey. "Here, put on your

harness." She handed me a contraption of nylon straps and buckles hung with aluminum D-rings. Attached to one side was a length of colorful rope that ended with a spring-loaded clip. I turned the thing round and round, trying to figure out how to put it on. "What do we do with this?"

"There's a cable strung above the ledge that's used by the window washing platform," said Thom. "We can clip our ropes onto that."

When I had finally struggled into my harness, I saw that Janey and Thom had already gotten into their gear and were advancing on the open hatch. "Have I got this right?" I asked.

Janey stepped back from the panel and gave my harness a couple of tugs. She tightened one of the buckles until it was painfully snug. "Looks good," she said. "Ready to go out?"

I walked over to the hatch. A strong wind was still gusting through the opening. "Can't we wait for the wind to calm down?"

"Wind never calms," volunteered the security guard. "It's the pressure . . ."

"Right," I said. "The pressure differential." I stuck my head out and looked down the ledge. At the corner of the building, through some whim of the architect's design, the ledge belled out into a platform at least thirty feet on a side. That was where the drake had built its nest. In between the nest and the hatch was fifty feet of ledge that was something less than a yard wide. And when I looked over the edge . . .

I jerked back inside, panting.

Janey was looking at me funny. "Don't tell me that William Mackie, ace pilot, is afraid of heights?"

"There is a big difference between flying a plane and hanging on the side of a building," I said.

"Yeah," said Thom, coming up beside us. "Planes can fall. Ropes are more trustworthy."

"Look," I said, "I've put in thousands of hours in the air and I've never had an accident."

"What about . . ." started Janey.

"Okay. One accident, but it wasn't the plane's fault."

"It's okay, Janey," said Thom. "I'll go out first."

"Oh no, you won't." I walked over to the hatch and leaned out, fighting my reeling stomach.

"Will you both just get out of the way?" said Janey. She reached through the hatch and snapped her rope onto the stout cable. Then she boosted herself through the opening and walked slowly away down the ledge.

Just watching her made me dizzy, but I reached up with numb fingers and buckled myself on. One last silent prayer and I followed her toward the nest.

The ledge was made of the same polished marble as the rest of the stonework. Not the best surface in the world to walk on. Add to that the attention it had obviously garnered from the city's pigeons, and it made for pretty unhealthy footing. I took a few moments to decide between facing the street or facing the wall. I decided I wanted the edge in front of me where I could keep an eye on it, so I slid along the ledge with the wall at my back.

One foot at a time, I moved toward the nest. Where we stood near the top of the building, the tower was stained red by the setting sun. When I risked a look down, I could see that the base of the building was already in darkness and the cars on the street below had turned on their lights. It seemed like I traveled miles down that ledge before my foot bumped against a chunk of driftwood that must have been dropped by the builder of the giant nest. The knot of wood tottered for a moment, then tipped and plunged off the ledge. "Oops," I said, hoping that no one chanced to be walking below.

A few more steps and I was away from the narrow part of the ledge and onto the relative safety of the wide corner platform. I looked around and saw Janey kneeling among the scraps of rotting wood and rusty metal that made up the nest.

"Any eggs," I asked.

She shook her head. "Not eggs. Babies." She lifted a tiny beast from the pile of debris. The hatchling moved slowly, holding its red-lined mouth open toward her. I noted that it already had a full complement of small, but wicked-looking, teeth. "There's five of them," she said. "They all seem to be healthy."

Thom stepped out onto the ledge. He moved with the assurance of a veteran rock climber, crossing the ledge in a few quick hops, and dropped easily into the nest. He reached for one of the babies. "See," he said, "told you it was a dragon."

The baby he was holding not only had a pair of wings, but four legs as well. Though I was no real expert on drakes, I knew enough to recognize the one clear characteristic that separated the two families of flying reptiles: wyverns have two legs, dragons have four.

The babies were about the size of adult cats, with droopy, wet-looking wings that were far too small to support their weight. They were emerald green, with stripes of yellow and red that looked artificial. If they hadn't been moving, I would have sworn they were the product of some toy company.

Janey was examining the intricate markings on their bellies. "From what I can remember of juvenile dragons, these are either one of the Welsh varieties or some African species."

"What are they doing here?" I asked.

"Somebody probably brought in the parents as pets," said Thom.

"We had some rich hotshot that actually smuggled in a pair of African Redeyes a few years back. Real conversation piece . . . until they ate him."

"Well, these little fellows must have all hatched within the last couple of hours," said Janey. "Their egg teeth are still attached." She stood up and brushed rotted wood from her jeans.

"Okay. Thom, you take one of the babies inside, get the cages set up, and come back for another. Bill and I will make some measurements out here, then bring in the rest."

Thom gave a casual salute and stepped out onto the ledge. In seconds, he was inside with the first baby.

Janey had me go through the nest, calling out the sizes of

the bits of refuse used in its construction. Among the items I found were a pair of wooden bar stools, a large number of old mattress springs, and a neat stack of chrome hubcaps. When Janey had gotten this information down in her note pad, we used a tape measure to get the diameter of the roughly circular nest.

We hadn't finished before the sun slipped behind the horizon and it was suddenly and almost completely dark. The only illumination was provided by the distant lights on the street below and by a sky that glowed with the yellow-brown reflection of those lights.

Thom came bouncing back along the window ledge with a flashlight in hand. "The first one's tucked away," he said. "Ready for another?"

"There's nothing else we can do here in the dark," said Janey. "Let's get the babies inside, and we can come back to finish looking at the nest in the morning."

I was none too excited about the idea of another day spent out on the ledge, but I was awfully anxious to get back inside. I handed one hatchling to Janey, and another to Thom. The last two had crawled under a length of rotting tree, and it took me a few seconds to work one loose.

Thom helped Janey back onto the ledge, giving her a little more assistance than I thought she needed. As Janey started her walk along the ledge, I noticed that the security guard had stuck his head through the hatch and was waving at us madly. He was shouting something, but the wind snatched his words away.

"What's he saying?" asked Thom.

"I think he's trying to tell us that their plan to trap the mother didn't pan out," I told him.

"How do you know?"

"Look." I pointed past his shoulder.

A shadow moved across the evening sky, an inky shape that was growing larger with frightening speed.

"Janey!" I shouted. "Run!" I turned to Thom. "Quick, get inside." Thom's eyes were fastened on the approaching shape. Not risking a glance myself, I shook him. "Come on, get moving!"

Thom snapped out of it and jumped out onto the ledge, encumbered by the baby under his arm. He took a step, overbalanced, whirled his free arm, and barely remained upright. He took another step toward the open hatch.

I climbed onto the ledge, the fourth baby tucked under my arm. The dragon came rushing past with a roar that made my bones vibrate. Just ahead of me, Thom took another step, but his eyes were on the dragon, not on the ledge, and his step took him into space.

I scrambled forward, falling to my knees as I approached the spot where Thom had vanished, and peered downward at the dizzying view. At first I didn't see Thom. A shout from my right showed me that his rope had held and he was swinging only a few feet below the ledge.

The dragon shot past again. The clawed tip of its wing struck the building above my head, gouging a path through a metal frame and showering me with chips of broken marble. The wind of its passage almost sent me down to join Thom, but I managed to crawl along the ledge to the hatch and shove the squalling baby drake into Janey's waiting hands.

The dragon was coming. I didn't have to look to know that, I could feel it, like a pressure coming down from above. I lay on my belly, reaching blindly downward, and managed to grasp Thom's upraised hand.

Thom came over the ledge with blood pouring from his swollen nose.

The dragon went screaming past just below us.

My arm was wrenched as some part of the dragon struck Thom. His face went pale, and his eyes rolled back. I heard glass shatter as the dragon hit the windows on the floor below. Another pull brought Thom's shoulders into view. Amazingly, the baby dragon was still with him, its tiny claws digging into his plaid shirt. I dropped his limp hand, grabbed his harness, and shoved him and the baby through the hatch. Then I dived through headfirst, landing between a pair of yowling baby dragons.

The mother dragon made another pass, its head sweeping just above the ledge. With a clatter of metal and the crack of breaking wood, it landed heavily in the nest. It stretched its long neck toward us and made a last bellow of protest. Then the horse-sized head fell into the nest.

For long minutes, no one moved. We sat there on the concrete floor in the dark, just breathing. I, for one, was glad to be breathing.

Janey got up and went over to Thom. She shone her flashlight into his eyes, and gingerly lifted the cuff of his jeans. "The wing must have struck him in the shin," she said. "There's a compound fracture here. It's not bleeding badly, but it's going to hurt like hell when he comes to."

"Uh, why don't I go call for an ambulance?" asked the security guard.

"Why don't you?" I said.

The guard walked away, and Janey took his flashlight over to the hatch. I followed, rubbing at the strained muscles in my left arm.

"Look," said Janey. The white circle of her light glinted off a metal bolt that protruded from the thick tail of the dragon. As she moved the light up the body, wounds could be seen in its back, its legs, its neck.

"Good God," I said.

Janey nodded. "Looks like their capture plan wasn't very neat."

I wrapped my aching arms across her shoulders, feeling her painful tension. "I'm sorry."

She pulled away. "We've got to get the last baby."

"What? Now?"

"Yes."

I looked out at the dark mass of the dragon. "Are you nuts? You want to go back onto a ledge, five hundred feet in the air, in the dark, and steal a baby dragon away from its mother. While the mother's there. Oh, and besides that, the dragon's hurt. Have I got it right?"

She put her hand on my arm. "Bill, that dragon is mortally wounded. It may even be dead already. If it's dead, the baby will starve before morning. If the mother's still alive, it could easily crush the baby in its death throes." She moved away from me, quickly inspected her harness, and began to climb through the hatch.

I knew that if I gave myself time to think, my knees would start shaking far too much to ever walk that slippery ledge, so I clambered through the hatch right behind her. It seemed quieter now. The traffic in the streets had diminished to a trickle, and many of the buildings were dark. Night birds flew past, and I saw a larger shape that might have been some small urban drake out to catch its evening meal. Out on the river, the tugboats had turned on their searchlights, and the wide beams swept endlessly across the brown water. I reached the nest and stepped carefully into the loose mass of material.

There were soft clanks of metal as Janey searched through the nest for the last baby. "I don't see it," she whispered. "I'm afraid the mother might have landed on it."

I edged forward, my eyes on the bulky form of the inert dragon. "I'll look." I tripped over a piece of wood and almost stepped on the dragon's tail.

"Careful!" hissed Janey.

"Right, right. Wait a minute, I see something. Shine your light over here."

She turned her flashlight where I pointed, and the light caught the brilliant green of the baby. It was sitting beside the foreleg of its fallen parent, its tiny claws scratching weakly at the adult dragon's scaly hide. When the light struck it, the baby turned toward us and let out a pitiful cry.

"Come here, little guy," I said. I stepped carefully through the debris of the nest and reached down for the tiny dragon. Its side was wet with the blood of its mother.

"Okay," said Janey. "Let's go."

The baby dragon bit me. Its needle-sharp teeth sliced into the tender skin between my thumb and index finger. I stumbled back with the baby dangling from my hand and fell against the mother dragon.

The big dragon surged to its feet. Its neck whipped around and the warm wash of its breath swept over me. For a moment I was staring into the fist-sized eye, then the jaws darted forward and yellow sparks flashed as the dragon's teeth closed on the metal rings of my harness. It lifted me from the ground and tossed me over the side.

The baby dragon screamed as we fell. There was an abrupt jerk as we hit the end of the belay, everything swung sideways, then I was through the window that the dragon had shattered in its attack on Thom. Either the dragon's teeth or the glass of the window must have weakened the rope. It parted and I fell to the floor.

I lay on my face in a carpeted office on the thirty-fifth floor, my hands and arms cut by broken glass. The baby dragon released its death-grip on my bleeding hand and crawled away. Behind me the mother dragon bellowed.

I climbed to my feet and went to the broken window. "Janey! You okay?" No answer.

There was a whistling sound from above. It started out high and distant, but the pitch went down and the volume went rapidly up. The dragon was coming. Fast. I turned, bent, grabbed the baby by its tail, and ran from the office.

The wall of windows imploded as the dragon smashed its way into the building.

I ran out into the hallway, trying to move and look back at the same time, stumbling against furniture, looking for some clue that would lead me toward the elevators. The dragon smashed easily through the plaster wall of the office. Wings folded, it came down the hall with rapid steps, its shoulders knocking pictures from the walls and its taloned feet tearing at the carpet. I slid around a corner as the dragon swatted aside desks and office chairs. The baby dragon clawed at the air as he swung by his tail from my hand. I started toward an open door when I spotted the white and red of an exit sign glowing in the distance. Putting everything I had into it, I sprinted toward the sign.

The exit sign didn't mark the elevators, it marked the door to the stairs. At the moment, the idea of going down thirty-five flights of stairs didn't sound bad at all—as long as the dragon wouldn't fit. I grabbed the door and pulled.

It was locked.

"You can't do this!" I shouted at the door. "There's a fire code!"

A copy machine went tumbling down the hall behind me, and I turned to see the dragon smashing its way through a series of flimsy partitions. I ran on.

Sure that I was heading toward the center of the building, I ran past dozens of offices and hallways. Then I turned through a wide door flanked with potted trees, passed a long conference table, and came to a dead end. It was a corner office, windows on two sides, with a huge glass-top desk, sparse arrogantly modern furniture, and a pair of fancy floor lamps. Obviously, it was the lair of some big-time executive. I would have preferred a broom closet.

The elevator bell sounded, tantalizingly near. I turned to retrace my steps.

The dragon turned the corner, blocking my path. It had slowed to a stumbling walk. Blood poured from the wounds on its head and neck, splashing on the tasteful carpet. It made a coughing noise, and bloody froth spilled from its mouth. With a shudder that sent nearby furniture flying, the dragon collapsed. The slit-pupiled eyes closed.

I leaned back against the glass desk, the adrenaline draining from my body and leaving me with painful fatigue. I could hear the faint sound of sirens from the street outside. By now every police car, fire truck, and ambulance in the city was probably on its way.

The baby dragon made a plaintive cry.

Immediately, the big dragon's head came up and it let out a hiss like a ruptured steam boiler. It pushed through the office door, widening the frame significantly. It snapped at me, its teeth coming within arm's length of my head.

I dropped the baby and looked frantically around the office for anything that could be a weapon. Grabbing one of the tall floor lamps, I made a major league swing, smashing the base of the lamp into the jaw of the dragon.

The dragon lifted a foreleg and slammed the lamp from my hands. A sideswipe of its head threw me against the glass wall, a fine spiderweb of cracks radiating out from my impact. The head lowered slowly, the bloody snout opening.

Janey ran into the room and snatched up the lamp. As the dragon started to turn her way, she jammed the business end of the lamp right down its throat.

The long neck snapped back, arching over the dragon's bleeding body. Blue fire played along its teeth, and smoke came from its dozens of wounds. The beast's eyes turned milky, then black.

Steam curling from its nostrils, the great head swung down.

I looked up, unable to move, as the head struck me, knocked me through the broken window, and sent me into the darkness.

I opened my eyes, stared at the ceiling, and said, "I'm not dead."

"Well, you're obviously as brilliant as you ever were." Janey leaned into my blurry, rotating field of view. She reached down and ran a hand softly over my cheek. "You've been out for almost twenty hours," she said. "How do you feel?"

I tried to sit up, but my stomach and head told me that lying down was a much better idea. "Terrible, but not as bad as I expected. I thought I was going to be a wet spot on Broadway."

Janey smiled. "You would have been, if the dragon's neck hadn't fallen across your legs and pinned you down."

I closed my eyes, hoping I could get back to sleep before the twinges of pain that I was beginning to feel became full-blown agony.

"Oh," said Janey. "I got a phone call while you were under. Another job offer."

"I hope it's studying butterflies," I said.

I feel asleep to the sound of her laughter.

Covenant with a Dragon
by
Susan Casper

Susan Casper made her first fiction *sale to Charles L. Grant's anthology* Fears *in 1983 (she sold several word search puzzles and logic problems to* Isaac Asimov's Science Fiction Magazine *all the way back to 1977, but she doesn't count those), and has subsequently gone on to sell short work to* Playboy, Amazing, The Magazine of Fantasy and Science Fiction, The Twilight Zone Magazine, Isaac Asimov's Science Fiction Magazine *(fiction this time!), and to many original horror anthologies such as* Shadows, Whispers, *and* Midnights. *She is co-editor, with Gardner Dozois, of the horror anthology* Ripper!, *and has just completed her first novel,* The Red Carnival. *Born in Philadelphia, she lives there still, although she has managed to move a number of blocks away from the actual hospital where she was born in the years gone by since then.*

Here she gives us a compelling look at a child caught quite literally between two worlds, a child who has powerful enemies—but, fortunately, also has powerful friends. . . .

* * *

She reached for him. It was not unusual for Richard to feel her hand slipping through the covers in that hazy time between sleep and wakefulness, a gentle touch to see if he, too, was awake and wanting, and knowing this, he feigned sleep. She made no attempt to wake him, merely rested her fingers against his thigh for just a moment and then slowly moved them away. As soon as her hand was gone he was sorry that he hadn't responded. He disliked disappointing her even in small ways, but he just couldn't bring himself to make love to her this morning. Carol had not been the woman he'd been dreaming of in the sultry heat of that lonely summer.

Too many times in the last few weeks he had given in to

the temptation and held Carol in his arms pretending that she was Thot. It never worked very well. The textures were wrong—skin and hair—and the scent. Carol was candy sweet compared to Thot's heady musk. Besides, Carol was his wife. Even if she never guessed, and he wondered sometimes if she might not already know, it wasn't right to use her as a substitute for long-dead dreams. Thot had been too much on his mind of late. More than she had been through all the last decade. More than she had when he first returned home. He had no idea why.

He reached up and clutched the little carving of a dragon that always hung on a leather thong around his neck. The memories came. Romantic ones at first—sweetly scented flowers, gentle heat, the laughter he shared with Thot as she gave him the carving and tried to convince him that it would help keep him safe—but he made an effort of will and slowly the reality began to penetrate. For the first time in a long time he saw the squalid house, ruined by war, invaded by insects. He could hear the baby cry and once again felt a desperate desire to go and comfort her . . . to assure her that things would be all right when he knew that there was no such assurance. The pain in his leg throbbed as he searched the debris while his world crumbled and hope collapsed within him. He grasped the dragon, holding it tightly in his fist, and allowed the pain to ease slowly away.

"Honey, are you okay? It's getting late." Carol's voice startled him back to reality. He noted the look of concern on her face and forced himself to smile.

"Of course I am," he said. He pounced, grabbing her suddenly by the shoulders and forcing her back against the pillows. "One for you," he said, kissing her cheek, "and one for Godzilla," he added, bending to kiss the barely noticeable bulge of her abdomen. He rolled out of the bed and began to get dressed. "Remember, Pop's coming home from the hospital tonight, so we're eating at Dom and Marie's."

He said good-bye to his son and went out into the early morning breeze. His brother Joey had often offered to pick him up with the truck on his way back from the food distribution center, but it was so beautiful in the mornings before the worst of the day's weather hit, and only a handful of people on the streets. Besides, it wasn't such a long walk.

The market was already a busy place when he got there. Angelina Lo Patto was emptying a bucket of ice into her display window, for the squid and porgies and filets of bluefish, cod, and flounder to rest on. Outside her store were barrels of live crabs and buckets of mussels and clams. Several of the butchers were laying out bright red cuts of meat delivered fresh from the slaughterhouse around the corner, and the poultry men were stacking crates of squawking birds and frantically scrabbling rabbits waiting to be selected for their moment of glory. Mrs. Ly, an elderly Vietnamese woman who was the newest vendor in his block of the market, had just let herself out of her son's station wagon to begin setting up her card table across the street.

Joey was late with the truck. There were no crates to be pried open, no oranges to tumble out onto the dusty gray planks of his rickety stand, no onions to rustle their brown paper skins in the cool morning breeze. He lit a cigarette and leaned back against the cool bricks of the spice store to wait. Across the street, Mrs. Ly's son piled boxes on the sidewalk so that the children with him could unpack their goodies onto the table. There were always groups of children around Mrs. Ly's stand in the mornings. So many, that he had been unable to keep himself from asking her once if they were all hers. How she had laughed. Two were her grandchildren, the rest belonged to the other families who shared the rented house with her. All came to help from time to time, and Richie loved to watch them as they stopped to play, got in each other's way, and occasionally broke some of the merchandise. When that happened, Mrs. Ly would cuff the offender soundly, yelling all the while in short, unintelligible, singsong bursts. Most of the children were very young, but today there was an older girl with them, wearing one of those purple balloon coats that had been the rage a year or so ago. She worked with her back to him, setting out rows of cheap, cut-glass bud vases, her hair swaying back and forth against the violet nylon as she moved. Thot had not been much older than that when he had first seen her, leaning over a small, magnetic chessboard behind the HQ. She had been so pathetically eager to learn to play the game, so charmingly anxious to improve her English that he had felt compelled to ask her father if he could give her lessons. He had never meant to become more than her teacher.

The girl in the purple coat reminded him of Thot; though she was of bigger build, she had the same delicateness of movement, as though the very air around her was made of crystal that she might shatter with an ungraceful move. Slowly, she turned and fixed on Richie a sad-eyed stare that made his chest ache and sent his cigarette rolling across the sidewalk in a flash of sparks. What was there about that face? It was not Thot's face. Only the child's eyes were Oriental. The rest of her features were very European. And yet . . .

"Well, are you gonna help or what?" Joey asked, punching Richie gently on the arm.

"Huh? Help what?"

"What the hell do you *think* I'm talking about?" Joey said disgustedly. "We gotta unload."

Richie looked into Joey's face, which was a younger mirror of his own. Vinnie, Dom, Joey, himself, Pop . . . there was no denying the relationship. All had the same squared-off jaw, that thin upper lip balanced against a much fuller lower one, a straight nose with slightly flared nostrils. Even the kids, Vinnie's four, Dom's three, and his own son, Jason, had that same Augustino face, looking more like sisters and brothers than cousins. He glanced back across the street in time to catch one more look at the girl as she followed the other children into the waiting car. Nose, mouth, chin . . . except for the eyes, she had the same face. His heart lurched. Without a word to his brother, he started across the street.

"Richie!"

He stopped and changed gears, noticing his brother through a haze of fog. It wasn't possible. He had checked it out very carefully. Thot and Mia were *both* dead.

"Okay, I don't need to work today if you don't," Joey said, tossing a crate of lettuce back on the ground.

"The hell you don't," Richie said, and grabbing the nearest crate, he began to pry open one of the wooden slats. He threw himself into the work, but thoughts of the child nagged at him through the early morning chores. There were few customers on the streets as yet; if he was going to talk to Mrs. Ly, there would be no better time. "Joey, I'm takin' a break," he called back over his shoulder.

"Good morning, Augustino," Mrs. Ly said, pronouncing his name as if it were four separate words.

"That girl," he said, without greeting. "That girl in the purple coat who was helping you unload this morning—who is she?"

"Very pretty, that one, but much too young for you." Mrs. Ly laughed.

"How old is she?" Richie asked, and something about his expression took the smile off of her face. She looked him over carefully, and then as if she too noticed something for the first time, she nodded gravely.

"The child was orphaned very young. We cannot be certain of her true age. None of her relatives have ever claimed her. Her age of record is fifteen. She may be younger, but not much. Some of these mixed-blood children tend to be a little bit bigger."

His temples throbbed and his neck ached, the dragon felt like a lead weight on its thong. Fourteen . . . She could be fourteen. "Tell me whatever you know about her? Or her family? How did you happen to find her . . . ?"

"Slow down, Augustino. This is not the place or time. We will talk later. You come back to my house for lunch. My daughter makes *bahn cuon*. . . . It is very good," she said.

He nodded. "When?" he asked.

"My daughter-in-law comes to watch the stand at twelve. We can go then," she said and turned to face her first customer of the morning.

The day dragged slowly, with just enough business to keep his mind from wandering completely out of the present, though he felt much more comfortable with his daydreams. He found it hard to keep the resentment out of his voice when some old lady would interrupt him by paying for her purchases. Joey was little help. Periodically, Richie looked up to see if Mrs. Ly's relief had come yet. What would she be able to tell him? Was there any way that he could know for sure? He touched the dragon through the thin cotton cloth of his T-shirt.

At exactly twelve-thirty Mrs. Ly's daughter-in-law turned onto Ninth Street and the old woman nodded to him from across the street.

Richie followed the old lady through the crowds and stalls of the market until she turned down a tiny row-house-lined street. All the while, his mind flooded with the memory of a tiny baby pressed briefly into his arms. For a long time he had hoped and searched, and then he had searched without hope until the word came back that they were dead. Now he could feel the warmth of hope radiate in his chest, right under the dragon; he could almost believe that the carving itself was glowing with its own warmth and sending the heat throughout his body.

They stopped in front of a shabby-looking brick house on Christian Street that would have been too small even for *one* large family. Mrs. Ly led him up the weatherworn stairs and through the aluminum screen door into a living room crammed with worn furniture and knickknacks. It was a noisy home. Voices came from every room, along with the cry of babies, and the high-pitched giggle and chatter of small children too young to be out playing on their own. But beneath the clutter of a house stuffed with more people than it was ever designed to hold, he could see that the place was spotlessly clean. Mrs. Ly left him seated on the sofa and went into the kitchen. He heard a long exchange of rapid-fire Vietnamese. It had never really sounded like a language to him, and he wished now that he had taken the trouble to learn it from Thot, as she had learned English from him. Whatever Mrs. Ly had said, a parade of people came out of the kitchen, passed quickly through the living room and up the stairway. One young woman smiled and nodded in Richie's direction, the other two completely ignored him. Mrs. Ly then motioned for Richie to follow her.

They ate first, with only occasional, polite bursts of conversation about business. The food was gone, but the smell of boiling cabbage that hung about the kitchen made it difficult for him to eat. Mrs. Ly finished first and waited patiently while he popped the last bite into his mouth. "Now, Augustino," she said at last, "tell me why you want to know about this child."

He told her what he could about himself and Thot, about the child they had had together, revealing more with his eyes and the tone of his voice about just how lost he had been when he had been forced to return home without them—about the painful readjustment to the life he had left.

She did not interrupt his speech. When he finished she took his hand and said, "Augustino, I am sorry. No one can give you the information you seek. The child herself knows nothing of her past. She was an orphan, a street child, when she was found. Phen Ngo worked for my husband many years ago in Saigon. Her own children were both killed in the war. It was said that single women with children were given preference in leaving the country, so she and the child adopted each other. This way it worked out better for both of them.

"As for the child's name, she has used many. She was content to take the name of Phen Ngo's oldest girl. And while it does seem likely that her father was an American soldier, there were so *many* soldiers there fifteen years ago, so many mixed-blood children left behind . . . This resemblance you see, it could be coincidence. You will never be more sure than you are at this moment. Is this enough for you? You must think about this thing carefully. Remember, it has been fourteen years."

Richie flipped a finger under the thong around his neck and tugged out the dragon. It felt warm and alive in his hand. "Thot gave me this," he said. "The child has one also."

Mrs. Ly studied the carving. "Lynn has such a thing,"

she said slowly, "but even that means very little. Such carvings are not uncommon in my country. Many have them."

"I think I might be her father," he said at last.

"You must not *think*. You must be certain in your heart. More than that, you must make a decision as to what you will do about it. The child is not unhappy here. This is a better life than the one she knew before. If you decide that she is your child, will you take her away? It will be very hard for her. She does not speak your language, she does not know your ways.

"And *your* family, Augustino. Will they be as eager to welcome this child that may or may not be yours?" She stared at him for a long time. "We will go back to work now. You must talk with your wife. You must talk with your brothers and your parents. When you are sure, then you can come back . . . if you still want to."

All the way home that night, Richie tried to think up ways of telling Carol. There didn't seem to be any way to avoid hurting her, but she was so damned maternal that—once she got over the shock—she would have no problem accepting the girl. Then, when he had Carol on his side, they could stand together against anything his family had to offer.

He was nervous when he entered the house, anxious to tell her and have done with it, but she was busy helping Jason with his day-camp project. Then Marge Braunstein called and Carol settled in for a nice long chat. He didn't get her alone until she was seated at the vanity getting ready to put on her evening's makeup. "Carol, I have something very important to talk to you about," he said.

"Go ahead," she said, brushing a thin dark line above the lashes on her upper eyelid.

"It's about when I was in 'Nam," he said, "and it's kind of hard for me to talk about. I know I never told you much about what went on over there, or why I stopped writing to you. It was very good of you, sweetheart, not to push me about things until I was ready, but now there's a reason why you have to know. So, please, be patient with me for a few minutes. You see, there was this girl—"

"Oh, spare me, Richie. True confessions . . . just what I need," she said angrily, blinking back a tear. "Did it ever occur to you to wonder *why* I never asked you about all this? Did you really think it was my overwhelming patience, or maybe that I just didn't care? I never thought that you were celibate the whole two years that you didn't write. I didn't ask because I didn't want to know about 'this girl.' As long as you didn't say anything, I could convince myself that it wasn't anything serious, that it was only because I wasn't around. Then it wasn't so bad. But now . . . now you're going to tell me that you were ready to throw me over for one of *them*, aren't you? Tonight; when I have to go over to your brother's house and play sweet adoring wife for your whole family." She slammed her hairbrush down on the vanity and stood up, her face tight and red-streaked with tears.

"You know, it wouldn't have been so bad back when we were kids and I had all those romantic notions of what *they* were like, but now . . . Now that I see them every day, sitting out in front of their foul-smelling apartments with their tight little monkey asses, gabbing together like a flock of turkeys, grabbing free this and free that off the government, while decent people have to work their asses off to get anything." She stood over him breathing heavily for a moment, then turned and walked out of the room.

He stared after her, shaking with rage. How dare she betray him like this. For the first time since they had been married, he wanted to hit her. But in a moment the feeling left him and he found himself strangely empty and lost. There was nothing left to do. This woman would *never* accept the child. He reached for his dragon and felt its warmth burning there beneath his cotton shirt, but this time it gave him no comfort. What good was it? It was a part of his past, like Thot, like the girl . . . like the woman he had thought he was married to. He would have to put it all behind him and get on with his life. He reached for the dragon and tugged it off, rubbing the back of his neck raw on the thong before it finally parted. He slipped the tiny carving from the leather string and stared at it in his palm.

It, too, had betrayed him. He took a deep breath and threw the dragon across the room.

"Darling," Carol whispered. He turned to see her standing in the doorway, looking much more controlled. "I'm sorry, honey. I know you didn't tell me just to hurt me. I know you're not that kind of person. There had to be a reason. Whatever it is, I want to help. Has she turned up in Philly? Is that it? Is she trying to hurt you, now, after all these years? Whatever it is, I'll stand by you," she said. She walked toward him with her hand outstretched to soothe him, but he couldn't bear to let her touch him. Not just yet. He brushed past her.

"I'll meet you at Dom's," he said.

Even a walk through his beloved South Philly streets didn't seem to be much help. The problem, as it unfolded in his mind, seemed to be an endless maze from which there was no exit. His parents would be worse than Carol. What a fuss they had made when Dom had started dating that Jewish girl.

He sat on an empty step for a while to watch a group of girls playing rope, until tears came to his eyes, then forced himself to move on. Guilt and worry were a terrible load on his mind. He began to feel as if he were being followed. Stalked, rather, like a deer during hunting season. But a look over his shoulder told him what he already knew—there was nobody there.

Dom's house was alive and crackling with the casual tension that overlaid most family gatherings. Poppa, the undisputed king of the castle, being thoroughly patronized by his sons. The women always found some excuse to go off together, leaving Mama in the kitchen by herself. Only Richie stood aloof, watching it all with mixed emotions. The children took their turns going to grandpa for their little tokens of affection—he would like to see Mia as part of that group. And yet, seeing how ill the old man was, how much he had aged in the last few weeks, Richie wondered if he had the right to disturb the old man's peace.

Carol went to bed as soon as they got home, but he couldn't bring himself to get that close to her. He stayed downstairs, awake most of the night, trying to concentrate on a movie. He awoke in the morning to find himself crumpled into the unopened recliner. Everything ached. The cut on his neck burned unbearably and the long-healed injury of his leg throbbed almost as badly as it had when the bone was broken. He could hear no signs of movement from upstairs, though his watch told him that it was an hour past their usual wake-up time. How could they sleep so long in this muggy and stifling heat? Summer seemed to have crept up on them during the night. He rubbed his gritty eyeballs and went about the painful business of disentangling himself from the chair.

The world wobbled. Noise; the nerve-wrenching noise of grinding metal and rock, human voices shrieking, shouting, glass shattering, desks, typewriters, chairs being flung against the walls. Heat, and the bitter smell of burning wood and flesh. Reaching out for something, anything solid, and his leg, almost with a will of its own, twisting in the opposite direction. A dull thump; an incredible burst of pain that momentarily took his vision, his arms working, vainly trying to pull himself out. Dust closed his eyes and choked his nose and throat. The endless hours that seemed like years waiting for anything, even death to free him from the pain.

His leg ached so badly that he almost didn't make it up the stairs, and his hands shook as he fumbled with the shower knobs. He'd read enough to know about flashbacks without ever having one before—but it had been so real that he had trouble placing himself in the present. His dragon, his only comfort during the long time waiting for rescue and the months in the hospital that followed, was gone. He couldn't remember what he'd done with it. He sank down until he was seated in the tub and let the stinging water wash away his tears.

He didn't bother to towel off after his shower, allowing the air to cool him as it dried. The day was so humid that this didn't work very well, sweat replacing the water before he ever reached the point of being dry. He limped into the bedroom and lay down on top of the sheet. Carol reached out for him and he took her hand, grateful for the warmth and companionship. She murmured sleepily and rolled into his arms. He held her tightly.

"Richie, are you . . . ?" He placed a finger over her lips, and she bit back the words. It was Carol in his arms, her short blond curls cushioning his shoulder from the weight of her head. This time he tried to picture Thot but found that he could not do it. This was the way it was supposed to be and yet it wasn't right. It was as though a piece of himself were missing. Without knowing why, he was afraid.

For a long time they lay there, without moving. The door opened and Jason stuck his head into the room.

"Good morning, Daddy," he said. Richie lifted his arms and the child crawled into bed. Richie clasped him tightly. What was the matter with him? He was a man of riches, his family surrounding him with love. How could he let a thing that had happened almost fifteen years ago—a thing that had not entered his thoughts in many years—shake his faith in that? He kissed his wife and his son, each on top of the head, and forced himself to dress.

The heat, dreadful for April when the day started, soared to temperatures that would have been bad in the dog days of August. Air currents moved down Ninth Street, but they were not cooling breezes. To Richie it felt more as if some giant, foul creature were breathing down his neck. So real was the image that he found himself continually looking over his shoulder, expecting to see . . . he wasn't sure what. Nothing there but the heavy, invisible heat. And as the day wore on, bright scarlet fruit turned brown and rich greens darkened and shriveled, until the whole market began to take on the sickly, sweet rotting smell of the jungle.

Only a very few people picked their way through the stalls, as if the unseasonal heat had made most folks afraid to venture out of the cool shade or away from their air-conditioning.

Once Mrs. Ly looked up and smiled at him from across the street, but he turned his head away, unable to answer with a smile of his own. He couldn't shake the feeling that something actually *was* coming, and he knew that whatever it was, it would be coming from that direction. He could almost make it out when he looked down the little street that entered Ninth Street from the east, right next to her stand. A vague white mist rolling down the street.

"You all right?" Joey asked.

"I'll manage," he answered coldly. "Heat's so bad I almost feel like I'm seeing things," he added half under his breath. He rubbed his eyes to clear the hallucination, and yet when he looked back it seemed even more detailed—a great white mass, visible, and yet so transparent that he could clearly see the street behind it.

Two old ladies came by, followed by a younger woman with children. Richie's mouth was so dry that he couldn't even wait on them. He grabbed one of his own overripe peaches and sucked the sickly sweet juice to clear his throat, but by the time he had finished, Joey had already taken care of them. "Why don't you go home, Richie," Joey said when he had finished with the customers.

"I'm okay," Richie shouted, his fists knotted, amazing himself with the force of his anger. He had to take a deep breath and calm himself down. Slowly, he would turn his head and look across the street. He would force himself to see it the way it really was, the way it rationally had to be. Slowly, he turned his head and raised his eyelids.

It was still there. Perhaps even a little more solid than it had been before. A white and terrible thing that seemed to be taking the shape of a giant beast.

Richie whirled around and pounded his fist on the stand, shattering an overripe cantaloupe into an explosion of orange pulp. He pulled off his fruit-stained T-shirt and wiped his face and neck with the damp material. "You're right, kid. Maybe I should go home," he said.

All the way home Richie paused at every corner to see if he was being followed, but if the creature was behind him, it was far enough away that he couldn't see it.

Carol must have been staring out the window, for she greeted him at the door with a look that he could have sworn was furtive and nervous. "Guess who came to see me today?" she said before she even kissed his cheek in greeting. The thought passed briefly through his mind that she was having an affair. He limped up to the top step to see his father sitting on the sofa.

"Hi, Pop," he said, but his disappointment amazed him. How convenient it would have been to find out she was cheating on him. How easy it would have made everything.

He made an effort not to limp as he entered the house, though the leg was hurting so badly that he was beginning to wonder if he hadn't reinjured it. "What brings you to see my wife in the middle of the day? Should I be jealous?"

"Ah, if it weren't for your mother . . ." the old man said.

"Honey, I have to pick up a few things for dinner. Pop, if you'll excuse me?" So *that* was the setup. Carol had asked Pop to come over and have a talk with him, and she was afraid that Richie would be angry. Well, far from it. Richie was glad to have a chance to speak to his father alone.

"Carol's worried about me?" Richie asked the moment she was out the door.

His father nodded. "And not just Carol. Your mother and I are a little worried, too. She says you've been acting funny."

"Acting funny?" Richie asked, raising his voice, feeling the old rage boil back up in him.

"Slow down, son." Frank Augustino patted him gently on the arm. "She's only concerned for your welfare. Your mother and I saw it, too, last night. Moody, short-tempered, staring into space, your mind a million miles away. Son, this isn't like you. What's bothering you?"

Richie wanted to tell him. While there were things they had never discussed, he had never actually lied to his father. Besides, he wanted the old man to take charge and make everything better—the way he had when Richie was a boy, but Pop was so sick. The heat alone was dangerous for a man in his state of health, and if he took the news badly . . .

"It's nothing, Pop," he said at last. He tried to keep his hands from trembling where his father could see, but the feeling was back. That same feeling of being watched, stalked, that he'd had all afternoon. Something was *out* there, just beyond his range of vision . . . just outside the window. He wanted to go and look and yet he knew that it was the worst thing that he could do. Looking at it, acknowledging its existence, seemed to give it form and substance—as if it were his own willingness to give it power over him that *gave* it that power.

"Richie?"

He wouldn't look. He wouldn't even think about it. He tried to find something that he could concentrate on.

"Richie, look at you. How can you tell me there's nothing wrong?"

"Damn it, Pop. It's nothing. I can handle it." He heard a noise. A low bass rumble that could have been a roar. He had to look. He got up and crossed to the window, forgetting to hide his limp.

It was there, outside the window, just as he knew that it would be. A great white beast, no longer featureless, and so familiar that he knew that if he could just lift the veils of gauze from his mind, he would know just what to do about it. He felt a moan escape his lips—and the next thing he knew, his father was at his side, helping him back to the sofa, the sick old man taking most of Richie's weight on his shoulders.

"Richard, if there's something wrong, you can't just ignore it and hope that it goes away. You can't just say, 'I can handle it.' You're a husband and a father. You have responsibilities. If you let your problems get out of hand—if something should happen to you—who will be there to take care of your wife and your children? Your mother and I won't be around much longer. Your brothers are barely supporting their own families. Think about Jason growing up without a father's guiding hand. Think about the coming baby who would never really even *know* you. It is a terrible thing for a child to grow up without a father."

Richie looked up, startled by his father's phrase, and his eye caught a shape at the window. It was visible, now, from where he sat, and its form was quite distinct. Scales scalloping down its back, red eyes that seemed to glow from within, snakelike white tendrils curling from the sides of its awful mouth . . . It might have been his own little dragon grown to mammoth size, except for a large yellow stain down its side. It stood outside in the street, so motionless that it might still have been carved of bone, and yet he could tell that the eyes were watching him, the ears taking in everything that he had to say. *His* dragon. He had forsaken it, and now it had turned on him. He didn't know if he could win it back, but he knew that he had to try.

"Pop, listen!" Richie said with sudden urgency. "There *is* a problem, but I have to tell you something about my life in 'Nam for you to understand.

"When I was stationed at headquarters, I worked with a local translator, a man named Pai Som Trinh. You know me, Pop. I was never one for hanging around the bars, chasing hookers and getting drunk, yet there wasn't much else for a man to do in his spare time. This man and his family sort of took me in. I missed you all so much, it was like having a second family. Anyway, Som had a daughter named Thot. She wanted to learn to speak English and she wanted to learn to play chess and she wanted to know all about America. I thought it would be fun to teach her. She was such a cute little kid. And then one day I realized she wasn't a kid anymore. I never meant to fall in love with her—there was her father, and there was Carol—but things just happened." He paused, trying to decide what kind of look it was that flitted briefly over his father's face.

"Things got pretty desperate after a while. Both of her parents were killed, and she was pregnant. I really wanted to marry her, to bring her and the child home with me when I came, but in the Army there was a lot of red tape involved in that sort of thing.

"I only saw the baby once. All leaves were canceled, and then we were bombed and I wound up in the hospital. When I finally got out, I tried to find them, but they were gone. I got word later that they were dead."

"All this you never told us?"

"I'm sorry, Pop. At first I couldn't bear to talk about it;

later there didn't seem to be any point. Carol was willing to forgive my long silence without asking questions and I found that I still had feelings for her. Why hurt her? I squeezed myself back into my old life and tried to pick up the pieces."

"And what has this to do with now? Have you found this woman again?" Pop asked.

"No. Thot is dead. I accepted that a long time ago, or I never would have married Carol. But I think I've found my child. I know I have. My daughter." The old man's eyes were closed; Richie could read nothing from his expression. "She's living right here in Philly—not more than five blocks from here—with a family of refugees. Pop, you should see her. She's a beautiful child with her mother's eyes and hair, but the rest of her face is pure Augustino."

"I can see why you've been so troubled. Does the child know that you're her father? Is she asking you for anything? What do you plan to do about it?"

"I wanted to tell her, but Carol . . ." He spat his wife's name bitterly. "How could she have become so prejudiced without my even knowing? Now I don't know what to do."

"You told Carol?"

"No, I didn't tell her about the girl. Not yet. Not after the reaction I got from telling her about Thot." Richie sighed and watched his father expectantly.

"How could you keep such a secret from your wife?" The elder Augustino sighed and shook his head. "Son, this is not an easy thing for me to say, but I think it would be best if we just kept this between ourselves. Best for everyone. I know that your mother and I raised you with a strong sense of family responsibility, but, I think you are being very selfish to want to bring that child here. You think you would be helping her, but she is almost grown. Her ways are not your ways. And could you really ask Carol to take in another woman's child, the child of a woman you had been prepared to leave her for? She would have to be a saint . . ." The old man kept on talking, but Richie was no longer listening. He had tried his best and he had failed.

And Thot's dragon was still standing outside the window.

Listening . . . Watching . . . Waiting until the moment was right . . . His leg throbbed, his mind was slow and foggy and the heat was almost unbearable, and Richie wasn't even sure he cared about anything anymore.

"Oh, Pop," he said weakly. "A moment ago you said it was a terrible thing for a child to grow up without a father. Now you tell me it's in my daughter's best interest to forget her."

"In some cases—"

"Please. I don't want to hear it anymore. Just go home, will you?" Without waiting for an answer, Richie got up and pulled himself up the stairs, leaning most of his weight on the banister. He was so tired. Much too tired to fight anymore. But even now, with everything against him, there was one final answer. One quick way to stop all of the pain and make everything right again. He reached up on the closet shelf and brought down a beat-up pink shoebox. With trembling hands he cleared away a stack of old photographs and greeting cards and pulled out his gun. It was an old .38 police special that Carol had bought for him to keep at the stand, but which he never remembered to take. He fished out the box of bullets and with gentle, almost loving fingers, he rolled out the cylinder and pressed a bullet into every chamber. Then he laid the gun down on the neat white bedspread and dropped to his knees on the floor.

Silently, he prayed. He said a prayer for his own redemption, for the future of those he left behind. He prayed that Jason would not be the one to find him. He prayed for the unborn child, but his father's words continued to haunt his prayers. It *was* a terrible thing for a child to grow up without a father, and he would be leaving three of them. But that left him no answer at all. Unless . . .

He wished that his mind would clear, that he could think things *out*. Yet even through the mist that shrouded his thoughts, he could see only one solution. He would have to take them all with him. No child left behind to suffer. God would open his waiting arms and take them all to his bosom.

He could not remember the walk to Mrs. Ly's house, the pause to sit and rest his leg on almost every block, or the fear of the thing that stalked behind him—so strong that he dared not even look around. Fear that it would get him before he could finish his work. Before he knocked he made an effort to straighten up, brushing his hair back from his face and tugging at his clothes. The man who answered the door did not speak English, but soon Mrs. Ly appeared behind him.

Her eyes widened for a moment and then she lowered her eyelids, nodding, and backed up to usher him inside. She barked out a strange word and a plump, dour-looking woman got up from the sofa and ran upstairs. If there were other people in the room, Richie failed to notice them.

"I've come for my daughter," he said. "I want her to meet my wife and son."

"Augustino, it is getting late. I cannot go with you and you will need a translator."

He shook his head. "Mrs. Ly, I hope you understand. This is a very delicate matter. It cannot be done with strangers present. I won't take very long."

"You are certain then that she is your child?"

"Mrs. Ly, I don't have any doubts."

Mrs. Ly sighed. "I think you may be right. Wait for just a moment, please." She shouted something into the other room and a moment later the girl appeared in the doorway.

"I want her with me," he said, his voice hoarse and dry. "It is a terrible thing for a child to be without a father." He took the child's hand and led her out the door.

The ease with which they let the girl go—and with someone who was practically a stranger—strengthened his belief that what he was doing was right. They cared nothing for her. She was just another mouth to feed, cast in with them by chains of circumstance.

They walked in silence. At first she would giggle when he stopped on someone's stoop to rest, but after the first few times it appeared to make her nervous. He quickened the pace in spite of the pain and heat, and did not stop again. When they got to the house, her expression changed and he could tell that she was frightened. She reached for something under her blouse. It was a gesture he knew quite well.

The dragon. Mrs. Ly had said that she had one. It would have to go. Nothing could interfere with his plan.

He moved behind her and swept the hair from the back of her neck. A silver chain gleamed against her pale skin. He undid the clasp and jerked it free of her clutching fingers, holding it high against her efforts to reclaim it. It was a tiny carved dragon, much like his own, except for a slight discoloration along one side. A yellow stain on the flank.

He froze. Then, slowly, he turned to look at the creature he knew was standing behind him. It was no longer still. It roared at him silently, pawing the air . . . a yellow discoloration matching the one on the carving he held in his hand. *Her* dragon!

Suddenly, there was hope. The child was jumping up and down, reaching for her necklace, but he couldn't let her have it back. Not yet. He grabbed her by the wrist and made her sit down on the front steps, then motioned for her to wait.

Carol was seated on the sofa. There was a book across her knees, but he could tell that she hadn't been reading. Used tissues littered the top of the cocktail table and dark mascara streaks soiled her eyes.

"Wait here," he shouted. "And whatever you do, don't come upstairs."

The dragon was still behind him. He could feel its breath on his back as he crossed the living room and forced his way painfully up the stairs. He wondered that the house didn't collapse under its ponderous weight as it mounted the stairs behind him.

Even knowing that such measures were a waste of time, he limped across the hall as fast as his useless leg permitted and slammed the bedroom door behind him.

It was here. It *had* to be. He remembered it quite clearly now, like a moment spotlighted in time. He had taken the dragon off and thrown it against the window; and heard the tiny clink as it hit the glass and bounced off into the cushioning draperies. He felt along the edge of the windowsill, ran his hand along the baseboard below—he even shook the drapes several times. No dragon . . . And he was running out of time.

"Richie! What is going on?" Carol was standing in the doorway. And the dragon was right behind her. Its terrible mouth opened, exposing a lash of bright red tongue. He watched her turn to follow his gaze, shrug, and turn around again.

"You don't see it, do you?" he asked almost calmly.

"Richie, what *are* you talking about?" She took a few steps into the room. Jason was right behind her.

"The dragon," he said, moving to interpose himself between them and the creature.

"This?" she asked, holding a small carved dragon on her outstretched palm. Gingerly, he reached out to touch it and felt its vitality like a spark running through his fingers. He took it in his hand. Instantly, he felt its power surging through him, easing his pain and lifting the clouds from his mind.

But the dragon was still there in the hallway, and now it was starting to move toward the bedroom door. Richie brushed past Carol and Jason out into the hallway and shut the door behind him, ignoring Carol's questions, her worried tears.

The dragon was walking toward him, its hot breath burning through his body. He looked toward the stairs on one side, the doorway to Jason's room on the other. He backed into Jason's doorway and laid the child's carving down on the dark gray carpet. His own dragon he kissed once for luck and laid it down too, facing the other. Then, like a miracle, he noticed a cloud of steam on the stairs, billowing and growing until it solidified into a creature very much like the first one.

The hallway was tiny, but walls seemed to be no problem for them. They circled each other tentatively. Two great paws raised, they probed at each other. And then they lunged. Two impossible creatures locked in battle, their bodies rearing on hind legs until he could no longer see their heads. And then they fell, rolling over through the banister, rolling down the stairs. He followed, unable to tear his eyes away.

They rolled, two distinct forms, across the living room floor. Then, suddenly, an even stranger thing happened. They stood, facing each other, paws raised and flailing, and yet, Richard realized, they were no longer fighting. They began to merge, sinking each into the other like one creature falling into a mirror. They slowly came together until there was only one great white dragon that thinned and faded even as he watched, until there was nothing left but a thin white mist . . . and then even that was gone.

He turned and saw Carol standing at the top of the stairs, her face a tortured mask of worry. He climbed the stairs and placed a comforting arm around her shoulder. "Carol, there's something I have to tell you," he said softly. He knew he would have to hurry because his child was waiting outside, and it was starting to rain.

Paper Dragons
by
James P. Blaylock

Here's one of the strangest and most strangely beautiful stories you are ever likely to read: as evocative, melancholy, and mysterious as a paper dragon soaring against the darkening sky of evening. . . .

James P. Blaylock was born in Long Beach, California, and now lives in Orange, California. He made his first sale to the now-defunct semi-prozine Unearth, *and subsequently became one of the most popular, literate, and wildly eclectic fantasists of the '80s and '90s. His critically acclaimed novels include* The Last Coin, Land of Dreams, The Digging Leviathan, Homunculus, The Elfin Ship, The Disappearing Dwarf, *and* The Stone Giant. *His most recent book is* The Paper Grail.

* * *

Strange things are said to have happened in this world—some are said to be happening still—but half of them, if I'm any judge, are lies. There's no way to tell sometimes. The sky above the north coast has been flat gray for weeks—clouds thick overhead like carded wool not fifty feet above the ground, impaled on the treetops, on redwoods and alders and hemlocks. The air is heavy with mist that lies out over the harbor and the open ocean, drifting across the tip of the pier and breakwater now and again, both of them vanishing into the gray so that there's not a nickel's worth of difference between the sky and the sea. And when the tide drops, and the reefs running out toward the point appear through the fog, covered in the brown bladders and rubber leaves of kelp, the pink lace of algae, and the slippery sheets of sea lettuce and eel grass, it's a simple thing to imagine the dark bulk of the fish that lie in deepwater gardens and angle up toward the pale green of shallows to feed at dawn.

There's the possibility, of course, that winged things,

their counterparts if you will, inhabit dens in the clouds, that in the valleys and caverns of the heavy, low skies live unguessed beasts. It occurs to me sometimes that if without warning a man could draw back that veil of cloud that obscures the heavens, snatch it back in an instant, he'd startle a world of oddities aloft in the skies: balloon things with hovering little wings like the fins of pufferfish, and spiny, leathery creatures, nothing but bones and teeth and with beaks half again as long as their ribby bodies.

There have been nights when I was certain I heard them, when the clouds hung in the treetops and foghorns moaned off the point and water dripped from the needles of hemlocks beyond the window onto the tin roof of Filby's garage. There were muffled shrieks and the airy flapping of distant wings. On one such night when I was out walking along the bluffs, the clouds parted for an instant and a spray of stars like a reeling carnival shone beyond, until, like a curtain slowly drawing shut, the clouds drifted up against each other and parted no more. I'm certain I glimpsed something—a shadow, the promise of a shadow—dimming the stars. It was the next morning that the business with the crabs began.

I awoke, late in the day, to the sound of Filby hammering at something in his garage—talons, I think it was, copper talons. Not that it makes much difference. It woke me up. I don't sleep until an hour or so before dawn. There's a certain bird, Lord knows what sort, that sings through the last hour of the night and shuts right up when the sun rises. Don't ask me why. Anyway, there was Filby smashing away some time before noon. I opened my left eye, and there atop the pillow was a bloodred hermit crab with eyes on stalks, giving me a look as if he were proud of himself, waving pincers like that. I leaped up. There was another, creeping into my shoe, and two more making away with my pocket watch, dragging it along on its fob toward the bedroom door.

The window was open and the screen was torn. The beasts were clambering up onto the woodpile and hoisting themselves in through the open window to rummage through my personal effects while I slept. I pitched them out, but that evening there were more—dozens of them, bent beneath the weight of seashells, dragging toward the house with an eye to my pocket watch.

It was a migration. Once every hundred years, Dr. Jensen tells me, every hermit crab in creation gets the wanderlust and hurries ashore. Jensen camped on the beach in the cove to study the things. They were all heading south like migratory birds. By the end of the week there was a tiresome lot of them afoot—millions of them to hear Jensen carry on—but they left my house alone. They dwindled as the next week wore out, and seemed to be straggling in from deeper water and were bigger and bigger. The size of a man's fist at first, then of his head, and then a giant, vast as a pig, chased Jensen into the lower branches of an oak. On Friday there were only two crabs, both of them bigger than cars. Jensen went home gibbering and drank himself into a stupor. He was there on Saturday though; you've got to give him credit for that. But nothing appeared. He speculates that somewhere off the coast, in a deepwater chasm a hundred fathoms below the last faded colors is a monumental beast, blind and gnarled from spectacular pressures and wearing a seashell overcoat, feeling his way toward shore.

At night sometimes I hear the random echoes of far-off clacking, just the misty and muted suggestion of it, and I brace myself and stare into the pages of an open book, firelight glinting off the cut crystal of my glass, countless noises out in the foggy night among which is the occasional clack clack clack of what might be Jensen's impossible crab, creeping up to cast a shadow in the front porch lamplight, to demand my pocket watch. It was the night after the sighting of the pig-sized crabs that one got into Filby's garage—forced the door apparently—and made a hash out of his dragon. I know what you're thinking. I thought it was a lie too. But things have since fallen out that make me suppose otherwise. He did, apparently, know Augustus Silver. Filby was an acolyte; Silver was his master. But the dragon business, they tell me, isn't merely a matter of mechanics. It's a matter of perspective. That was Filby's downfall.

There was a gypsy who came round in a cart last year. He couldn't speak, apparently. For a dollar he'd do the most amazing feats. He tore out his tongue, when he first arrived, and tossed it onto the road. Then he danced on it and shoved it back into his mouth, good as new. Then he pulled out his entrails—yards and yards of them like sausage out of a machine—then jammed them all back in and nipped shut the hole he'd torn in his abdomen. It made half the town sick, mind you, but they paid to see it. That's pretty much how I've always felt about dragons. I don't half believe in them, but I'd give a bit to see one fly, even if it were no more than a clever illusion.

But Filby's dragon, the one he was keeping for Silver, was a ruin. The crab—I suppose it was a crab—had shredded it, knocked the wadding out of it. It reminded me of one of those stuffed alligators that turns up in curiosity shops, all eaten to bits by bugs and looking sad and tired, with its tail bent sidewise and a clump of cotton stuffing shoved through a tear in its neck.

Filby was beside himself. It's not good for a grown man to carry on so. He picked up the shredded remnant of a dissected wing and flagellated himself with it. He scourged himself, called himself names. I didn't know him well at the time, and so watched the whole weird scene from my kitchen window: His garage door banging open and shut in the wind, Filby weeping and howling through the open door, storming back and forth, starting and stopping theatrically, the door slamming shut and slicing off the whole embarrassing business for thirty seconds or so and then sweeping open to betray a wailing Filby scrabbling among the debris on the garage floor—the remnants of what had once been a flesh and blood dragon, as it were, built by the ubiquitous Augustus Silver years before. Of course I had no idea at the time. Augustus *Silver*, after all. It almost justifies Filby's carrying on. And I've done a bit of carrying on myself since, although as I said, most of what prompted the whole business has begun to seem suspiciously like lies, and the whispers in the foggy night, the clacking and whirring and rush of wings, has begun to sound like thinly disguised laughter, growing fainter by the months and emanating from nowhere, from the clouds, from the wind and fog. Even the occasional letters from Silver himself have become suspect.

Filby is an eccentric. I could see that straightaway. How he finances his endeavors is beyond me. Little odd jobs, I don't doubt—repairs and such. He has the hands of an archetypal mechanic: spatulate fingers, grime under the nails, nicks and cuts and scrapes that he can't identify. He has only to touch a heap of parts, wave his hands over them, and the faint rhythmic stirrings of order and pattern seem to shudder through the crossmembers of his workbench. And here an enormous crab had gotten in, and in a single night had clipped apart a masterpiece, a wonder, a thing that couldn't be tacked back together. Even Silver would have pitched it out. The cat wouldn't want it.

Filby was morose for days, but I knew he'd come out of it. He'd be mooning around the house in a slump, poking at yesterday's newspapers, and a glint of light off a copper wire would catch his eye. The wire would suggest something. That's how it works. He not only has the irritating ability to coexist with mechanical refuse; it speaks to him too, whispers possibilities.

He'd be hammering away some morning soon—damn all crabs—piecing together the ten thousand silver scales of a wing, assembling the jeweled bits of a faceted eye, peering through a glass at a spray of fine wire spun into a braid that would run up along the spinal column of a creature which, when released some misty night, might disappear within moments into the clouds and be gone. Or so Filby dreamed. And I'll admit it: I had complete faith in him, in the dragon that he dreamed of building.

In the early spring, such as it is, some few weeks after the hermit crab business, I was hoeing along out in the garden. Another frost was unlikely. My tomatoes had been in for a week, and an enormous green worm with spines had eaten the leaves off the plants. There was nothing left but stems, and they were smeared up with a sort of slime. Once when

I was a child I was digging in the dirt a few days after a rain, and I unearthed a finger-sized worm with the face of a human being. I buried it. But this tomato worm had no such face. He was pleasant, in fact, with little piggy eyes and a smashed-in sort of nose, as worm noses go. So I pitched him over the fence into Filby's yard. He'd climb back over—there was no doubting it. But he'd creep back from anywhere, from the moon. And since that was the case—if it was inevitable—then there seemed to be no reason to put him too far out of his way, if you follow me. But the plants were a wreck. I yanked them out by the roots and threw them into Filby's yard too, which is up in weeds anyway, but Filby himself had wandered up to the fence like a grinning gargoyle, and the clump of a half-dozen gnawed vines flew into his face like a squid. That's not the sort of thing to bother Filby though. He didn't mind. He had a letter from Silver mailed a month before from points south.

I was barely acquainted with the man's reputation then. I'd heard of him—who hasn't? And I could barely remember seeing photographs of a big, bearded man with wild hair and a look of passion in his eye, taken when Silver was involved in the mechano-vivisectionist's league in the days when they first learned the truth about the mutability of matter. He and three others at the university were responsible for the brief spate of unicorns, some few of which are said to roam the hills hereabouts, interesting mutants, certainly, but not the sort of wonder that would satisfy Augustus Silver. He appeared in the photograph to be the sort who would leap headlong into a cold pool at dawn and eat bulgar wheat and honey with a spoon.

And here was Filby, ridding himself of the remains of ravaged tomato plants, holding a letter in his hand, transported. A letter from the master! He'd been years in the tropics and had seen a thing or two. In the hills of the eastern jungles he'd sighted a dragon with what was quite apparently a bamboo ribcage. It flew with the xylophone clacking of windchimes, and had the head of an enormous lizard, the pronged tail of a devilfish, and clockwork wings built of silver and string and the skins of carp. It had given him certain ideas. The best dragons, he was sure, would come from the sea. He was setting sail for San Francisco. Things could be purchased in Chinatown—certain "necessaries," as he put it in his letter to Filby. There was mention of perpetual motion, of the building of an immortal creature knitted together from parts of a dozen beasts.

I was still waiting for the issuance of that last crab, and so was Jensen. He wrote a monograph, a paper of grave scientific accuracy in which he postulated the correlation between the dwindling number of the creatures and the enormity of their size. He camped on the cliffs above the sea with his son Bumby, squinting through the fog, his eye screwed to the lens of a special telescope—one that saw things, as he put it, particularly clearly—and waiting for the first quivering claw of the behemoth to thrust up out of the gray swells, cascading water, draped with weeds, and the bearded face of the crab to follow, drawn along south by a sort of migratory magnet toward heaven alone knows what. Either the crab passed away down the coast hidden by mists, or Jensen was wrong—there hasn't been any last crab.

The letter from Augustus Silver gave Filby wings, as they say, and he flew into the construction of his dragon, sending off a letter east in which he enclosed forty dollars, his unpaid dues in the Dragon Society. The tomato worm, itself a wingless dragon, crept back into the garden four days later and had a go at a half-dozen fresh plants, nibbling lacy arabesques across the leaves. Flinging it back into Filby's yard would accomplish nothing. It was a worm of monumental determination. I put him into a jar—a big, gallon pickle jar, empty of pickles, of course—and I screwed onto it a lid with holes punched in. He lived happily in a little garden of leaves and dirt and sticks and polished stones, nibbling on the occasional tomato leaf.

I spent more and more time with Filby, watching, in those days after the arrival of the first letter, the mechanical bones and joints and organs of the dragon drawing together. Unlike his mentor, Filby had almost no knowledge of vivisection. He had an aversion to it, I believe, and as a

consequence his creations were almost wholly mechanical—
and almost wholly unlikely. But he had such an aura of
certainty about him, such utter and uncompromising con-
viction, that even the most unlikely project seemed inexpli-
cably credible.

I remember one Saturday afternoon with particular clarity. The sun had shone for the first time in weeks. The grass
hadn't been alive with slugs and snails the previous
night—a sign, I supposed, that the weather was changing for
the drier. But I was only half right. Saturday dawned clear.
The sky was invisibly blue, dotted with the dark specks of
what might have been sparrows or crows flying just above
the treetops, or just as easily something else, something
more vast—dragons, let's say, or the peculiar denizens of
some very distant cloud world. Sunlight poured through the
diamond panes of my bedroom window, and I swear I could
hear the tomato plants and onions and snow peas in my
garden unfurling, hastening skyward. But around noon great
dark clouds roiled in over the Coast Range, their shadows
creeping across the meadows and redwoods, picket fences,
and chaparral. A spray of rain sailed on the freshening
offshore breeze, and the sweet smell of ozone rose from the
pavement of Filby's driveway, carrying on its first thin
ghost an unidentifiable sort of promise and regret: the
promise of wonders pending, regret for the bits and pieces
of lost time that go trooping away like migratory hermit
crabs, inexorably, irretrievably into the mists.

So it was a Saturday afternoon of rainbows and umbrel-
las, and Filby, still animated at the thought of Silver's
approach, showed me some of his things. Filby's house was
a marvel, given over entirely to his collections. Carven
heads whittled of soapstone and ivory and ironwood populated the rooms, the strange souvenirs of distant travel.
Aquaria bubbled away, thick with water plants and odd,
mottled creatures: spotted eels and leaf fish, gobies buried to
their noses in sand, flatfish with both eyes on the same side
of their heads, and darting anableps that had the wonderful
capacity to see above and below the surface of the water
simultaneously and so, unlike the mundane fish that swam

beneath, were inclined toward philosophy. I suggested as much to Filby, but I'm not certain he understood. Books and pipes and curios filled a half-dozen cases, and star charts hung on the walls. There were working drawings of some of Silver's earliest accomplishments, intricate swirling sketches covered over with what were to me utterly meaningless calculations and commentary.

On Monday another letter arrived from Silver. He'd gone along east on the promise of something very rare in the serpent line—an elephant trunk snake, he said, the lungs of which ran the length of its body. But he was coming to the west coast, that much was sure, to San Francisco. He'd be here in a week, a month, he couldn't be entirely sure. A message would come. Who could say when? We agreed that I would drive the five hours south on the coast road into the city to pick him up: I owned a car.

Filby was in a sweat to have his creature built before Silver's arrival. He wanted so badly to hear the master's approval, to see in Silver's eyes the brief electricity of surprise and excitement. And I wouldn't doubt for a moment that there was an element of envy involved. Filby, after all, had languished for years at the university in Silver's shadow, and now he was on the ragged edge of becoming a master himself.

So there in Filby's garage, tilted against a wall of roughcut fir studs and redwood shiplap, the shoulders, neck, and right wing of the beast sat in silent repose, its head a mass of faceted pastel crystals, piano wire, and bone clutched in the soft rubber grip of a bench vise. It was on Friday, the morning of the third letter, that Filby touched the bare ends of two microscopically thin copper rods, and the eyes of the dragon rotated on their axis, very slowly, blinking twice, surveying the cramped and dimly lit garage with an ancient, knowing look before the rods parted and life flickered out.

Filby was triumphant. He danced around the garage, shouting for joy, cutting little capers. But my suggestion that we take the afternoon off, perhaps drive up to Fort Bragg for lunch and a beer, was met with stolid refusal.

Silver, it seemed, was on the horizon. I was to leave in the morning. I might, quite conceivably, have to spend a few nights waiting. One couldn't press Augustus Silver, of course. Filby himself would work on the dragon. It would be a night and day business, to be sure. I determined to take the tomato worm along for company, as it were, but the beast had dug himself into the dirt for a nap.

This business of my being an emissary of Filby struck me as dubious when I awoke on Saturday morning. I was a neighbor who had been ensnared in a web of peculiar enthusiasm. Here I was pulling on heavy socks and stumbling around the kitchen, tendrils of fog creeping in over the sill, the hemlocks ghostly beyond dripping panes, while Augustus Silver tossed on the dark Pacific swell somewhere off the Golden Gate, his hold full of dragon bones. What was I to say to him beyond, "Filby sent me." Or something more cryptic: "Greetings from Filby." Perhaps in these circles one merely winked or made a sign or wore a peculiar sort of cap with a foot-long visor and a pyramid-encased eye embroidered across the front. I felt like a fool, but I had promised Filby. His garage was alight at dawn, and I had been awakened once in the night by a shrill screech, cut off sharply and followed by Filby's cackling laughter and a short snatch of song.

I was to speak to an old Chinese named Wun Lo in a restaurant off Washington. Filby referred to him as "the connection." I was to introduce myself as a friend of Captain Augustus Silver and wait for orders. Orders—what in the devil sort of talk was that? In the dim glow of lamplight the preceding midnight such secret talk seemed sensible, even satisfactory; in the chilly dawn it was risible.

It was close to six hours into the city, winding along the tortuous road, bits and pieces of it having fallen into the sea on the back of winter rains. The fog rose out of rocky coves and clung to the hillsides, throwing a gray veil over dew-fed wildflowers and shore grasses. Silver fencepickets loomed out of the murk with here and there the skull of a cow or a goat impaled atop, and then the quick passing of a half-score of mailboxes on posts, rusted and canted over toward the cliffs along with twisted cypresses that seemed on the verge of flinging themselves into the sea.

Now and again, without the least notice, the fog would disappear in a twinkling, and a clear mile of highway would appear, weirdly sharp and crystalline in contrast to its previous muted state. Or an avenue into the sky would suddenly appear, the remote end of which was dipped in opalescent blue and which seemed as distant and unattainable as the end of a rainbow. Across one such avenue, springing into clarity for perhaps three seconds, flapped the ungainly bulk of what might have been a great bird, laboring as if against a stiff, tumultuous wind just above the low-lying fog. It might as easily have been something else, much higher. A dragon? One of Silver's creations that nested in the dense emerald fog forests of the Coast Range? It was impossible to tell, but it seemed, as I said, to be struggling—perhaps it was old—and a bit of something, a fragment of a wing, fell clear of it and spun dizzily into the sea. Maybe what fell was just a stick being carried back to the nest of an ambitious heron. In an instant the fog closed, or rather the car sped out of the momentary clearing, and any opportunity to identify the beast, really to study it, was gone. For a moment I considered turning around, going back, but it was doubtful that I'd find that same bit of clarity, or that if I did, the creature would still be visible. So I drove on, rounding bends between redwood-covered hills that might have been clever paintings draped along the ghostly edge of Highway One, the hooks that secured them hidden just out of view in the mists above. Then almost without warning the damp asphalt issued out onto a broad highway and shortly thereafter onto the humming expanse of the Golden Gate Bridge.

Some few silent boats struggled against the tide below. Was one of them the ship of Augustus Silver, slanting in toward the Embarcadero? Probably not. They were fishing boats from the look of them, full of shrimp and squid and bug-eyed rock cod. I drove to the outskirts of Chinatown and parked, leaving the car and plunging into the crowd that swarmed down Grant and Jackson and into Portsmouth Square.

It was Chinese New Year. The streets were heavy with the smell of almond cookies and fog, barbecued duck and gunpowder, garlic and seaweed. Rockets burst overhead in showers of barely visible sparks, and one, teetering over onto the street as the fuse burned, sailed straightaway up Washington, whirling and glowing and fizzing into the wall of a curio shop, then dropping lifeless onto the sidewalk as if embarrassed at its own antics. The smoke and pop of firecrackers, the milling throng, and the nagging senselessness of my mission drove me along down Washington until I stumbled into the smoky open door of a narrow, three-story restaurant. Sam Wo it was called.

An assortment of white-garmented chefs chopped away at vegetables. Woks hissed. Preposterous bowls of white rice steamed on the counter. A fish head the size of a melon blinked at me out of a pan. And there, at a small table made of chromed steel and rubbed formica, sat my contact. It had to be him. Filby had been wonderfully accurate in his description. The man had a gray beard that wagged on the tabletop and a suit of similar color that was several sizes too large, and he spooned up clear broth in such a mechanical, purposeful manner that his eating was almost ceremonial. I approached him. There was nothing to do but brass it out. "I'm a friend of Captain Silver," I said, smiling and holding out a hand. He bowed, touched my hand with one limp finger, and rose. I followed him into the back of the restaurant.

It took only a scattering of moments for me to see quite clearly that my trip had been entirely in vain. Who could say where Augustus Silver was? Singapore? Ceylon? Bombay? He'd had certain herbs mailed east just two days earlier. I was struck at once with the foolishness of my position. What in the world was I doing in San Francisco? I had the uneasy feeling that the five chefs just outside the door were having a laugh at my expense, and that old Wun Lo, gazing out toward the street, was about to ask for money—a fiver, just until payday. I was a friend of Augustus Silver, wasn't I?

My worries were temporarily arrested by an old photograph that hung above a tile-faced hearth. It depicted a sort of weird shantytown somewhere on the north coast. There was a thin fog, just enough to veil the surrounding countryside, and the photograph had clearly been taken at dusk, for the long, deep shadows thrown by strange hovels slanted away landward into the trees. The tip of a lighthouse was just visible on the edge of the dark Pacific, and a scattering of small boats lay at anchor beneath. It was puzzling, to be sure—doubly so, because the lighthouse, the spit of land that swerved round toward it, the green bay amid cypress and eucalyptus was, I was certain, Point Reyes. But the shantytown, I was equally certain, didn't exist, couldn't exist.

The collection of hovels tumbled down to the edge of the bay, a long row of them that descended the hillside like a strange gothic stairway, and all of them, I swear it, were built in part of the ruins of dragons, of enormous winged reptiles—tin and copper, leather and bone. Some were stacked on end, tilted against each other like card houses. Some were perched atop oil drums or upended wooden pallets. Here was nothing but a broken wing throwing a sliver of shade; there was what appeared to be a tolerably complete creature, lacking, I suppose, whatever essential parts had once served to animate it. And standing alongside a cooking pot with a man who could quite possibly have been Wun Lo himself was Augustus Silver.

His beard was immense—the beard of a hill wanderer, of a prospector lately returned from years in unmapped goldfields, and that beard and broad-brimmed felt hat, his Oriental coat and the sharp glint of arcane knowledge that shone from his eyes, the odd harpoon he held loosely in his right hand, the breadth of his shoulders—all those bits and pieces seemed almost to deify him, as if he were an incarnation of Neptune just out of the bay, or a wandering Odin who had stopped to drink flower-petal tea in a queer shantytown along the coast. The very look of him abolished my indecision. I left Wun Lo nodding in a chair, apparently having forgotten my presence.

Smoke hung in the air of the street. Thousands of sounds—a cacophony of voices, explosions, whirring pinwheels, Oriental music—mingled into a strange sort of harmonious silence. Somewhere to the northwest lay a village built of the skins of dragons. If nothing else—if I discovered nothing of the arrival of Augustus Silver—I would at least have a look at the shantytown in the photograph. I pushed through the crowd down Washington, oblivious to the sparks and explosions. Then almost magically, like the Red Sea, the throng parted and a broad avenue of asphalt opened before me. Along either side of the suddenly clear street were grinning faces, frozen in anticipation. A vast cheering arose, a shouting, a banging on Chinese cymbals and tooting on reedy little horns. Rounding the corner and rushing along with the maniacal speed of an express train, careered the leering head of a paper dragon, lolling back and forth, a wild rainbow mane streaming behind it. The body of the thing was half a block long, and seemed to be built of a thousand layers of the thinnest sort of pastel-colored rice paper, sheets and sheets of it threatening to fly loose and dissolve in the fog. A dozen people crouched within, racing along the pavement, the whole lot of them yowling and chanting as the crowd closed behind and in a wave pressed along east toward Kearny, the tumult and color muting once again into silence.

The rest of the afternoon had an air of unreality to it, which, strangely, deepened my faith in Augustus Silver and his creations, even though all rational evidence seemed to point squarely in the opposite direction. I drove north out of the city, cutting off at San Rafael toward the coast, toward Point Reyes and Inverness, winding through the green hillsides as the sun traveled down the afternoon sky toward the sea. It was shortly before dark that I stopped for gasoline.

The swerve of shoreline before me was a close cousin of that in the photograph, and the collected bungalows on the hillside could have been the ghosts of the dragon shanties, if one squinted tightly enough to confuse the image through a foliage of eyelashes. Perhaps I've gotten that backward; I can't at all say anymore which of the two worlds had substance and which was the phantom.

A bank of fog had drifted shoreward. But for that, perhaps I could have made out the top of the lighthouse and completed the picture. As it was I could see only the gray veil of mist wisping in on a faint onshore breeze. At the gas station I inquired about a map. Surely, I thought, somewhere close by, perhaps within eyesight if it weren't for the fog, lay my village. The attendant, a tobacco-chewing lump of engine oil and blue paper towels, hadn't heard of it—the dragon village, that is. He glanced sideways at me. A map hung in the window. It cost nothing to look. So I wandered into a steel and glass cubicle, cold with rust and sea air, and studied the map. It told me little. It had been hung recently; the tape holding its corners hadn't yellowed or begun to peel. Through an open doorway to my right was the dim garage where a Chinese mechanic tinkered with the undercarriage of a car on a hoist.

I turned to leave just as the hovering fog swallowed the sun, casting the station into shadow. Over the dark Pacific swell the mists whirled in the seawind, a trailing wisp arching skyward in a rush, like surge-washed tidepool grasses or the waving tail of an enormous misty dragon, and for a scattering of seconds the last faint rays of the evening sun shone out of the tattered fog, illuminating the old gas pumps, the interior of the weathered office, the dark, tool-strewn garage.

The map in the window seemed to curl at the corners, the tape suddenly brown and dry. The white background tinted into shades of antique ivory and pale ocher, and what had been creases in the paper appeared, briefly, to be hitherto unseen roads winding out of the redwoods toward the sea.

It was the strange combination, I'm sure, of the evening, the dying sun, and the rising fog that for a moment made me unsure whether the mechanic was crouched in his overalls beneath some vast and finny automobile spawned of the peculiar architecture of the early sixties, or instead worked beneath the chrome and iron shell of a tilted dragon, frozen in flight above the greasy concrete floor, and framed by tiers of heater hoses and old dusty tires.

Then the sun was gone. Darkness fell within moments, and all was as it had been. I drove slowly north through the village. There was, of course, no shantytown built of castaway dragons. There were nothing but warehouses and weedy vacant lots and the weathered concrete and tin of an occasional industrial building. A tangle of small streets comprised of odd, tumble-down shacks, some few of them on stilts as if awaiting a flood of apocalyptic proportions. But the shacks were built of clapboard and asphalt shingles—there wasn't a hint of a dragon anywhere, not even the tip of a rusted wing in the jimsonweed and mustard.

I determined not to spend the night in a motel, although I was tempted to, on the off chance that the fog would dissipate and the watery coastal moonbeams would wash the coastline clean of whatever it was—a trick of sunlight or a trick of fog—that had confused me for an instant at the gas station. But as I say, the day had, for the most part, been unprofitable, and the thought of being twenty dollars out of pocket for a motel room was intolerable.

It was late—almost midnight—when I arrived home, exhausted. My tomato worm slept in his den. The light still burned in Filby's garage, so I wandered out and peeked through the door. Filby sat on a stool, his chin in his hands, staring at the dismantled head of his beast. I suddenly regretted having looked in; he'd demand news of Silver, and I'd have nothing to tell him. The news—or rather the lack of news—seemed to drain the lees of energy from him. He hadn't slept in two days. Jensen had been round hours earlier babbling about an amazingly high tide and of his suspicion that the last of the crabs might yet put in an appearance. Did Filby want to watch on the beach that night? No, Filby didn't. Filby wanted only to assemble his dragon. But there was something not quite right—some wire or another that had gotten crossed, or a gem that had been miscut—and the creature wouldn't respond. It was so much junk.

I commiserated with him. Lock the door against Jensen's crab, I said, and wait until dawn. It sounded overmuch like a platitude, but Filby, I think, was ready to grasp at any reason, no matter how shallow, to leave off his tinkering.

The two of us sat up until the sun rose, drifting in and out of maudlin reminiscences and debating the merits of a stroll down to the bluffs to see how Jensen was faring. The high tide, apparently, was accompanied by a monumental surf, for in the spaces of meditative silence I could just hear the rush and thunder of long breakers collapsing on the beach. It seemed unlikely to me that there would be giant crabs afoot.

The days that followed saw no break in the weather. It continued dripping and dismal. No new letters arrived from Augustus Silver. Filby's dragon seemed to be in a state of perpetual decline. The trouble that plagued it receded deeper into it with the passing days, as if it were mocking Filby, who groped along in its wake, clutching at it, certain in the morning that he had the problem securely by the tail, morose that same afternoon that it had once again slipped away. The creature was a perfect wonder of separated parts. I'd had no notion of its complexity. Hundreds of those parts, by week's end, were laid out neatly on the garage floor, one after another in the order they'd been dismantled. Concentric circles of them expanded like ripples on a pond, and by Tuesday of the following week masses of them had been swept into coffee cans that sat here and there on the bench and floor. Filby was declining, I could see that. That week he spent less time in the garage than he had been spending there in a single day during the previous weeks, and he slept instead long hours in the afternoon.

I still held out hope for a letter from Silver. He was, after all, out there somewhere. But I was plagued with the suspicion that such a letter might easily contribute to certain of Filby's illusions—or to my own—and so prolong what with each passing day promised to be the final deflation of those same illusions. Better no hope, I thought, than impossible hope, than ruined anticipation.

But late in the afternoon, when from my attic window I could see Jensen picking his way along the bluffs, carrying with him a wood and brass telescope, while the orange glow of a diffused sun radiated through the thinned fog over the sea, I wondered where Silver was, what strange seas he sailed, what rumored wonders were drawing him along jungle paths that very evening.

One day he'd come, I was sure of it. There would be patchy fog illuminated by ivory moonlight. The sound of Eastern music, of Chinese banjos and copper gongs would echo over the darkness of the open ocean. The fog would swirl and part, revealing a universe of stars and planets and the aurora borealis dancing in transparent color like the thin rainbow light of paper lanterns hung in the windswept sky. Then the fog would close, and out of the phantom mists, heaving on the groundswell, his ship would sail into the mouth of the harbor, slowly, cutting the water like a ghost, strange sea creatures visible in the phosphorescent wake, one by one dropping away and returning to sea as if having accompanied the craft across ten thousand miles of shrouded ocean. We'd drink a beer, the three of us, in Filby's garage. We'd summon Jensen from his vigil.

But as I say, no letter came, and all anticipation was so much air. Filby's beast was reduced to parts—a plate of broken meats, as it were. The idea of it reminded me overmuch of the sad bony remains of a Thanksgiving turkey. There was nothing to be done. Filby wouldn't be placated. But the fog, finally, had lifted. The black oak in the yard was leafing out and the tomato plants were knee-high and luxuriant. My worm was still asleep, but I had hopes that the spring weather would revive him. It wasn't, however, doing a thing for Filby. He stared long hours at the salad of debris, and when in one ill-inspired moment I jokingly suggested he send to Detroit for a carburetor, he cast me such a savage look that I slipped out again and left him alone.

On Sunday afternoon a wind blew, slamming Filby's

garage door until the noise grew tiresome. I peeked in, aghast. There was nothing in the heaped bits of scrap that suggested a dragon, save one dismantled wing, the silk and silver of which was covered with greasy hand prints. Two cats wandered out. I looked for some sign of Jensen's crab, hoping, in fact, that some such rational and concrete explanation could be summoned to explain the ruin. But Filby, alas, had quite simply gone to bits along with his dragon. He'd lost whatever strange inspiration it was that propelled him. His creation lay scattered, no two pieces connected. Wires and fuses were heaped amid unidentifiable crystals, and one twisted bit of elaborate machinery had quite clearly been danced upon and lay now cold and dead, half hidden beneath the bench. Delicate thises and thats sat mired in a puddle of oil that scummed half the floor.

Filby wandered out, adrift, his hair frazzled. He'd received a last letter. There were hints in it for extensive travel, perhaps danger. Silver's visit to the west coast had been delayed again. Filby ran his hand backward through his hair, oblivious to the harrowed result the action effected. He had the look of a nineteenth-century Bedlam lunatic. He muttered something about having a sister in McKinleyville, and seemed almost illuminated when he added, apropos of nothing, that in his sister's town, deeper into the heart of the north coast, stood the tallest totem pole in the world. Two days later he was gone. I locked his garage door for him and made a vow to collect his mail with an eye toward a telling, exotic postmark. But nothing so far has appeared. I've gotten into the habit of spending the evening on the beach with Jensen and his son Bumby, both of whom still hold out hope for the issuance of the last crab. The spring sunsets are unimaginable. Bumby is as fond of them as I am, and can see comparable whorls of color and pattern in the spiral curve of a seashell or in the peculiar green depths of a tidepool.

In fact, when my tomato worm lurched up out of his burrow and unfurled an enormous gauzy pair of mottled brown wings, I took him along to the seaside so that Bumby could watch him set sail, as it were.

The afternoon was cloudless and the ocean sighed on the beach. Perhaps the calm, insisted Jensen, would appeal to the crab. But Bumby by then was indifferent to the fabled crab. He stared into the pickle jar at the half-dozen circles of bright orange dotting the abdomen of the giant sphinx moth that had once crept among my tomato plants in a clever disguise. It was both wonderful and terrible, and held a weird fascination for Bumby, who tapped at the jar, making up and discarding names.

When I unscrewed the lid, the moth fluttered skyward some few feet and looped around in a crazy oval, Bumby charging along in its wake, then racing away in pursuit as the monster hastened south. The picture of it is as clear to me now as rainwater: Bumby running and jumping, kicking up glinting sprays of sand, outlined against the sheer rise of mossy cliffs, and the wonderful moth just out of reach overhead, luring Bumby along the afternoon beach. At last it was impossible to say just what the diminishing speck in the china-blue sky might be—a tiny winged creature silhouetted briefly on the false horizon of our cove, or some vast flying reptile swooping over the distant ocean where it fell away into the void, off the edge of the flat earth.

Up the Wall
by
Esther M. Friesner

Esther M. Friesner's first sale was to Isaac Asimov's Science Fiction Magazine *in 1982; she's subsequently become a regular contributer there, as well as selling frequently to markets such as* The Magazine of Fantasy and Science Fiction, Amazing, Pulphouse, *and elsewhere. In the years since 1982, she's also become one of the most prolific of modern fantasists, with thirteen novels in print, and has established herself as one of the funniest writers to enter the field in some while. Her many novels include* Mustapha and His Wise Dog, Elf Defense, Druid's Blood, Sphinxes Wild, Here Be Demons, Demon Blues, Hooray for Hellywood, Broadway Banshee, Ragnarok and Roll, *and* The Water King's Daughter. *She's reported to be at work on her first hard science fiction novel. She lives with her family in Madison, Connecticut.*

Here she takes us to ancient Briton, to a time when the power of the Roman legions is on the wane, for a surprising and very *funny look at the roots of legend.*

* * *

A gust of northcountry air swept over the undulating hump of Hadrian's Wall, still bearing with it the chill of the sea. The northcountry was the hard country—even the starveling sheep had the grim air of failed philosophers—but worse land yet lay north of the wall, in wild Caledonia, if the word of tribal Celts and travelers could be believed. Two figures in the full finery of the Roman legions paced the earthworks as dusk came on. The last rays of the setting sun struck gold from the breast of the eagle standard jammed into the soil between them. In looks, in bearing, in the solemn silence folded in wings around them, they carried a taste of eternity.

It all would have been very heroic and poetical if the shorter man had not reached up under his tunic and *pteruges*, undone his *bracae*, and taken a long, reflective pee in the direction of Orkney. His comrade affected not to notice.

Rather by way of distraction than conversation, the taller fellow broke silence almost simultaneously with his mate's breaking wind. In a good, loud, carrying voice he declaimed, "Joy to the Ninth, Caius Lucius Piso! The days of the beast are numbered. It shall be today that the hero comes; I feel it. This morning all the omens were propitious." He had the educated voice and diction a senator's son might envy. His Latin was high and pure, preserved inviolate even here, at the northernmost outpost of the legions. He turned to his mate. "What news from the south?"

"News?" his companion echoed. Then he placed a stubby tongue between badly chapped lips and blew a sound that never issued from the wolf's-head bell of any bucina. "Sweet sodding Saturn, Junie, how the blazes would *I* have any more news from the friggin' south than you, stuck up here freezin' me cobblers off, waitin' on the relief—see if *them* buggers ever show up, bleedin' arse-lickers the lot of 'em, and everyone knows Tullius Cato's old lady's been slippin' into the commander's bedroll, so *he* never pulls the shit-shift, wish *my* girl'd show half as much support for me career, but that's women for you—only women ain't so much to your taste, now as I remember the barrack-room gab, are they, no offense taken, I hope?"

His Latin was somewhat less than that of his hawk-faced comrade-in-arms.

Junius Claudius Maro regarded the balding, podgy little man with a look fit to petrify absolutely that fellow's already chilled cobblers. "You presume too much upon our training days, Caius Lucius Piso. Were I to report the half of what you have just said, our beloved commander could order the flesh flayed from your bones." He settled the drape of his thick wool mantle more comfortably on his shoulders, then suffered a happy afterthought: "With a steel-tipped knout. However, for the love that is between us,

I will say nothing." He looked inordinately pleased with himself.

"Right, then," said Caius Lucius Piso. His own afterthought bid him add: "Ta." He uprooted the Imperial eagle, hoisted it fishpole-wise over one shoulder, and casually commenced a westerly ramble. "I'll just be toddling on down the wall, eh? Have a bit of a lookabout? Keep one peeper peeled for this hero fella you say's coming, maybe kindle a light, start a little summat boiling on the guardroom fire, hot wine, the cup that cheers, just the thing what with a winter like we're like to have, judging by the misery as's crept into me bones. Bring you back a cuppa, Junie?" This last comment was flung back from a goodly distance down the wall, went unheard, and received no reply.

The nearest guardroom along that section of the wall where the ill-matched pair patrolled had once been a thing of pride, to judge by its size. It was large enough to have housed sheep, for whatever purpose. Years and neglect had done their damnedest to bring pride to a fall. Hares and foxes took it in turn to nest in the tumbledown sections of the derelict structure, but there was still a portion of the building with a make-do roof of old blankets and sod. In the lee of the October winds, surrounded by shadows, Caius Lucius Piso knelt to poke up the small peat fire in the pit.

The flame caught and flared, banishing darkness. Caius gasped as his small fire leaped in reflection on the iron helmet and drawn sword of the man hunkered on his hams in the dingy guardroom. The image of a slavering wild boar cresting his helmet seemed to leap out at the trembling Roman. Beneath the brim, two small, red, and nasty orbs glared. From porcine eyes to bristly snout, there was a striking family resemblance between boar crest and crest-wearer.

There was also the matter of the man's sword. Caius Lucius Piso's initial impression of that weapon had not been wrong. It was indeed as large, keen, and unsheathed as it had seemed at first glance. It was also leveled at the crouching Roman. The man snarled foreign words and raised the sword several degrees, sending ripples through his thickly corded forearm muscles. Many of his teeth were broken, all were yellow as autumn crocus, and the stench emanating from him, body and bearskin, was enough to strike an unsuspecting passer-by senseless. He looked like a man to whom filth was not just a way of life, but a religious calling:

Caius Lucius Piso knew a hero when he saw one.

"Oh, *shit*," he said.

"*That's* him?" Goewin knotted her fists on her hips and studied the new arrival. "*That's* our precious hero?"

"Hush now, dear, he'll hear you." Caius Lucius Piso made small dampening motions with his hands, but the lady of his hearth and heart was undaunted. She had been the one who'd taught him how to make that obnoxious tongue-and-lips blatting sound, after all.

"Hush yerself, you great cowpat. Who cares *does* he hear me? Stupid clod don't speak *fly*speck of honest Gaelic." She smiled sweetly at the visitor, who stood beside the oxhide-hung doorway, arms crossed. He appeared to disapprove of everything he saw within the humble hut, and, without a word, somehow conveyed the message that he had sheathed his fearsome sword under protest.

"Who'd like a bit of the old nip-and-tuck with any ewe he fancies, then?" Goewin asked him, still smiling. "Whose Mum did it for kippers?"

"Goewin, for Mithra's sake, the man's a guest. *And* a hero! He's only biding under our roof until they're ready to receive him formally at headquarters."

"*Hind*quarters, you mean, if it's the Commander yer speaking of."

"Epona's east tit, woman, mind your tongue! If word gets back to the commander that you've been rude to his chosen hero . . ." Caius Lucius turned chalky at the thought.

"A *hero?*" Goewin cocked her head at the impassive presence guarding her doorway. "*Him?*" She clicked her tongue. "If *that's* the sort of labor we're down to bringing into Britain, just to take care of a piddling beast *you* lot could handle, weren't you such hermaphros, *well*—"

"That's not fair and you know it, Goewin. You can't call a monster big enough to carry off five legionaries any sort of piddler."

"Oh, pooh. 'Tisn't as if it carried all five off in one go. I've not seen it anymore than you have, but I know different. You Romans *always* exaggerate, as many a poor girl's learned to her sorrow on the wedding night or 'round the Beltaine fires. Probably no more'n a newt with glanders, but straightaway you lot bawl 'Dragon!' and off for help you run. Bunch of babes. And if *that* piece propping up the doorpost's the best you could drum up on the Continent—" She shrugged expressively. "This country's just going to ruin, Cai, that's all." She slouched over to grasp the stranger's impressive left bicep. "Look 'ee here. Shoddy goods, that is. Scrawnier than—"

There was a flicker of cold steel. The man's dagger was smaller than his sword, lighter, far handier, with a clean line that would never go out of style. It was almost the size of a Roman legionary's shortsword, but he handled it with more address. Presently it addressed Goewin's windpipe.

"*Ave*, all," said Junius, pulling back the oxhide and stepping unwittingly into the midst of this small domestic drama. "The commander is now prepared to greet our noble visitor with all due—"

The noble visitor growled something unintelligible and dropped his dagger point from Goewin's throat. Caius Lucius rather supposed that his guest disliked interruptions. Junius stared as the blade turned its attention to him.

"Now just a moment—" Junius objected in his flawless Latin.

A moment was all Caius Lucius wished. His wife was safe, but now his messmate was in danger. Dragon or no, and never mind that Junie Maro was the biggest prig the Glorious Ninth had ever spawned, the bonds of the legion still stood for *some*thing. While trying to remember precisely what, he picked up a small wine jug and belted the noble visitor smack on top of his iron boar.

Junius Claudius Maro looked down at the crumpled heap of clay shards, fur, and badly tanned leather at his feet, then gave Caius Lucius a filthy glare by way of thanks for his life. "You *idiot*," he said.

"You're welcome, I'm sure," Caius replied. Sullen and bitter, he added, "Didn't kill 'im. Didn't even snuff his wick."

That much was true. The man was not unconscious, just badly dazed and grinning like a squirrel. Caius Lucius watched, astounded, as old Junie knelt beside the stunned barbarian and spoke to him in a strange, harsh tongue. Still half loopy, the man responded haltingly in kind, and before long the two of them were deep in earnest conversation punctuated by bellowing laughter.

"You—you *speak* that gibberish, Junie?" Caius Lucius ventured to ask when his comrade finally stood up.

"*Geatish*, not gibberish," Junius replied, wiping tears of hilarity from his eyes. "Gods, and to think I never believed the *pater* when he told me it's the only tongue on earth fit for telling a really *elegant* latrine joke! Later on, you must remind me to tell you the one about—but no. The pun won't translate, and, in any case, Ursus here says he's going to kill you in a bit. If our commander doesn't have you crucified first, for nearly doing in our dragon-slayer."

Caius Lucius gaped. "*Crucified?*"

His wife sighed. "Didn't me Mum just *warn* me you'd come to a bad end. Now I'll have to listen to the old girl's bloody I-told-you-so's 'til Imbolc. *Honestly*, Cai—!"

"Caius Lucius Piso, you are accused of damaging legion property." The Commander of the Ninth slurped an oyster and gave the accused the fish-eye. "This man has been brought into our service at great *personal* expense to deal with our—ah—little problem, and you make free with his cranial integrity." The commander grinned, never loath to let his audience know when he'd come up with an especially elegant turn of phrase. Marcus Septimus, the commander's secretary, toady, and emergency catamite, applauded dutifully and made a note of it.

"Bashed him one on the conk, he did," Goewin piped up from the doorway. "I *saw* 'im!"

Caius could not turn to give his wife the killing look she deserved. He was compelled to stand facing his commander, head bowed, and hear Goewin condemn him with one breath, then, with the second, titter, "Ooooh, Maxentius, you keep your hands to *yourself*, you horrid goat! And me not even a widow yet!" Her pleased tone of voice belied her harsh words. Obviously, Goewin did not believe in waiting until the last minute to provide for her future.

Caius scuffed his already worn *perones* in the packed earthen floor of the commander's hut, and tried to think of something besides death. It didn't help to dwell on the thought of killing old Junie, for that specific fantasy always veered over to the general theme of *thanatos*, which by turns yanked his musings back to his own imminent fate. The commander was not happy, and all the way back to the first generation, the Commanders of the Ninth had had a simple way of dealing with their discontent.

"Right. Guilty. Crucify him," said the commander.

Junius looked smug. He stood at the commander's left hand while the man he had dubbed Ursus sprawled on a bench to the right. He still wore the boar's head helm, but now the eyes beneath the brim no longer showed murderous rage. Instead they roved slowly around the hut, silently weighing the worth and transportability of every even vaguely valuable item they spied. They only paused in their mercantile circuit when Junius leaned around the back of the commander's chair to whisper a translation of Caius' sentence in the barbarian's shaggy ear.

Something like a flint-struck spark kindled in the depths of those tiny eyes. "NEVER!" Ursus bawled—and then all Hades broke loose.

Afterwards, Caius could not say whether he was more shocked by the barbarian's reaction, or by the fact that he had understood the man's exclamation precisely.

He quickly shelved linguistic musings in favor of survival. It really *was* an impressive tantrum the barbarian was throwing; he also threw the bench. Everyone in the commander's hut who could reach an exit, did so, in short order. The commander and all members of the makeshift tribunal held their ground, but only because they were cut off from the sole escape route by the rampaging dragon-slayer himself.

Ursus was on his feet, each clenched fist the size of a toddler's skull. He gave a fierce kick, knocking over a little tabouret bearing a bowl of windfalls and a silver wine jug with matched goblets. He picked up the fallen objects one by one and flung them at the hut's curved walls. Though his sword and dagger had perforce been laid aside before coming into the commander's presence, he still looked able to reduce the population barehanded, *ad libitum*. Throughout this demonstration, he continued to chant, "Never, never, *never!*"

The commander's face resembled an adolescent cheese. His jowls shuddered as much as his voice when he inquired so very delicately of his guest, "What? *Never?*"

When Junius went to translate this into Geatish, the hero seized him by the throat and shook him until his kneecaps rattled. He pitched the Roman javelin-fashion at the open doorway of the commander's house. Unfortunately, he missed his aim by a handspan. Junius came up face-first against a doorpost and knocked one of the severed heads out of its niche. The commander's woman, a hutproud lady, fussed loudly as she dusted it off and tucked it back where it belonged.

Junius received no such attentions.

Ursus glowered at the fallen foe.

"Far though my fate has flung me,
Weary the whale-road wandering,
Still shall I no stupidity stomach,
Butt and baited of boobies!"

All this he spat at his retired translator. He used a sadly corrupt version of Latin, admixed higgledy-piggledy with a sprinkling of other tongues. Like most bastards, it had its charm, and was able to penetrate where purebreds could not follow. It took some concentration, but every man of the Ninth who heard Ursus speak so, understood him.

Caius took a tentative step towards his unexpected champion. "You haven't half got a bad accent, mate. For a bloody foreigner, I mean. Pick up the tongue from a trader, then?"

Ursus' eyes narrowed, making them nigh invisible. He motioned for Caius to approach, and when the little man complied, he grabbed him and hoisted him onto tip-toe by a knot of tunic.

"Hear me, O halfling halfblood,
Lees of the legion's long lingering
Here hard by Hadrian's human-reared hillock!
Your lowly life I love not.
Murder you might I meetly,
Yet you are young and useful.
Wise is the woman-born warrior
Dragons who dauntless dares;
Smarter the soul who sword-smites serpents
Carefully, in company of comrades."

Caius was still puzzling this out when Marcus Septimus inched up behind him and whispered, "I think he wants a sword-bearer or something to stand by while he does in the dragon for us."

"Want *my* opinion," Caius growled out of the corner of his mouth, "the bugger's just as scared as the rest of us. Sword-bearer, my arse! What he wants is *bait!*"

"We could still crucify you," Marcus suggested.

Caius got his hands up and delicately disengaged the barbarian's hold on his tunic. Once there was solid earth under his feet again, he said, "All right, Ursus. You've got me over the soddin' barrel. I'll go."

Everyone left in the hut smiled, including Junius, who had just rejoined the sentient.

Ursus clapped the little legionary on the shoulder and declaimed: "Victory velcomes the valiant!"

Marcus raised one carefully plucked brow and clucked. "'Velcomes?' Hmph. If they're going to come over here and take our coin, they might at *least* learn to speak our language properly!"

"Silly Geat," Junius agreed, rubbing his head.

Ursus was neither deaf nor amused, and his smattering of Latin was enough to parse personal remarks. He gathered up the two critics as lesser men might pick strawberries. Marcus cast an imploring glance at the commander, who was suddenly consumed by a passion to get to know his toenails better.

"Sagas they sing of swordsmen," Ursus informed them.
"Hymn they the homicidal.
Geats, though for glory greedy,
Shame think it not to share.
Wily, the Worm awaits us.
Guides will I guard right gladly!
And, should the shambler slay you,
Sorrow shall I sincerely."

Caius leered at the two wriggling captives. "In other words, gents, we've *all* been bloody drafted."

"Oh, I hate this, hate this, *hate this*," Marcus whined as they trudged along Hadrian's Wall, fruitlessly trying to keep pace with Ursus.

"Put a *caliga* in it, you miserable cow! It's not like he'd tapped *you* to be his weapons bearer." Caius gave Marcus an encouraging jab with the bundle of spears that had been wished on him by his new boss. "All *you've* got to do is lead him to the fen where the monster's skulking and take off once the fun starts. Shouldn't be too hard for you."

"We're all going to *die*," Marcus moaned. "The dragon will be all stirred up, and it will slay that great brute before you can say *hic ibat Simois*, and then it will come after *us*. I can't outrun a dragon! Not in *these* shoes."

At the head of the line where he marched beside Ursus, a spare eagle standard jouncing along on his shoulder, Junius overheard and gave them a scornful backwards glance. He said something that Caius did not quite catch, but which caused Marcus to make an obscene gesture.

"Soddin' ears going on me," Caius complained. "What'd he say, then?"

"*That*—" Marcus pursed his ungenerous mouth "—was *Greek*."

"Greek to *me*, all right," Caius agreed. "Junie always was a bloody show-off."

"He said we were both slackers and cowards, and when we get back and he tells the Commander how badly we've disgraced the Glorious Ninth in front of the hired help, we'll both be crucified."

"Not *that* again." Caius shifted the spears. "I'm fucking sick and tired of Junie and his thrice-damned crucifixions. Mithra, it's like a bally religion with him. What's he need to get off, then? A handful of sesterce spikes and a mallet?"

"He also said that he was going to warn Arctos to keep a weather eye on us so we don't bolt."

Caius flung down his bundle, exasperated. "*Now* who's been wished on us for this little deathmarch, eh? Bad enough we're to split two men's rations four ways—sod the commander for a stone-arsed miser—but who's this fifth wheel coming to join us?"

The clatter of falling spears made the rest of the party draw up short. Marcus was totally bewildered. "*What* fifth wheel?"

"This Arctos bastard who'll be baby-minding us, that's who!" Caius shouted.

Junius regarded the angry little man with disdain. "I will thank you to keep a civil tongue in your head when speaking of our *pro tempore* commander, Caius Lucius Piso." He then turned to the barbarian and added, "Do not kill him yet, O august Ursus. We will need him to carry the spears."

"Arctos *is* Ursus, Cai, old boy," Marcus whispered. "Greek, Latin, same meaning, same name. So sorry if I confused you. The drawbacks of a really good classical education." He tittered behind his hand.

"Sod off," Caius growled, gathering up the armory.

It was some three days later that the little group finally stepped off on the northern side of the wall and reached their goal. Gray and brown and thoroughly uninviting, the fen stretched out before them. Mist lay thick upon the quaking earth. A few scraggly bushes, their branches stripped of foliage, clung to the banks of the grim tarn like the clutching hands of drowning men going under for the last time.

"—and the best freshwater fishing for miles about." Caius sighed as he viewed the haunt of their watery Nemesis. "If the commander wasn't half such a great glutton, we could leave the fish to the dragon and eat good boiled mutton like honest folk. But *no*. Off he goes, filling our ears with endless, colicky speeches about the honor of the Ninth and all that Miles Gloriosus codswallop, when the *truth* is that he just fancies a sliver of stuffed pike now and again. So in he brings this hero fella, and now our lives aren't worth a tench's fart."

"I heard that!" Junius called. "And when the commander finds out—"

"Junie, love, why don't you go nail your balls to a board?" Marcus Septimus remarked over-sweetly.

Caius patted the former secretary on the back. "You know, Marc, old dear, you're not a bad sort for a catamite."

The barbarian directed his helpers to pitch camp, which they did in swift, efficient, legion fashion. Despite their internal bickerings, proper training made them work well together. Even Marcus did not manage to get too badly underfoot. When the lone tent was pitched and dinner on the boil, Caius flopped down on the damp ground without further ceremony.

"Oh, me aching back! Mithra knows how many friggin' *milia pasuum* we've covered, and for what? Just so's we'd be on time to be ate tomorrow morning!"

A gaunt shadow fell across his closed eyes. "Get up, Caius Lucius Piso," Junius said, using the tip of his foot to put some muscle behind the order. "The food is ready and we can't find Ursus anywhere."

"Can't we now?" Caius did not bother to open his eyes. "Here's me heart, bleeding like a stuck pig over the news. Run off, has he? Jupiter, I never figured the big ox to have a fraction so much sense as *that*. Commander shouldn't've paid him in advance."

"He was paid nothing." Junius' words were as dry as Goewin's onion tart. "Nor has he run off. Ursus is a *hero*."

"Says who? Himself?"

Junius tucked his hands tightly into the crooks of his elbows. "Our commander is not without his sources of information, nor would he engage such an important hireling blind. He heard nothing but the most sterling reports of our man's prowess at disposing of supernumerary monsters. Granted, the fellow's one of those Ultima Thule types who hails from where they've the better part of the year to work on polishing their lies for the spring trade, but even discounting a third of what they say he's done—"

Caius made that blatting sound again.

"In any case, our noble commander is not the sort to make a bad bargain, and were he to hear *you* so much as *implying* that he might, he would—"

"Yes, yes, I know, crucify me." Caius forced himself to stand. "I'll go fetch 'im, then, before you get yer hands all over calluses from nailing me up."

Caius didn't have far to go before he found his temporary leader. The barbarian squatted on a little hummock of high ground overlooking the fen, his sword jammed into a large, moldy-looking log some short distance away. His helmet was off, propped upside-down between his ankles, and his left hand kept dipping into it, then traveling to his mouth. Caius smelled a penetrating sweetness above the fetid reek of the marshland.

"Hail, heart-strong helper!" Ursus beamed at the little Roman. Viscous golden brown strands dripped from his beard and moustache.

"Hail yerself," Caius replied. He sauntered up the hummock and scrooched down beside the barbarian. "Got something good, have we?" He peered into the upended helm.

Ursus nodded cheerfully, his expression miraculously purged of any bloodlust. He jerked one thumb at the log, while with the other hand he shoved the helmet at Caius.

"Hollow this harvest's home,
Fallen the forest friend
Ages ago, several seasons spent.

Rotten and rent, core and root,
Toppled to turf the tall tree.
Gilded the gliding gladiators,
Plying their pleasant pastime,
Sweetness sun-gold instilling,
Honey they heap in hives.
Noisy their nest they name,
Daring and daunting dastards,
Stabbing with stings to startle
Thieves that their treasure try taking.
Came then the conquering caller,
Scorning their scabrous squabbles,
Their dire drones disdaining,
Helping himself to honey.
Right were the runes they wrought
When saw he first the sunlight,
Bidding the birthed boy Bee-wolf
Never another name know."

"Boy? Who gave birth to what boy hereabouts?" Caius' eyes darted about suspiciously.

The barbarian struck his own chest a fearsome thump.

"Oh." Caius dipped into the honey. Through gummy lips he added, "Going on about yerself, then, were you?"

The barbarian bobbed his head eagerly.

"Nice bit o' puffery, that. Bee-wolf, eh? That'd be yer common or garden variety bear, ain't it? So that's why Junie stuck you with Ursus, leave it to *him* not to have more imagination than a badger's bottom. Kind of a circumlocutionariatory way to go about naming a sprat, don't ask *me* why you'd want yer kid associated in decent folks' minds with a horrid great smelly beast what hasn't the brains of a turnip, though it does make for a tasty stew, especially *with* a turnip or two, gods know *I* hope you didn't smell like one from the minute you were born—a bear, I mean, not a turnip; *nor* a stew—but you can't bloody tell about foreigners, now can you? Never one word where twenty'll do, no offense taken, I hope?"

Bee-wolf nodded, still grinning. His find of wild honey had sweetened his temper amazingly well.

"'Course, not that a name like that don't have its poetry to it, mate. A man needs a bit of poetry in his life now and again." Caius chewed up a fat hunk of waxy comb and spat dead bees into the fen with casual accuracy. "'Mongst my Goewin's folk—Goewin's the jabbery little woman you came near to filleting with yer dagger—they keep a whole *stable* of bards plumped up just to natter on about how this chief slew that one and made off with his cattle. It's a wonder to me the poor beasties have a bit o' flesh left on their bones, the way those mad Celts keep peaching 'em back and forth, forth and back, always on the move. Savagery, *I* call it; not like us Romans. Compassionate, we are—one of the refinements of civilization. Cruelty to dumb brutes makes me want to spew."

Caius leaned forward, encouraged to this intimacy by the barbarian's continued calm. "Now if it were up to *me*," he confided, "I'd leave this poor soddin' dragon alone, I would. Live and let live, I say—that's the civilized way to go about it. It's not as though he's ate up more'n *five* of our men, after all, and we've just got guesses to go by even for that. Only one witness ever come back to tell us it *were* the dragon for certain as ate 'em , or even *was* they ate, and *that* man was our *signifer* Drusus Llyr, what no one knew his parents was first cousins 'till it was too late, and *he* died stark bonkers that very night. You want me considered opinion, them fellers went over the Wall, they did, fed up to their gizzards with the commander and the whole glorious Ninth fucking Legion." He drew a deep sigh. "Can't say as I blame 'em. Can't even rightly say as I wouldn't do the same."

Ursus looked puzzled.

"Came the commander's call.
Summoning my sword to serve him.
Nobly the Ninth he named,
Home and haven of heroes."

"Arr, that's just recruitment blabber." Caius waved it all aside. "Lot of fine talk, all of it slicker than goose shit, just to rope in the young men as are half stupid, half innocent, and t'other half ignorant, no offense meant. Once in a while he manages to gammon a few of the local brats into uniform, but mostly it's sons of the legion following in their Da's footsteps because a camp upbringing's ruined 'em for honest work stealing cattle. Na, the Ninth's not what she used to be."

"When, I do wistful wonder,
  Was this, thy lonesome legion
  More than a muddle of men
  Prowling the piddling plowlands,
  Wandering the Wall's wide way?"

"Wozzat? Oh, I get yer. Well, truth to tell—" Caius leaned in even closer and nearly rested his elbow in the honey "—I haven't the foggiest. See, mate, *used* to be as the Ninth was as fine a lot of pureblood Roman soldiers as ever you'd fancy—and didn't our commander just! But then, well . . . you know as how *things* have this narsty way of just . . . *happening*, like?"

"Fate do I fear not.
  Still, circumstances stun stalwarts.
  Here, have more honey."

Caius did so. "Like I been saying, what with the wild upcountry folk the Ninth was first sent here to deal with, always on the march, camp here today, there tomorrow, try to keep the Celtic chieftains in line or even learn to tell 'em *apart* one from the other, and what with the odd carryings-on back home in dear old Roma Mater, inside the city, out in the provinces, up 'crost the German frontier with them as must be yer kissin' cousins, Saxons and Goths and that lot, *well*, in comes one rosy-fingered dawn and gooses our then-commander with the fact that there ain't no orders come through from Rome or even Londinium to tell us arse from elbow. No *orders*, mate! You know what *that* means to a professional soldier and bureaucrat like our commander?"

"No, that knowledge I know not."

"Small wonder you would, you being a hero and all. Stand up for yerself, do what you like, go where the fancy takes you. But *regular army?* We don't dare take a *shit* without proper orders to wipe off with after. So when there *wasn't* none coming through, we dug in where we was, up by the Wall, took up with the local ladies, bred our boys to the Legion and our girls to bribe any tribes we couldn't beat in a fair fight, and we waited." Caius rested his face on one hand, forgetting it was the one he'd been using to dip into Ursus' helmet. "We're still waiting, man and boy, father to son, can't *tell* you how bloody long it's been."

The barbarian tilted his helmet and slurped out the last of the plundered honey. He wiped his gooey whiskers on the back of an equally hairy forearm, then said:

"Strangely this strikes me as scoop-skulled.
Why do you wait and wonder?
Beneath your brows lurk brains or bran?
Sit you thus centuries? Shitheads."

Caius made a hand-sign that translated across any number of cultures. "Look, mate, so long as our bleedin' commander, latest in a long line of Imperially appointed shitheads, has got more than three like old Junie there to lick his tail and say *please, sir, what's for afters?* it's no use running off. There's precious little as *is* to keep the men occupied. Hunting down a deserter'd be a rare treat for any of 'em. And it's as much as my life's worth to speak up and say let's break camp and head south like sensible folk, try to scare up some news from Rome as isn't staler than week-old pig piss. See, so long as we're up *here*, our commander's the law. Go *south*, and he could find out that the only thing he's got a right to control is his own bladder, and not too strict a say over *that*. So if a man's fool enough to suggest a move off the Wall, 'Orders is orders,' he'd say, 'and traitors is traitors. And we of the Glorious Ninth know what to do with *traitors*, don't we, Junie, me proud beauty?'"

"Crudely crucify the creatures," Ursus supplied.

"You're not just talking through yer helmet there, mate," Caius agreed. "Speaking of which, it's in a proper mess. Give 'er here to me, and you go fetch that boar-sticker of yours out of the log. We'll have a proper wash-up—me for the helmet, you for the blade, before she rusts silly, doesn't anybody ever teach you barbarians respect for a good bit of steel?—then we'll go back to camp and get some oil for the pair of 'em. Supper's ready, and if we let it go to the bad, Junie'll be off crucifying us left and right again."

"Dares he the deed to do,
Sooner my sword shall steep its steel,
Blood-drinker, blade and brother,
Entirely in his entrails."

Caius took up the helmet, beaming. "You're a decent sort, Bee-wolf, for a bleedin' hero." He toddled down the slope to rinse out the helmet.

As he squatted to his task in the shallows, a tuneless ditty on his lips, a loud, wet, crunch hard by his right foot made him start and keel over into the murky water. The helmet went flying out over the fenland, landing with an echoing *plop* in a nearby pool.

Junius Claudius Maro leaned hard on the eagle standard and observed the helm's trajectory with a critical eye. "*Now* you shall not escape punishment, Caius Lucius Piso."

"*Punishment?*" Caius spluttered, scarcely feeling the cold water that seeped through his clothes. Rage kept him warm. "After *you* was the one as scared the *bracae* off me, sneaking up and chunking that whopping great standard into the sod like you was trying to spit me foot with it?" He picked himself up out of the shoreline muck and hailed the hummock. "Oi! Bee-wolf! You saw him do that, didn't you? You saw as it wasn't no fault of *mine* that your helmet—"

But Bee-wolf was not paying attention to the angry little Roman. He stood on the high ground, honey still gumming his beard, and stared out across the fen to the spot where his boar-crest helmet had gone down. He made no move to yank his sword free of the fallen log where it still stood wedged in the heart of the ruined beehive. Something in the barbarian's sudden pallor and paralysis stilled Caius' own tongue. From the corner of one eye, he saw that Junie was likewise rapt with terror. He did not *want* to see what had frightened them so, but, at last, look he did.

The fen bubbled. The slimy surface heaved. Slowly, seemingly as slender as a maiden's arm, a snakey form broke the face of the stagnant water. On and on it came, climbing even higher into the clear air, until Caius thought that there simply could *not* be any more to come without ripping reality wide open and sending all the world plunging down into the gods' own nightmares. He was only half aware of the eagle standard toppling over into the mud as Junie whirled and fled. This sudden movement galvanized the lazily rising length of serpentine flesh. The spade-shaped head darted within arm's length of Caius, ignoring the petrified little man as if he were part of the scenery. A maw lined with needle-like teeth gaped open, impossibly wide, and sharp jaws clamped shut around Junie, hauberk, shriek, and all.

"Oh, I *say!*" Caius exclaimed, as his comrade's scream knocked his own tongue free. Automatically, he stooped to retrieve the fallen standard, then turned to the hummock and bawled, "*There's* your bloody fen-monster, Bee-wolf, old boy! Do for 'er now while she's busy with poor Junie and you've got surprise on yer . . ." His words dribbled away.

The high ground was bare, the hero nowhere to be seen.

"*Coward!*" came Marcus' angry shout from the direction of camp. "You pusillanimous, recreant, craven, dastardly, caitiff—Oooooh, you *rabbit*, come back with Cai's *sword!*" The commander's secretary came stomping into sight of the fen just as the monster commenced reeling in a struggling Junie.

Caius heard Marcus's yips of shock blend nicely with Junie's continued screaming and blubbering. The dragon was imperturbable, allowing the bulk of his still-submerged and leisurely sinking body to drag his prize into the fen. Caius watched as span after span of sequentially decreasing neck slipped past him. It would not be long before Junie followed, down into the fen, without so much as a last *vale* for his old messmate.

"Bloody foreigners," Caius grumbled, and, raising the eagle standard high, he brought it crunching down as hard as he was able, just at the moment when the monster's head came by.

BONK.

The dragon froze, its wicked mouth falling open. Junius

flopped out. He wasted no time in questioning deliverance, but hauled his body free. He was breathing hoarsely—no doubt he had a rib or two the worse for wear—but he was able to pull himself a little ways up the shore.

Caius smashed the beast in the head again with the eagle of the Ninth, putting all his weight in it. He and Junie looked at each other. "One bloody word out of you about damaging legion property, Junie," he shouted, "and it's back in the fen I'll toss you myself!"

"Not a word, not one!" Junie wheezed, pulling himself farther up the bank. Marcus came running down, holding his tunic well out of the mud, and tried to hoist the injured man without soiling himself. It was an impossible endeavor.

"Cai, leave that horrid creature alone and come here *right now* and help me with Junius!" he called. "Go on, let it be, it's had enough."

"Stop yer gob, will you?" Caius was panting with the effort of using the legion standard as a bludgeon, but he lofted it for a third blow anyhow. "If this bugger's just stunned, *I'm* nearest, and I'll be twigged if I'll be the tasty pud to tempt an invalid monster's palate when it comes to. Not just to keep *your* tunic clean, Missy Vestal!"

"Well, who died and made *us* Jupiter Capitolinus?" With a peeved sniff, Marcus slung Junie's arm around his neck, letting the mud slop where it would. "If you're still speaking to the *plebs*, Cai, we'll be back in camp." He hustled Junie out of sight without waiting to see the eagle descend for the third time.

The beast had been hissing weakly, but the final smash put paid to that. There was a sickening crunch that Caius felt all the way up his arms and shoulders, and then it was no longer possible to tell where the monster's skull ended and the bogland began. Caius wiped his sweating brow, getting honey all over his face. "*That's* done," he said, "and damned if anyone'll credit it. Goewin won't, for one; not without proof, and that means the head." He felt for his sword, then remembered that not only had he left it in camp, but the barbarian had made off with it.

"Vesta's smoking hole!" He thrust the standard deep

into the sodden ground, cradling it in the crook of one arm as he raised cupped hands to lips and bellowed, "Oi! Marcus! Fetch me back Junie's sword when yer at a loose end, there's a dear!" He waited. Not even an echo returned.

Caius called again, then another time, until he felt a proper fool. He left the standard rooted where it was and trudged back to the camp, only to find that all of it—tent, packs, gear, cookpots and dinner—was gone. In the failing light, he spied two rapidly retreating figures headed in the direction of the Wall.

"Plague rot 'em, lights and liver," Caius muttered. "Look at the buggers run! I never saw Junie move *that* fast, even when he wasn't chawed over by a dragon." He patted his legion dagger, still firmly tucked into his belt. "Well, old girl, it'll be a long saw, but you and me, we'll have that bleeder's head off right enough, even does it take us all night. After all, it's *my* dragon."

Caius' chest inflated with pride as he realized the full measure of his deed. "Didn't even need a sword to kill 'im," he told the air. "And if there's any man likes to fancy that means I did for the monster *barehanded*, who's to tell the tale any different?" He was fairly swaggering by the time he returned to the scene of his triumph.

His mood of self-congratulation quickly soured to outrage when he beheld the tableau awaiting him at the fenside. The eagle had fallen again, knocked down by the hopeless struggle of a raggedy, gray-bearded relic who had the dragon by the narrowest bit of its neck and was obviously trying to yank the whole enormous carcase out of the water, hand over hand. The head, already pulpy, could not long stand such cavalier treatment. It squashed into splinters of bone and globs of unidentifiable tissue in the old man's grasp.

"Here, now!" Caius barked, rushing forward too late to preserve his trophy. He shouldered the gaffer aside, stared at what once might have been the full price of Goewin's respect—to say nothing of that of the commander and the Ninth—and burst into tears.

The old man cowered and wrung his hands, squeezing out

little pips of blood and brain matter from between the palms. "Noble Chieftain, forgive this worthless fool for having dared to presume you had abandoned your lawful kill!" He spoke Gaelic, a dialect slightly different from Goewin's folk.

"Oh, you pasty old fiend, you've bally ruined *everything*!" Caius wailed, kicking the goo that had once been the dragon's head. "How am I ever going to prove I slew the beast without the head to show for it? I can't bloody well tow the whole fucking corpse down the Wall, can I now?"

"You might take a handful of the teeth with you, my lord," the old man suggested timidly, awed by Caius' passion.

"Oh, yes!" Caius did not bother to trim his sarcasm. "Dragon's teeth'll do, *won't* they? When every peddler the length and breadth of Britain's got *bags* full of such trumpery—grind 'em up and slip 'em in yer wine when yer woman wants cheering and you can't afford unicorn's horn or a legionary's pay—each and *all* culled from the mouths of any great fish luckless enough to wash up dead on the seacoast?" He gulped for breath, then spat, "Think the commander don't know *that* much? He's one of their biggest customers. You stupid sod!"

"High Chief, do but calm your wrath against me." The old man pointed a palsied finger at the pool that still concealed the bulk of the beast. "Together we can surely pull the monster's body onto land, and then you have but to cut out its heart and eat it and then—"

Caius stopped crying and frowned. "You off yer nut *entire*, or are you just senile? Eat a beastly dragon's *heart*? Whuffo?"

"Why, High Chief, then you shall be wiser than any wizard and understand the speech of all the birds of the air!" The old man flung his arms wide. He wore no more than a mantle of red deer hide, with a knot of anonymously colored cloth doing up his loins. His expansive gesture wafted the full power of his personal aroma right into Caius's face.

The legionary wiped his nose, then pinched it shut. "Is

thad whad you was doing? Trying to beach this creature so as to ead id's heart and have yerself a chat with the birdies?" The old man nodded. Caius dropped his pinching fingers. "Mithra, what sort of cuckoo hatched you?"

The oldster hung his head. "My mother was a wise woman, my father I never knew. At my birth, the bards of our tribe tell that two dragons coupled in a field hereabouts and—"

"Right, right." Caius waved him silent. "Serve me right, asking for the straight story from a Celt," he said to himself. Aloud he added, "You one of them wizard fellers yerself, then? Or can't you afford decent clothes, just?"

A sly glint came into the old man's eye. When he smiled, Caius beheld a mouthful of the memories of decent teeth. "King and lord, you are as all-seeing as you are all-valiant. I am indeed privy to the occult forces of nature."

"Well, I knew there was summat of the privy about you," Caius riposted. He chortled over his own sally until he caught the look the old man was giving him. He decided to return to his wrathful pose; folk treated you with more honor if they feared you were going to send their conks down the same route he'd shown the dragon.

Thoughts of the beast forced him to consider the ruined trophy and his present position. Although he glared doom at the old man, in his heart he knew that he would not be able to afford the luxury of such a killing look when he faced his commander again.

Junie and Marcus, they'll make camp before I do, what with the time I'm wasting on this geezer and the thought of what I've got to say, he reflected. *Even with Junie banged up like he is, they'll stir their stumps to be first in line with the tale of what happened to the dragon. Think for a tick they'll make it truthful? Huh! That'd mean old Junie'd have to admit as he was near ate and saved by me.* Me! *He'd sooner—Well, he'd sooner crucify hisself, given there was a way to see that stunt through.*

Caius scraped his chin with fingers still sticky from the honey harvest and regarded the self-styled wizard thoughtfully. "Here," he said. "You called that great wallopin' beast me lawful kill, didn't yer?"

"Oh, aye, that I did, most awful lord."

"Saw the whole thing happen, did yer?"

The old man grinned like a death's head and nearly bobbed the head off his meager neck in agreement as he pointed to the paltry stand of scrub that had been his hiding place throughout the epic conflict.

"That's all right, then." Caius was better than satisfied. "You'll just nip along back to the legion camp with me and tell anyone as I points you at just exactly what happened here, how I stepped up bold to that 'ere dragon and—"

The old man's eyes rolled back in his head and he sank cross-legged to the ground. A horrid gurgling welled out of his throat as he tilted his face skywards. "Bold came the high king, master of men, open-handed to the least of his servants, and the golden eagle flew before him, symbol of his might and fame. Fled they all three, the cowards who had served him, leaving him lone to fight the unwholesome beast of the bogland. Terrible was his ire against the fainthearted. Cursing, he killed one man for his shameful act, striking him down like a dog—"

"Now just a minute, you old rattlebrain, I never killed no one but the *dragon*!"

The old man opened his eyes so sharply that Caius thought he heard a whipcrack. "Now you've made me lose the sacred thread of creation, O High Chief." He managed to make the highflown title sound like a synonym for *numbskull*.

"Arr, that don't signify. There wasn't half the truth in what you were saying—leave it to you Celts—and if the commander's not drunker than Silenus when he hears you out, he'll rule as *all* of what you have to say is pure horseshit."

An uneasy inspiration creased Caius' brow. "Excepting for the part as where you says I killed someone. Bee-wolf, curse him, *he's* gone. Who's to say what's become of him? That Junie and Marcus, they're clever as a brace of seaport whores, the pair of 'em. Shouldn't take 'em long to club together and tell the commander that *I* murdered the hero while *they* did for the dragon. Nodens' nuts, Junie's got the battle scars to prove it! And what've *I* got? What in bloody Hades have *I* got?" The gristle of reality stuck in his throat and he crumpled down beside the old man, sniveling.

"Does this mean that my noble lord will not help his sworn servant to cut out the dragon's heart?" the graybeard asked by way of comfort.

"Oh, go help yerself to the soddin' heart, you old fool!" Caius sobbed. "Can't you see I've me own troubles?"

"The burden of rule falls heavy on the uncounseled," the old man intoned with due solemnity. "Yet, by my head, I swear never to give you ill-considered advice, nor to let aught but wise words pour from my lips into your ears."

"You try pouring anything into *my* ears, grizzlepate, and I'll cosh you a good one!" Caius raised his fists to the darkening sky. "Oh gods, not even a place to lay me head tonight, and odds are it won't be many days before the commander sends out a patrol to hunt me down!"

"Over the dead bodies of your guardsmen, my lord." The old man looked grim but determined.

"Over—*what*?" Caius asked.

Even allowing for oral decoration and a useless genealogical sidebar tracing the ancestry of the dragon's last-but-one victim, it did not take the old man too long to inform Caius that the beast had caused the death of his tribe's chieftain, a man of sterling character and many cattle. An upstart stripling named Llassar Llawr of the Lake Country had tried to avenge the chief's consumption, but he too had been dragged into the fen for his troubles.

"Is that why you were here, skulking about?" the Roman asked. "Waiting to see was anyone *else* fool enough to have a go at the monster, so's you could leap out and ask for a gob of heart did they succeed?"

"I was not *skulking*." The old man puffed up like an infected wound. "Wizards have no need to skulk. I was in trance, communing with the gods, awaiting a sign to foretell the coming of a hero to defeat the dragon and take the right of kingship over our tribe. Since the beast took the life of our lawful lord, it was only right that its death provide us with a replacement."

"So you were waiting for a hero?" Caius snorted. "Been there meself. Had one *on* me, I did, in fact, but he bolted." To himself he thought, *Wonder what did become of old Bee-wolf? Nothing too bad, I hope. Can't judge him too harsh, getting the monster sprung on him like that. How was he to know the beast wouldn't bide quiet 'til morning, then come be slaughtered all polite and planned? Luck to you, mate, wherever you are! Could be as you'll still make a hero, some day. Mithra knows there's fens aplenty in this wicked world, and maybe a dragon or two to be getting on with.*

To the old man he said, "I guess you'll have to make do with *me*, then. Kingship, eh? Well . . . it's bound to bring me no worse than the Glorious Ninth ever did, they can kiss me glorious bum goodbye, see if *I* care." He paused in his diatribe. "'Course, there's Goewin . . ."

"This Goewin, is she your woman?" the old man asked.

Caius suddenly recalled Goewin's voice, alternately throwing him to the figurative lions during his trial and slyly encouraging Maxentius' advances. His mouth set hard. "Not any *more* she's not; not after all the slap-and-tickle she's no doubt been up to soon's as I got fairly out of sight. Just you tell me one thing: If I'm yer new chieftain, like you say, this don't mean I've got to be forever riding about, stealing other folks' cows, now does it? I'm strictly infantry, you know."

"You need lead no cattle-raids, my lord." The old man smiled beneficently, if a trifle smugly. "Not if you tell the tribesmen that your faithful servant and all-wise wizard has counseled you that the gods are against it." Softly he added, "I could be even *more* all-wise if you'd give me a hand with the dragon's heart, Noble Chief. Unless you'd like to eat it yourself . . . ?"

Caius gagged.

By the light of a hastily kindled fire, the two men managed to haul a length of the dragon's dead body onto the shore a little after nightfall. Caius made some exploratory excavations with his dagger in the region of the beast's chest, but quickly saw that this was a futile game as well as a messy one.

"Like a field mouse trying to rape a lion," he complained. "This job wants a man-sized blade. Bugger all, if only that Bee-wolf bastard hadn't run off with—"

Caius remembered something. He glanced up at the hummock, where the departed barbarian's sword still stood at attention in the rotten log. "Hang on a mo', Granddda," he told the wizard. "Won't be gone but a shake."

The old man watched him ascend the high ground. The years, and the diet that had cost him most of his teeth, had been even less charitable to his eyes. The night, the wizard's nearsightedness, and the uncertain firelight all conspired to obscure just what happened next. The wizard wiped a small bit of rheum from his eyes, blinked, and looked again just in time to see Caius' hand close around one end of a long, thickish object standing upright in a second, far more massive, object. Just as the old man had mentally discounted a number of things those distant articles *might* be, Caius gave a heave and brandished something long and gleaming overhead with both hands.

There was only one possible object for a sane man to brandish in this fashion: a *sword*. As for what it had been sheathed *in* . . .

"A stone!" the wizard shouted. "He pulled the sword from a stone!"

By the time Caius came back down to the fire, the awe-smitten old man was groveling in the mud and gibbering about magical strength and miraculous proof of kingship.

"Say, O Highest of the High Chiefs," the wizard babbled, "Say what this, your humblest servant and counselor, shall name you before the tribe! Speak, and I shall fly swifter than the hunting merlin-hawk to spread your name among your waiting people!"

Caius rubbed his chin again. He was not sure what he had done to merit this, but he was not fool enough to question Fortuna's little pranks. "I am called Cai—" he began, then stopped. It would not take much for word to reach the Commander of someone with a Roman name jumped-up to chieftancy of a native tribe—not the way these Celts talked. It would take less time for the bastard to then dispatch the whole legion after him. The Glorious Ninth had gone to pot, true, but the strength of their old training still made them a bad enemy. Until Caius could give his new subjects the once-over and gauge their mettle as soldiers, he would do well to lay low.

"I mean, Cai, that's just me *milk*-name, as I was raised with," he said hastily. "What I'm *really* called is—" He cudgeled his brains for a moment, desperately trying to come up with a name that was not Roman and would not ring familiar in the Commander's ears.

He found one.

"—Arctos."

He settled down to clean his sword, completely forgetting his promise to cut out the dragon's heart.

"Lord," the old man prompted. "Lord, if you do not remove the beast's heart soon, it will lose all virtue."

"Sod off," said Arctos.

The old man scowled. "Bloody foreigners," he grumbled.

Still, it would make a good story.

Lan Lung
by
M. Lucie Chin

Here's an evocative and fascinating look into a world as alien to most of us as many an SF writer's distant planet: ancient China . . . a place which, as the engrossing and suspenseful story that follows will amply demonstrate, might well be marked on the maps with that ancient cartographer's warning, Here Be Dragons. . . .

Born in Oakland, California, M. Lucie Chin now lives in Brooklyn, New York, where she works in community theater as a fight choreographer and properties manager for the King's County Shakespeare Company. She made her first sale in 1980 to Galileo, *where she became a frequent contributor, and later also sold fiction to markets such as* Ares, Elsewhere, Faery!, Devils and Demons, *and* Masterpieces of Terror and the Supernatural. *Her first novel,* The Fairy of Ku-She, *was published in 1988, and she is currently at work on a new novel.*

* * *

Hsu Yuen Pao was a Taoist monk; an eccentric wanderer, an educated man, a poet and a magician. To me he was mentor, protector, companion and friend. He was sometimes called by the peasants we encountered The Man Who Walks With Ghosts.

I am the ghost.

Or so I have been told. So often in fact that after all the time I have been here that alone might be enough, but there is more. I remember dying. That is, I remember the event; the time, the place, the circumstances, the stupidity . . . but not the moment itself. Sometimes I think I am still falling; it was a long way from the top of the Wall, and all my life since that asinine mistake is just a dream, one long last thought between living and dying. But only sometimes. It is hard to believe when the night is cold enough to freeze dragon fire. It is hard to believe when drought turns rivers to muddy washes and rice fields to wastelands and a poor traveler must become a thief to eat. At such times it is easier to believe I have always been here, following Hsu Yuen Pao across the land, that the first thirty years of my life as I recall them are the dream.

But in the end that too is utterly unbelievable. I know too much of another place and time. In my childhood mankind reached for the stars. The Sons of Han have yet to reach across the sea.

I do not know the date by any measure of time I was ever taught. I can not translate the lunar calendar into the Gregorian of my memory. It is ancient China, the women have not yet begun to bind their feet, and no man in this land has ever seen a European. That is what I know of now. What of then?

I was born in Boston, Massachusetts on the 12th of June 2010, a fourth-generation American of Chinese descent. My name was Daniel Wing and my ethnic education was limited to the salutations exchanged on Chinese New Year and the names of my favorite edibles. Barefoot on the road I stand five feet nine and a half inches, and at the time of the accident atop the Great Wall of China I was as much a tourist as any of the obvious Caucasians who made up my group, following the polite guide who filled our heads with images of the past.

It was early April atop the Wall. Somewhere on the way down, as I exchanged one reality for another, it became warm and balmy late spring and I became *gwai* . . . the ghost. Towering above that diminutive ancient population, dressed strangely, babbling incomprehensibly, understanding nothing and no one, I was a perfect candidate for ghosthood; a non-person, inhuman. *Gwai*. It is the only word the Chinese have for those who are not of the Sons of Han, the True People, the Chinese themselves. It expresses, more than a lack of life, a lack of *reality*. It suits perfectly, these days, my own concept of myself.

It is said that a ghost grows faint when touched by the breath of a living man. To spit upon him robs him of his powers to change form and vanish. I was spit upon often in the days before Hsu Yuen Pao found me. He was a wise man. He understood about ghosts far better than the peasants who harried and chased me from their villages and fields. I did not trust him particularly, but he was quiet and patient and fed me and talked for me until I learned enough to speak for myself.

He was a small man, even among his own people, and he wore his garments oddly and in a most casual manner. He was young in appearance, though generally travel-worn, but his obsidian eyes seemed old as time, deep as wells, seeming to hold yet conceal the knowledge of great age. Villagers sometimes whispered that he had found the secret of eternal life, the personal immortality the ancient Taoist monks sought relentlessly. His hair was very black and carefully braided into the longest queue I have ever seen, which he wore looped through his sash in back for convenience. There hung about his person and around his neck an array of bags, pouches and containers of many types and sizes, and across his back was slung a long, narrow sheath. It was curved, seemingly to better fit the line of his body, and nearly a yard long, black and slim enough to house only the most needle thin of blades. A most unusual and impractical weapon I felt, but surely one of great value, for the hilt was the purest and clearest of pale pink crystal, and in gossamer script of gold upon the scabbard were the two characters *yü* and *yu*, one the ideograph for abundance, the other the symbol for fish.

He was afraid of nothing. Brave, in my opinion, to the edge of foolishness, mischievous as a child when the mood struck him, and we were frequently in trouble of one sort or another.

There was not a dialect we encountered which he did not speak with fluency and command, and he wrote poems I have never gained the skill to appreciate. I loved them though I could not read them.

In the quiet of night or as we walked the endless land, migrating more or less with the seasons, he would tell me of ghosts, and he would tell me of dragons.

"The face of the earth is covered with the endless, invisible trails of the dragon Lung Mei. To build a house or bury the dead upon such a spot is a great fortune."

He often said he felt that he and I had met upon such a spot.

In the second summer of my new existence we made a leisurely journey toward the western mountains. At the convergence of certain mountain streams there is a cataract called The Dragon Gate. The great carp of the rivers migrate yearly to this spot to make the valiant but usually futile attempt to leap the falls. Those fish who succeed and gain the higher waters are immediately rewarded and transformed into dragons. They then climb to the highest peaks, mount the passing clouds and are borne off into the heavens.

The Dragon Gate and the slopes around it are also the site of rare dragon bones of the finest quality, and Hsu Yuen Pao had made this journey often to collect them for geomancy and medical uses. Among the bags and pouches he wore were several in which he carried such things in small shards or ground into powders. I had seen him use them on occasion in the villages we passed through, sometimes to good effect, sometimes not. I think that if there is *any*thing to be said for the power of belief to heal, those bones have worked miracles.

I had my suspicions about them; not that I could positively identify them. That was the point. They could have been anything. They were not abundant except at the foot of the falls (where the implications to me were obvious) but Yuen Pao picked through such as we found with selective care.

In the evenings as we sorted our small hoard, setting some to dry by the fire and grinding the more fragile ones into fine powders, he would instruct me as best he could, considering the still simple state of my vocabulary.

"Small bones marked with wide lines are female," he said. "Rough bones with narrow lines are male. The variegated colors are most esteemed, while yellow and white are of medium value, and black are inferior. The light, yellow, flesh-colored, white and black are efficacious in curing diseases of the internal organs having their respective colors. If bones are impure or gathered by women, they should not be used.

"Dragons occasionally change their bones, regularly shed their skins and horns. The lofty peaks of mountains, cloud-shrouded or misty, contain the bones of great and venerable dragons which attract moisture and passing clouds.

"Remember, Little Brother, Lung is the god of all waters and the lord of all scaled creatures. When Lung is small, all fish are small. When he is of great size and well pleased with himself, there is abundance in all the land."

He was patronizing and often condescending. But he was also totally fascinating; no less so for believing himself everything he told me. And I learned. Sifting through the convoluted speech patterns the Chinese love, the multiple meanings and implications, carefully sorting fact from myth and tradition, anecdote from parable, I slowly built a body of knowledge I could rely on . . . in one way or another. My preconceptions and skeptical nature frequently got in the way, however, and my memories of another place and time. The first severe blow to these notions came at the end of a month on the slopes around the falls.

There had been a great display of heat lightning far off on the eastern plain during the night, and I had been amused by Yuen Pao's suggestion that it was an omen of some sort, by the seriousness with which he sat up much of the night watching the patterns of light and the scanty film of clouds hovering above the mountain tops looking for interpretations. He found none, though.

We spent the morning descending to lower slopes through forests of hardwood and conifers and rhododendrons. Farther north and west the giant panda roamed these mountain ranges. Below on the plain bamboo and catalpa and a great diversity of flora had not yet been obliterated by the demands of cultivation. It had been a lush world we passed through on our way up to the Dragon Gate. On our way down we became increasingly aware that the character of the vegetation had changed.

In the afternoon we passed a village nestled where three mountain streams converged. In spite of this the crops which had earlier promised abundant yields were now only mediocre and that at the cost of great labor to irrigate. At the next village we spent the night.

Their situation was much the same but there was word that the central flatlands were suffering badly. What had been scanty rain upon the mountain slopes and valley in the past month had not reached the plains at all. Even here there was fear that the harvest would be disastrously poor if, indeed, the crop would be harvestable before the monsoon. Every morning the woman and girls offered sweet rice steamed with sausages and nuts, bound in leaves, to the rain god, tossing them into the streams by the dozens. Beside the fields and in the bamboo groves braces of swallows hung from poles with long banners of red paper inscribed with respectful prayers.

Hsu Yuen Pao looked about nodding sagely as we walked and did not bother to explain. But I got the gist of things pretty well by that time. The Chinese system of education by osmosis was quite workable . . . if it was the only thing you had to *do* with your life, which in my case was literally true.

He marked our course southeast as we continued toward the plain. It was his contention that we must reach the coastal lands before the monsoon season. For transients such as we the semitropical climate of the southern coast was a necessity of life. That had not occured to me the year before. Then I had simply followed. The journey would take weeks on foot, and in a rarely used corner of my mind I wondered how long it would have taken by car.

Things were not yet so bad in the lowlands as we had expected to find on that first day, and at noon we stopped in a bamboo grove, still delicately lovely in the motionless air. No breeze rattled the stalks or stroked the leaves, but there is something inherently cooling about bamboo groves, especially the fresh yellowgreen shoots which we collected to boil with a little rice for our meal. I took the pack, which I had become accustomed to carrying, from my back and went about collecting the youngest shoots. When I returned with my pockets full I found Yuen Pao standing across the grove looking at me so oddly it stopped me in my tracks.

"Brother Gwai," he said somberly. "The night of the lightning was indeed an omen. But it was not for me to understand."

I have never been an endlessly patient man. Occasionally the obliqueness of his technique exasperated me. "Brother Pao," I said. "I do not understand. I am not a prophet. I know nothing of dreams or omens. I am ignorant. Please speak more plainly." I had learned to talk humbly in this land.

"Lan Lung," he said in a low tone.

The lazy deaf one? I was perplexed. Colloquialisms are confusing in any language. Particularly so in Chinese. But lung is also the word for dragon. Being unable to hear, the dragon came to be known by the word for its only handicap. Lan Lung, then, was also a lazy dragon. I had heard the term as an epithet hurled at street beggars. It made utterly no sense in a bamboo grove. I did not understand and said so.

Yuen Pao instructed me to stay exactly where I was till he returned; then he seemed literally to vanish. When he returned there was a brace of swallows in his hand, and the odd look was still on his face.

I went to my pack as he told me, folded back the flap, stepped aside and waited. Yuen Pao approached the pack cautiously, slowly swinging the dead birds by their feet, wings trussed with red cord.

At first I watched Yuen Pao. Then I watched what he watched. There was the smallest ripple of movement within my bag. Hsu Yuen Pao said one word.

The creature that emerged was tiny, palm-sized. It seemed, as the young of many reptiles may, exquisitely perfect in miniature.

"*This,*" I said, my smile broad with delight, "is a *dragon?*"

"Do not deceive yourself, Little Brother, Lan Lung is dragon enough for any man."

Gesturing for me to move farther aside, he offered the swallows before him and backed slowly away. Within the shadow of the pack tiny eyes flashed incandescently orange, bobbed up and down and were extinguished by daylight as it crept from cover.

It was not as tiny as I had at first thought, though still small and precious. A large handful then, perhaps a foot long head to tail. It had a vaguely bovine head with a long, broad-nostrilled snout. Scalloped plates of scale—white rimmed in blue, green and orange—lay flat against the head, three rows deep behind the eyes and below the jaw. Its muzzle bristled with catlike lavender whiskers, and upon its crown were short, blunt, double branching horns.

Eyeing the birds greedily, the little lizard arched his sinuous, serpentine body and rose upon his haunches stroking the air with four clawed paws. The sleek body was covered with lacelike scales, white edged in pale blue, and the curved claws were deep cobalt. There were flat plates of scale similar to those about his head at each shoulder and hip. It had no wings nor was the spine serrated, but there played about the body a vague bright aura.

As the little dragon's muscles bunched and he sank down upon his haunches, tail braced, he opened his mouth, but instead of a hiss there was a sound like the chiming of small brass bells. Hsu Yuen Pao swung the birds in a gentle arc, tossing them several feet into the grove. The dragon sprang, covering incredible distance in a single leap, as though gravity had no meaning for him. And as he moved he seemed to grow. He was cat-sized when he landed upon the swallows and began to devour them quickly.

With the dragon thus occupied, Yuen Pao, moving carefully, collected our few belongings and steered me with deliberate lack of hurry from the grove.

We shortly came upon a road and followed it for a couple of hours in silence before stopping to prepare the bamboo shoots still in my pockets. Yuen Pao was deeply contemplative, but for the first time in my admittedly limited experience he also seemed burdened by a weight of uncertainty. As we ate he told me a story.

Lung is the greatest of all creatures living in the world besides man himself. But as there are lazy men, so too are there lazy dragons. They do not like to exert themselves in the task of directing rain clouds about the sky. So they make themselves small and drop to earth where they hide in trees, under the roofs of houses and even in the clothing of unsuspecting men. Lung Wang, the dragon king, learning of their desertion from duty, sends messengers into the world to search for them. Lung may also make himself invisible, as is usually the case when man is present. These messengers are seldom seen, but when Lan Lung is found then Lung Wang, in fury, raises a great storm, killing the deserter with lightning bolts. This explains what might often seem a wanton destruction of life and property during such storms.

The convenient logic with which these stories usually ended invariably amused me, and I made the mistake of smiling. Hsu Yuen Pao became indignant and proceeded to tell me more about dragons in the next hour than I truthfully cared to know.

"It's a great puzzle," he said as we finally walked the road again. "It is rare that Lung allows himself to be seen by the eyes of mortal man. Such sightings are auspicious occasions and would normally be related directly to the emperor. But this is Lan Lung. It is not clear to me what this could mean."

I squinted up at the bright, cloudless sky. What did *any* thing mean in this place? My whole existence was a mystery. Alice down the rabbit hole. But as for the dragon, I had to admit the little fellow was fascinating. He had displayed an interesting degree of mutability, and he *did* look strikingly like the creatures I had seen in Chinese artworks. Hardly the beast of legend—but a little dragon and a lot of imagination, persistently applied, can leave behind legends larger than life. Hsu Yuen Pao *believed* this was a dragon capable of all he claimed for it.

When I looked back Yuen Pao was also contemplating the sky.

"Yes," he said, "this must be so, though I am still unsure what it means."

I pleaded ignorance.

"Lung is territorial," he said in an uncharacteristically straightforward manner, still looking into the sky. "Each is responsible for the rainfall upon his own lands." The rest was obvious enough. This time I managed not to smile.

The next two days on the road provided clear enough evidence that the tales we had heard in the hills were true. The drought extended severely as we entered the central plain and it promised to worsen. It was said that the rice crop was already unsalvageable, it being too late to plant again even if rain came soon, and despair was growing over the other, less fragile sorts of produce. And everywhere the people shook their heads and wondered what they had done to offend such a powerful dragon, for the area of the drought was wide.

In the villages we passed Hsu Yuen Pao bartered geomancy and spells and prayers for roots and dried preserves and goat bladder water bags (which were lighter to carry when full), and we amended our course to follow the streams and rivers more closely. He had seen Lan Lung and did not expect rain soon.

On the evening of the fourth day we camped on the bank of a muddy stream. Yuen Pao dug for roots. He would forage as long as possible to save our stores of dried goods for harder times. Those he found were pulpy and shriveled, but we boiled them in the water I had spent over an hour straining again and again. It made a bitter, unpleasant broth. The tubers were nearly tasteless but edible, and we supplemented the meal with a small handful of dried plums.

The fire was to have been extinguished as soon as the meal was prepared. Everything around us was dry as tinder, and a fire of any size was perilous in the open. Yet when I moved to put it out, Yuen Pao stopped me with a silent gesture. As I peered intently into the dark, it was several seconds before I saw what he saw. At first I thought it was a shadow by my pack, but when it moved, two iridescent orange eyes flashed in the firelight, and it had my complete attention.

Yuen Pao took up his small copper bowl and his chopsticks and began to eat with the same deliberate, unhurried movements with which he had steered me from the bamboo grove. I did the same, dividing my attention between Yuen Pao and the flickering eyes. Eventually the creature moved into the light, and I saw that this "dragon" too was white and roughly the same size as the other. This, Yuen Pao insisted, was because it was the same dragon.

We finished our meal and sat watching the little lizard prowl about our belongings while Yuen Pao recited poetry (ostensibly to keep the two of *us* tranquil, since the dragon could not hear them) till the fire went out on its own. He told me to lie down and sleep, which I eventually managed to do, but for a long time I could see his silhouette against the stars as he sat in contemplation of his dragon.

In the morning the little creature was gone, but Yuen Pao continued to conduct himself with the same care as the night before. It was his belief that Lung had been with us all along. He had simply been invisible as he may well have been at that very moment.

I tried to take the matter seriously. For him this was an important event, and he had been allowed to participate, if only he could understand in what way. Personally, I envisioned the little fellow either sleeping quietly beneath a rock or curled up among our foodstuffs out of the heat of the sun. The notion that he might be happy feasting on dried mushrooms and plums which we would later need bothered me a great deal, but Yuen Pao would not let me sort the contents of my pack before we set out.

In the evening as I laid our small fire the dragon appeared again. I could not tell from where. He was simply there, sitting on my pack on the ground in the smothering, breezeless heat. Again he was white. I, too, was beginning to believe it was the same dragon.

The next morning he was nowhere to be seen. This time, however, I sorted my pack. All our belongings were in order, and no food had been disturbed. Perhaps he ate bugs, or a pair of swallows would last him a week. I did not bring the subject up with Yuen Pao.

Again the night and morning were the same. We were getting used to him. Yuen Pao was no longer quite so careful in his movements, and he had decided that the key to the riddle was to wait for the ending. This day, however at our noon meal (little more than mushrooms and lotus root soaked in stale water) our companion showed himself. I caught Yuen Pao staring at me and, looking down, found Lan Lung curled up in the shadow of my left knee. When we finally stood to go, the little dragon scampered to my pack and vanished beneath the flap.

From that time on I seemed to take on a different dimension in Yuen Pao's eyes. But since I was never quite sure how he regarded my ghosthood, the new status was equally unclear.

In the following weeks the dragon established himself as a permanent member of our party and my own special companion. It was impossible to say what attracted him to me. Perhaps my smell. Perhaps it was my ghosthood. He and I were both fantasies, Lung and *gwai*; dragons and ghosts; stories to frighten children into obedience. It seemed appropriate that the myths of our existence should keep each other company.

He developed a habit of riding upon whatever part of my body shaded him from the sun, taking to my pack less and less frequently. Sometimes he would ride in one of the pockets of my loose, sleeveless coat or slither down my chest beneath my shirt and curl up next to my belly, a small bulge above my belt. He was smooth and dry to the touch, and the strange aura rippling over his body (Yuen Pao called it dragon fire) was almost like a cool breeze against my skin. When he climbed a leg or arm or scampered across my shoulders, his tiny claws prickled and his whiskers tickled. He seemed to absorb the moisture of my sweat, leaving a trail of dry skin in his wake. He was virtually weightless.

From time to time he would vanish but rarely for more than a day or two. Hsu Yuen Pao said he was simply invisible, but I believed he was hunting since he left our dwindling supply of food strictly alone. Our water was the only thing we shared with him. In proportion to his size, in face, he received a greater share than we did, and even that little was nearly enough to undo us.

The hardships of the summer were incredible. The people were ravaged as badly as the land and during the passage of the weeks became increasingly hostile to transients, guarding their stores of food and water jealously. Gaunt water buffalo stood about in the shade of tinder dry houses, and the mortality rate among the very old and the very young grew steadily. It became impossible to barter *any*thing we possessed for the things we needed, especially water. And to find a village with a good, deep, spring-fed well was a great fortune. Obtaining fresh water, however, even from *these* places, became an exercise in stealth.

For the most part I was unaware of the methods of pilferage employed. I was the decoy on most occasions, playing my ghostly role to the fullest. Sometimes I was convinced he actually did procure our ill-gotten gains by magic. He was able to come and go in the blink of an eye, sometimes seeming literally to vanish, and his skill at sleight of hand was astounding. In another place and time he would have been a masterful pickpocket.

At such rare times as we passed other travelers or stopped at a town or village, Lan Lung would disappear from sight. A bit addled by the heat, perhaps, I actually began to think of his as invisible myself.

We made progress slowly. The heat became a weighty burden, requiring us to stop often for rest. The rivers were reduced to muddy sludge, and many streams had vanished entirely. For a time we took to traveling by night. Not that it was noticeably cooler, but it spared us the direct assault of the sun.

I lost count of the weeks; could not make out even the slightest progress toward our goal. The mountains of the southern coast looked as far away as ever. Yet there came a time when Yuen Pao changed our course away from the last river, and we struck out directly for the hazy blue and gray peaks shimmering and dancing on the horizon. We crossed few roads on the last leg of our trek and passed no more villages. Our rate of travel by then could have been little more than ten miles per day, and Yuen Pao guessed we had another five or six days to go. We had been on diminishing rations for a long time, and foraging had long ago become useless. Two days out from the river there was so little food left that any attempt to ration it further was a useless illusion, and we finished it off without further pretense. The water was in no better shape, but that illusion we maintained as long as we could.

Lan Lung had settled into my right pocket and for over a week had barely stirred. When Yuen Pao and I shared our small bowl of water, a bit was always left for the little dragon who would crawl into the bowl and curl up into a ball rolling over and over in an attempt to bathe himself as best he could. On the evening our food ran out I found it was necessary to help him. I carefully lifted him from my pocket with both hands, placing him in the bowl. He moved a bit, tucking his tail feebly but did not roll over. When Hsu Yuen Pao was not looking, I wet my palm from the last goat bladder bag and stroked his dry body. He felt brittle to my touch, and it seemed days since I had seen his aura about him.

Looking up from the bowl, I found Yuen Pao watching me and realized he had seen what I had done. He did not disapprove. Days before, when I had mentioned that Lan Lung seemed to be suffering from thirst even more than we, he had explained that it was not thirst. It is the *presence* of moisture which preserves his powers of motion and mutability. Without this, Lung becomes powerless and dies.

The following evening there was not enough water to preserve that illusion either.

The next two days became an exercise in placing one foot before the other. We moved when we could move and stopped when we could do nothing else. I believed I had begun to hallucinate when we at last reached the foothills where we at least found shade and the vaguest hint of motion in the air. The leaves on the trees were not shriveled here, and farther up the slopes the grass was almost green.

We rested there, digging up a half decent root or two and locating a few edible berries. In my pocket Lan Lung was very still.

The next morning we made our way slowly into the foothills. The heat was still oppressive and the going even slower since we now had to climb and frequently had to help each other, but the world seemed fresher around us, and things were making a reasonably successful attempt to grow. There was hope of water here, if only we could find it. Yuen Pao crushed leaves and grasses and put the broken vegetation into my pocket with the little dragon in the vain hope that there might be enough moisture to preserve him.

I wondered what would preserve *us*, but Yuen Pao felt if there was any great import to this dragon it was our duty to do all that was possible. I think it kept him going far longer than even the need to save his own life. As for me, I could only reflect that dying the first time had been far easier than the second seemed destined to be.

On the afternoon of the third day, amid green grass and cool shady trees, we came upon a swiftly flowing stream, very deep and clear. Snow-fed, I realized, raising my cupped hands, aching from the frigid water. The long-prayed-for moisture was more pain than comfort in my mouth and throat and transformed my stomach into a clutch of knots.

Yuen Pao filled our two copper cooking bowls from the stream and set them on a warm rock in the sun. Then he set about filling our water bags before drinking himself. As he did these things and I tried to contain my eagerness for the water, I felt a feeble stirring in my pocket. I reached in and carefully removed Lan Lung with both hands, but Yuen Pao would not let me place him in one of the bowls. The water was still too cold for his enfeebled condition. So I put the limp little lizard back into my pocket and removed the garment, hanging it on a tree branch in the shade. When the water was warmed, Yuen Pao dribbled some of it into the pocket, and he and I shared the rest, refilling the bowl before starting the next. By the time we had drunk two bowls each and given as many to my pocket, the activity within had increased and it began to swell even as the water soaked through and ran off.

"It is enough," Yuen Pao said. "The belly is better filled with food."

"If we *had* any," I agreed.

"Look in the stream," he said.

There were fish in the deep swiftness of the current. Brown and white and golden orange carp, large and sleek, flashed by too rapidly for my weary eyes to follow. There was an abundance of food within reach but how to obtain it? I had neither the strength for speed nor the courage against the bone-biting cold to consider seriously trying to catch fish by hand.

Pointing out a far tree, Yuen Pao sent me to hang my dripping garment there, dragon and all, which I did while he took our water bags from the stream. As I watched, he raised both hands, gripping the crystal hilt above his right shoulder. Murmuring in low tones, eyes closed, he uttered an incantation I could not properly hear and slowly moved his hands up and forward. What he drew forth was not a sword. I was surprised to realized that in the time I had known him I had never actually seen this object before.

Amazingly flexible, too long to be withdrawn straight, the shaft whispered from its sheath and sprang free, whipping back and forth in supple, diminishing strokes. A yard long, it was less thick at the hilt than the stem of a flower, tapering away to nothing. It shone in the sun, lustrous and brilliantly purple. Yuen Pao's face was set and serious as he gazed up and down the length of the shaft, his voice hushed and reverent as he said, "Dragon whisker."

I thought of Lan Lung, his tiny whiskers tickling my neck or hand, and was dumbfounded.

Yuen Pao stepped to the bank, the crystal hilt in his right hand and murmured a few more barely audible words. Slipping the dragon whisker into deep water, he and I knelt upon the brink and watched.

"Come, brother Yu," he said. "Come seek your master, Lung Wang."

The fish and eels came from all directions, massing about

the purple wand till it was no longer visible among the bodies. Even from downstream they came, fighting the current to reach the dragon, master of all scaled things upon the earth. They crushed together from bank to bank till there was barely room to move, and those closest to the surface could be picked up by hand, barely wetting the fingers.

That night we feasted on eel and fish roasted upon flat rocks about a large fire. Others were prepared for drying to be carried with us for future meals. Finally, fed and watered and rested, I began to feel human again as we slowly climbed the foothills, following the course of the water upstream. Then there was a road and villages again, nestled in the mountain valley. The people in this land had not suffered drought at all. The crop here was good, though it could not begin to make up for the devastation upon the plains, and the people were willing to barter for Yuen Pao's skills. There were many dialects here, and they seemed to vary from valley to valley. Travelers were few, especially in the higher villages and, after an initial period of suspicion, for which my own appearance was no great help, the stories of our journey and the news of the lowlands were as much in demand as spells or medications.

It would have been nice to linger in a village here or there. Our strength returned to us slowly, and we tired sooner than we would have liked; the increasing altitude was no doubt a factor, but Yuen Pao would not permit delays. Inquiring after particular roads and passes he plotted our course, explaining that it would still require many days to cross the mountains and be safely on the southern slopes before the monsoon stopped all travel, and we had not much time now.

Lan Lung once again took to riding upon my shoulder or occasionally on top of my head. As we reached the highest passes, however, he once again took to my pocket or to nestling beneath my shirt. It was cold here, but Hsu Yuen Pao, in his infinite wisdom, proclaimed that was not the reason. We were too close to heaven here. The clouds were thickening on the southern horizon, and puffy white ships sailed close over our heads. The messengers of the Lung

Wang would be watching. During the last days of our crossing Lan Lung rarely betrayed his presence even to me. Only when he rode in my pocket was I truly aware of him.

Then we were climbing down. Though we were still high on the slopes, I was jubilant. It was almost like coming home.

Yuen Pao was known in many of the villages we passed, a fact I had come to realize was not particularly unusual. But one pleasant, near autumn afternoon as we passed a mile or so from the outer wall of a large town Yuen Pao stopped short in the road, nearly causing me to run him over. In my pocket, Lan Lung squirmed unhappily for a moment. Then we abruptly changed course, away from the wall and the town. He would not tell me why. At dusk, when we stopped to lay our fire, he told me a story from his seemingly inexhaustible fund.

There was once a Taoist monk (I wondered who) traveling through the mountain passes where he came upon six men bearing baskets or oranges northward, bound for a high official in the emperor's court. The baskets were very heavy and in return for the protection of their company the monk agree to help bear the loads.

He took a basket and carried it for an hour, then another till all the loads had been shared and the monk took his leave.

Some time later, at a lavish feast in honor of the emperor, the court official presented the fat oranges; a rare and expensive delicacy from the south. But when the emperor lifted one it seemed oddly light, and when the skin was broken . . . it was empty. Another was opened and another, but they were all the same.

The bearers were sent for and charged upon pain of death to explain the mystery; whereupon they told the tale of the Taoist monk and exclaimed that he had surely tricked them by magic. Since the peasants were too stupid to have conceived of such a skillful theft, the emperor was inclined to believe them. But rather than gaining favor, as the official had hoped, he found himself rewarded with a reduced income and the government of a poor province in the south, far from the court and power.

Yuen Pao claimed to have been told the story by one of the bearers only a year or two before he found me, implying that all travelers in this land were suspect and monks most especially. Sometimes I wondered exactly how gullible he thought I *was*.

It was not yet mid-morning of the next day when they caught up with us, even though we had been prudent enough to stay off the road. There were eight armed men on horseback. Any argument would have been utter stupidity and, though we proceeded at a fast forced march, it was dusk before we reached the great gate of the town wall. Our belongings were confiscated and we spent the night in a hovel on the edge of town. By the smell and the consistency of the floor, I judge it was a structure frequently used to house swine, which was a clear statement of what the magistrate thought of us.

Lan Lung, who had been in my pocket that morning, was gone. He had vanished, as was his habit when strangers were about. But this time, Yuen Pao said, he would not return. Lung has no love for men and their communities. When I naively suggested he might join us again on the road, Yuen Pao did not reply.

In the end, even I was acute enough to realize what a man seeking status would consider proper satisfaction for the affronted dignity of his emperor, though I still did not believe the business about the oranges. The fact that I had had nothing to do with anything was unimportant. By now the magistrate had heard all he required from the nearby villages. In his mind I would be an integral part of Hsu Yuen Pao and the Taoist magic.

There was no sleep that night. This time it was I who stood in the dark watching the lightning far to the south as the monsoons gathered at the coast, wondering about omens and dragons.

At dawn we were ushered out and made to stand waiting like penned sheep in the town square throughout the dismal gray morning and on into afternoon. Awaiting Pei Tae Kwan's pleasure. Waiting to die at his leisure.

It was unclear to everyone, including myself, whether a ghost could be killed, though I had a pretty good notion by now. But as there was no answer, Pei Tae Kwan had willingly accepted for himself the honor of discovering the facts.

The executioner arrived well before noon and stood like a statue among his swords. A dozen guards, stoic and heavily armed, encircled us. Beyond them, curious villagers and bold little boys eyed us carefully, pointing and talking loudly. Old women peered between the shoulders of the guards and railed at us. Yuen Pao was unmoved by the abuse. I simply did not understand the dialect.

From time to time he would send a child or old woman scurrying away with an upraised hand and a few words. It seemed to occur to none of them that if his magic were really so potent we would not have remained the captives we were.

The murky overcast had grown dense and slate gray by early afternoon. The air was a sullen broth of humidity, and water droplets occasionally fell out of suspension creating a fine mist. Though they threatened heavily, hanging low and pregnant overhead, the clouds did not open and drown us.

Pei Tae Kwan showed his face at last about midafternoon, making his way slowly down the street from the ornate monumental gate. The men in the drum towers signaled his approach, and a wave of silence fell upon the villagers as he passed. He took his time quite deliberately, and I had to admit it was finally beginning to get on my nerves.

Entering the armed circle he walked around slowly, looking us over with obvious contempt. When he spoke the tone of his voice was unmistakable; insulting, berating, humiliating. Two servants who had followed him into the guarded circle now began rummaging through our belongings which had been dumped on the ground several feet away. They smashed our rice bowls under foot and broke our chopsticks, throwing the pieces in our faces. They opened Yuen Pao's boxes and containers at the magistrate's command, spilling the dust to show his contempt for us. We could not buy him. We had hardly expected to.

The boys opened the black lacquered container and spilled out the shards of variegated bone we had collected at the Dragon Gate. They broke the lid from the carved box of red cinnabar and emptied the pale yellow dust of ground dragon bones into the dirt, shouting and picking out small round rubies (petrified dragon blood, Hsu Yuen Pao had called them).

Alarmed, the magistrate left us and took the gems from the boys, sending them out among the villagers. He laughed at Yuen Pao, placing the stones in a pocket of his gown, and called out mockingly as he kicked our belongings about. He spied the black scabbard and drew out the shining purple whisker which quivered in his hand like a stiff whip. There was silence for a moment, then more loud chatter. He bellowed, holding the prize aloft for all to see and looked at Hsu Yuen Pao, his eyes alight with greedy triumph. He brandished it like a sword and advanced upon us, kicking my pack out of his way. I saw it moved aside by his foot with an odd jerk which seemed more like a lurch to my eye, and it suddenly began to writhe and swell on the ground.

At the collective cry from the crowd Pei Tae Kwan turned and, seeing the churning form within the cloth, beat at it with the dragon whisker, then backed away and fled beyond the line of his guards as the bag swelled again.

Weapons drawn, the soldiers formed rank around the magistrate and one man sprang forward, striking a blow to the bag with his sword. There was a muffled sound like the distant toll of a bell and the pack split to shreds as Lung burst forth, growing to immense size in an instant. His serpentine body writhed, his tail lashing about, massive cowlike head high, four clawed forepaws slashing air. He was an explosion of silver and blue in the darkness of afternoon, fifty feet long. His voice was the booming of a gong. In the damp air his breath shone bright. Dragon fire played over his body. Beneath his chin was the great blue pearl of the sea, and upon his left shoulder was a long, ragged wound of red.

So rapidly did Lung grown to his full, terrible size, that the soldier who had struck the blow was crushed beneath the scaled belly without even the time to scream. Then Lung leapt, much as I had seen him do that first day in the bamboo grove, but now his body blotted out the sky. When he landed among the terrified screams of the people, men died beneath his huge feet and thrashing tail. The living fled in panic—villagers, soldiers and dignitaries—but the magistrate Pei Tae Kwan, the dragon whisker still clutched in his hand, lay beneath the right fore foot of the great saurian, a foot-long claw imbedded in his chest.

The gong of his voice beat again, and Lung moved around the tree dragging the body of Pei a step or two before it dropped from his claw. I watched, numb but fascinated, only slowly becoming aware of a persistent tugging at my arm. When I looked at Yuen Pao I was surprised to see the fear so plainly on his face, but I recognized it to be the fear of a prudent man. As the thunder began to rumble above and a hot wind came at our backs, I looked once more at Lan Lung, my little pet, and realized the magnitude of my folly. This was no pet; had *never* been one. I perhaps, had been his. This was Tsao Lung, a great scaled dragon, Lord of Rain, Ruler of Rivers, Commander of the Floods. The monsoons at our backs were under his control as were the clouds above our heads. He was deaf to the voice of man and paid no heed to the puniness of his life. Had I expected obedience from this creature? Affection? At that moment I would count myself lucky if he did not even notice me.

The town wall preventing retreat, the dragon between us and the street, Yuen Pao and I moved slowly about the tree, keeping it between us and the dragon as we maneuvered toward the door of the nearest house.

Lightning startled me, and the dragon turned, watching us. His breath was a bright haze about his head, and he favored his left leg. Out beyond the tree the house seemed very far away. Behind the great reptilian body we could see a knot of people, the boldest of the curious, peering from the shelter of the memorial gate. The lightning and thunder came again and Lung turned end to end, facing in our direction now. Body arched, head waving high, his voice boomed once more. Yuen Pao tensed beside me as my own muscles set for a bolt to the door, but there was no time to run. The dragon sprang in the air, his arc long and flat, looming even larger as he hurtled toward us.

My muscles jerked in an attempt to run, but I fell instead as the dragon dropped to ground barely ten feet from me, twisting his head and body away to confront what I suddenly saw falling from the sky to land farther up the street. Another dragon, this one gold and orange. He was five-clawed, and the pearl beneath his chin was the color of honey.

Sheltered behind the wall-like back of Lan Lung we scrambled for the house, but as we moved, he moved, leaping away up the street. A moment later there was an ear-ringing crash of lightning, shattering the tree across the square, barely a yard from the tip of his tail.

I thought of Yuen Pao's story. Lan Lung, the lazy dragon. For desertion of his post and duty, Lung Wang would send messengers to seek him and, when found, would destroy him with lightning bolts.

The two dragons confronted each other, rearing on their hind legs, their breath at last turning to fire as the rain came. Their voices beat upon the ear, and when they leapt to each other the ground shook beneath their bodies. They changed size rapidly and often, looking for advantage. Scales as big as a man's hand littered the street like fallen leaves as the dragons, red-clawed, red-fanged, rolled about in each other's embrace. Lightning struck twice more, gouging the road and shattering the wall. The rain poured down in dark sheets till all that could be seen was the fiery glow of their bodies and breath. They could no longer be told apart.

Then, as Yuen Pao and I sheltered in the doorway of the house, the quaking earth stilled, the brightness diminished, and there came a great quiet beneath the beating of the rain.

Slowly, as the torrent thinned, a mountainous form could be seen lying in the street, motionless, fireless, and beyond it, burning faintly, another dragon stood, its head waving slowly in the air, upturned to the clouds.

I wiped rain from my eyes, straining for a glimpse of color through the sheets of gray. I could not help but care. I had been his refuge till the end, even after I believed he had left me, and, in spite of all I had just seen, if he had scampered, mouse-sized, toward the door where I hid, I would have sheltered him again, foolish as it doubtless would have been. But in the thinning rain I could identify neither the dead dragon nor the live one.

Then the final bolt of lightning struck.

Hours later, when the rain stopped, there was not so much as a splintered bone in the muddy, cratered sheet. But beneath the blasted tree Yuen Pao found one large round scale of silver scalloped in blue. I wear it on a braided cord about my neck like an amulet. It marks me, though that is hardly necessary these days. Word of mouth travels swiftly in this land. The villagers saw from whence the dragon came. They knew whose pack it was. It was never established whether or not a ghost could die a second death (and I am still not sure about the oranges) but no one questioned the power of ghostly magic. It has been mainly to my advantage, I suppose; only occasionally have I resented it. I wear the reputation as I wear my "amulet" and the name the people gave me.

I am called Lung Gwai.

The Dragon Ghost.

Climacteric
by
Avram Davidson

One of the most eloquent and individual voices in modern SF and fantasy, Avram Davidson is also one of the finest short story writers of our times. He won the Hugo Award for his famous story "Or All the Seas with Oysters," and his short work has been assembled in landmark collections such as Strange Seas and Shores, The Best of Avram Davidson, Or All the Seas with Oysters, The Redward Edward Papers, *and* Collected Fantasies. *His novels include* The Phoenix and the Mirror, Masters of the Maze, Rork!, Rogue Dragon, *and* Vergil in Averno. *He has also won the Edgar and the World Fantasy Award. His most recent book is one of the best collections of the decade, the marvelous* The Adventures of Doctor Eszterhazy.

Here he gives us a typically wry and biting new take on a very old story. . . .

* * *

They had driven up, just the two of them, to a place in the mountains he had spoken of—store, garage, hotel, all in one—it was a rare day, a vintage day, with no one to bother them while they ate lunch and shared a bottle of wine. She spoke most; the things she said were silly, really, but she was young and she was lovely and this lent a shimmer of beauty to her words.

His eyes fed upon her—the golden corona of her hair, the green topazes of her eyes, exquisitely fresh skin, creamy column of neck, her bosom (O twin orbs of sweet delight!)—

"But never mind that," she said, ceasing what she had been saying. "I want to forget all that. You: What were you like as a boy? What did you dream of?"

He smiled. "Of a million beautiful girls—all like you," he added, as she made a pretty pout with her red little mouth—"and how I would rescue them from a hideous dragon, piercing through its ugly scales with my lance," he said, "while its filthy claws scrabbled on the rocks in a death agony . . . And the girl and I lived happily ever after, amid chaste kisses, nothing more."

She smiled, touched him. "Lovely," she said. "But—chaste kisses? Now, I used to dream—but never mind. It's funny how our dreams change, and yet, not so much, isn't it?" They looked swiftly about, saw nothing but a distant bird, speck-small in the sky; then they kissed.

Very soon afterward, they drove up a side road to the end, then climbed a path. "You're quite sure no one can see us here?" she asked.

"Quite sure," he said. He stepped back. There was a noise of great rushing, then a short scream, then—other noises. After a while he drew nearer and ran his hands lovingly over the sparkling and iridescent scales. The beautiful creature hissed appreciatively, and continued to clean its gorgeous and glittering claws with its shining black bifurcated tongue.

The Man Who Painted the Dragon Griaule

by

Lucius Shepard

The brilliant story that follows was one of the most popular and most-talked-about pieces of short fiction of the '80s. It takes place in a land dominated by the immobile but still-living body of an immense, mountain-huge dragon, enchanted into stillness in some sorcerous battle in the unimaginably distant past, so long ago that forests and villages have sprung up along the dragon's mountainous flanks. But, as we shall see, even into the lifetime of such a creature, change must come—sometimes even change of the most elemental and revolutionary sort. . . .

Lucius Shepard was perhaps the most popular and influential new writer of the '80s, rivaled for that title only by William Gibson, Connie Willis, and Kim Stanley Robinson. Shepard won the John W. Campbell Award in 1985 as the year's Best New Writer, and no year since has gone by without his adorning the final ballot for one major award or another, and often for several. In 1987, he won the Nebula Award for his landmark novella "R & R," and in 1988 he picked up a World Fantasy Award for his monumental short story collection The Jaguar Hunter. *His first novel was the acclaimed* Green Eyes; *his second the bestselling* Life During Wartime; *he is at work on several more. His latest books are a new collection,* The Ends of the Earth, *and a new novel,* Kalimantan. *Born in Lynchburg, Virginia, he now lives in Seattle, Washington.*

* * *

Other than the Sichi collection, Cattanay's only surviving works are to be found in the Municipal Gallery at Regensburg, a group of eight oils-on-canvas, most notable among them being Woman With Oranges. *These*

*paintings constitute his portion of a student exhibition
hung some weeks after he had left the city of his birth and
traveled south to Teocinte, there to present his proposal
to the city fathers; it is unlikely he ever learned of the
disposition of his work, and even more unlikely that he
was aware of the general critical indifference with which
it was received. Perhaps the most interesting of the group
to modern scholars, the most indicative as to Cattanay's
later preoccupations, is the* Self-Portrait, *painted at the
age of twenty-eight, a year before his departure.*

*The majority of the canvas is a richly varnished black
in which the vague shapes of floorboards are presented,
barely visible. Two irregular slashes of gold cross the
blackness, and within these we can see a section of the
artist's thin features and the shoulder panel of his shirt.
The perspective given is that we are looking down at the
artist, perhaps through a tear in the roof, and that he is
looking up at us, squinting into the light, his mouth
distorted by a grimace born of intense concentration. On
first viewing the painting, I was struck by the atmosphere
of tension that radiated from it. It seemed I was spying
upon a man imprisoned within a shadow having two
golden bars, tormented by the possibilities of light
beyond the walls. And though this may be the reaction of
the art historian, not the less knowledgeable and therefore more trustworthy response of the gallery-goer, it
also seemed that this imprisonment was self-imposed,
that he could have easily escaped his confine; but that he
had realized a feeling of stricture was an essential fuel to
his ambition, and so had chained himself to this arduous
and thoroughly unreasonable chore of perception.* . . .

—FROM *MERIC CATTANAY:*
THE POLITICS OF CONCEPTION
BY READE HOLLAND, PH.D.

I

In 1853, in a country far to the south, in a world separated
from this one by the thinnest margin of possibility, a dragon
named Griaule dominated the region of the Carbonales

Valley, a fertile area centering upon the town of Teocinte and renowned for its production of silver, mahogany, and indigo. There were other dragons in those days, most dwelling on the rocky islands west of Patagonia—tiny, irascible creatures, the largest of them no bigger than a swallow. But Griaule was one of the great Beasts who had ruled an age. Over the centuries he had grown to stand 750 feet high at the midback, and from the tip of his tail to his nose he was six thousand feet long. (It should be noted here that the growth of dragons was due not to caloric intake, but to the absorption of energy derived from the passage of time.) Had it not been for a miscast spell, Griaule would have died millennia before. The wizard entrusted with the task of slaying him—knowing his own life would be forfeited as a result of the magical backwash—had experienced a last-second twinge of fear, and, diminished by this ounce of courage, the spell had flown a mortal inch awry. Though the wizard's whereabouts was unknown, Griaule had remained alive. His heart had stopped, his breath stilled, but his mind continued to seethe, to send forth the gloomy vibrations that enslaved all who stayed for long within range of his influence.

This dominance of Griaule's was an elusive thing. The people of the valley attributed their dour character to years of living under his mental shadow, yet there were other regional populations who maintained a harsh face to the world and had no dragon on which to blame the condition; they also attributed their frequent raids against the neighboring states to Griaule's effect, claiming to be a peaceful folk at heart—but again, was this not human nature? Perhaps the most certifiable proof of Griaule's primacy was the fact that despite a standing offer of a fortune in silver to anyone who could kill him, no one had succeeded. Hundreds of plans had been put forward, and all had failed, either through inanition or impracticality. The archives of Teocinte were filled with schematics for enormous steam-powered swords and other such improbable devices, and the architects of these plans had every one stayed too long in the valley and become part of the disgruntled populace. And so they went on with their lives, coming and going, always returning, bound to the valley, until one spring day in 1853, Meric Cattanay arrived and proposed that the dragon be painted.

He was a lanky young man with a shock of black hair and a pinched look to his cheeks; he affected the loose trousers and shirt of a peasant, and waved his arms to make a point. His eyes grew wide when listening, as if his brain were bursting with illumination, and at times he talked incoherently about "the conceptual statement of death by art." And though the city fathers could not be sure, though they allowed for the possibility that he simply had an unfortunate manner, it seemed he was mocking them. All in all, he was not the sort they were inclined to trust. But, because he had come armed with such a wealth of diagrams and charts, they were forced to give him serious consideration.

"I don't believe Griaule will be able to perceive the menace in a process as subtle as art," Meric told them. "We'll proceed as if we were going to illustrate him, grace his side with a work of true vision, and all the while we'll be poisoning him with the paint."

The city fathers voiced their incredulity, and Meric waited impatiently until they quieted. He did not enjoy dealing with these worthies. Seated at their long table, sour-faced, a huge smudge of soot on the wall above their heads like an ugly thought they were sharing, they reminded him of the Wine Merchants Association in Regensburg, the time they had rejected his group portrait.

"Paint can be deadly stuff," he said after their muttering had died down. "Take Vert Veronese, for example. It's derived from oxide of chrome and barium. Just a whiff would make you keel over. But we have to go about it seriously, create a real piece of art. If we just slap paint on his side, he might see through us."

The first step in the process, he told them, would be to build a tower of scaffolding, complete with hoists and ladders, that would brace against the supraorbital plates above the dragon's eye; this would provide a direct route to a seven-hundred-foot-square loading platform and base station behind the eye. He estimated it would take eighty-one thousand board feet of lumber, and a crew of ninety men should be able to finish construction within five months. Ground crews accompanied by chemists and geologists would search out limestone deposits (useful in priming the scales) and sources of pigments, whether organic or minerals such as azurite and hematite. Other teams would be set to scraping the dragon's side clean of algae, peeled skin, any decayed material, and afterward would laminate the surface with resins.

"It would be easier to bleach him with quicklime," he said. "But that way we lose the discolorations and ridges generated by growth and age, and I think what we'll paint will be defined by those shapes. Anything else would look like a damn tattoo!"

There would be storage vats and mills: edge-runner mills to separate pigments from crude ores, ball mills to powder the pigments, pug mills to mix them with oil. There would be boiling vats and calciners—fifteen-foot-high furnaces used to produce caustic lime for sealant solutions.

"We'll build most of them atop the dragon's head for purposes of access," he said. "On the frontoparietal plate." He checked some figures. "By my reckoning, the plate's about 350 feet wide. Does that sound accurate?"

Most of the city fathers were stunned by the prospect, but one managed a nod, and another asked, "How long will it take for him to die?"

"Hard to say," came the answer. "Who knows how much poison he's capable of absorbing? It might just take a few years. But in the worst instance, within forty or fifty years, enough chemicals will have seeped through the scales to have weakened the skeleton and he'll fall in like an old barn."

"Forty years!" exclaimed someone. "Preposterous!"

"Or fifty." Meric smiled. "That way we'll have time to finish the painting." He turned and walked to the window and stood gazing out at the white stone houses of Teocinte. This was going to be the sticky part, but if he read them right, they would not believe in the plan if it seemed too easy. They needed to feel they were making a sacrifice, that they were nobly bound to a great labor. "If it does take forty or fifty years," he went on, "the project will drain your resources. Timber, animal life, minerals. Everything will be used up by the work. Your lives will be totally changed. But I guarantee you'll be rid of him."

The city fathers broke into an outraged babble.

"Do you really want to kill him?" cried Meric, stalking over to them and planting his fists on the table. "You've been waiting centuries for someone to come along and chop off his head or send him up in a puff of smoke. That's not going to happen! There is no easy solution. But there is a practical one, an elegant one. To use the stuff of the land he dominates to destroy him. It will *not* be easy, but you *will* be rid of him. And that's what you want, isn't it?"

They were silent, exchanging glances, and he saw that they now believed he could do what he proposed and were wondering if the cost was too high.

"I'll need five hundred ounces of silver to hire engineers and artisans," said Meric. "Think it over. I'll take a few days and go see this dragon of yours . . . inspect the scales and so forth. When I return, you can give me your answer."

The city fathers grumbled and scratched their heads, but at last they agreed to put the question before the body politic. They asked for a week in which to decide and appointed Jarcke, who was the mayoress of Hangtown, to guide Meric to Griaule.

The valley extended seventy miles from north to south, and was enclosed by jungle hills whose folded sides and spiny backs gave rise to the idea that beasts were sleeping beneath them. The valley floor was cultivated into fields of bananas and cane and melons, and where it was not cultivated, there were stands of thistle palms and berry thickets and the occasional giant fig brooding sentinel over the rest. Jarcke and Meric tethered their horses a half-hour's ride from town and began to ascend a gentle incline that rose into the notch between two hills. Sweaty and short of breath, Meric stopped a third of the way up; but Jarcke kept plodding along, unaware he was no longer following. She was by nature as blunt as her name—a stump beer keg of a woman with a brown weathered face. Though she appeared to be ten years older than Meric, she was nearly the same age. She wore a gray robe belted at the waist with a leather band that held four throwing knives, and a coil of rope was slung over her shoulder.

"How much farther?" called Meric.

She turned and frowned. "You're standing on his tail. Rest of him's around back of the hill."

A pinprick of chill bloomed in Meric's abdomen, and he stared down at the grass, expecting it to dissolve and reveal a mass of glittering scales.

"Why don't we take the horses?" he asked.

"Horses don't like it up here." She grunted with amusement. "Neither do most people, for that matter." She trudged off.

Another twenty minutes brought them to the other side of the hill high above the valley floor. The land continued to slope upward, but more gently than before. Gnarled, stunted oaks pushed up from thickets of chokecherry, and insects sizzled in the weeds. They might have been walking on a natural shelf several hundred feet across; but ahead of them, where the ground rose abruptly, a number of thick greenish-black columns broke from the earth. Leathery folds hung between them, and these were encrusted with clumps of earth and brocaded with mold. They had the look of a collapsed palisade and the ghosted feel of ancient ruins.

"Them's the wings," said Jarcke. "Mostly they's covered, but you can catch sight of 'em off the edge, and up near Hangtown there's places where you can walk in under 'em . . . but I wouldn't advise it."

"I'd like to take a look off the edge," said Meric, unable to tear his eyes away from the wings; though the surfaces of the leaves gleamed in the strong sun, the wings seemed to absorb the light, as if their age and strangeness were proof against reflection.

Jarcke led him to a glade in which tree ferns and oaks crowded together and cast a green gloom, and where the earth sloped sharply downward. She lashed her rope to an oak and tied the other end around Meric's waist. "Give a yank when you want to stop, and another when you want to be hauled up," she said, and began paying out the rope, letting him walk backward against her pull.

Ferns tickled Meric's neck as he pushed through the brush, and the oak leaves pricked his cheeks. Suddenly he emerged into bright sunlight. On looking down, he found his feet were braced against a fold of the dragon's wing, and on looking up, he saw that the wing vanished beneath a mantle of earth and vegetation. He let Jarcke lower him a dozen feet more, yanked, and gazed off northward along the enormous swell of Griaule's side.

The scales were hexagonals thirty feet across and half that distance high; their basic color was a pale greenish gold, but some were whitish, draped with peels of dead skin, and others were overgrown by viridian moss, and the rest were scrolled with patterns of lichen and algae that resembled the character of a serpentine alphabet. Birds had nested in the cracks, and ferns plumed from the interstices, thousands of them lifting in the breeze. It was a great hanging garden whose scope took Meric's breath away—like looking around the curve of a fossil moon. The sense of all the centuries accreted in the scales made him dizzy, and he found he could not turn his head, but could only stare at the panorama, his soul shriveling with a comprehension of the timelessness and bulk of this creature to which he clung like a fly. He lost perspective on the scene—Griaule's side was bigger than the sky, possessing its own potent gravity, and it seemed completely reasonable that he should be able to walk out along it and suffer no fall. He started to do so, and Jarcke, mistaking the strain on the rope for a signal, hauled him up, dragging him across the wing, through the dirt and ferns, and back into the glade. He lay speechless and gasping at her feet.

"Big 'un, ain't he," she said, and grinned.

After Meric had gotten his legs under him, they set off toward Hangtown; but they had not gone a hundred yards, following a trail that wound through the thickets, before

Jarcke whipped out a knife and hurled it at a racoon-sized creature that leaped out in front of them.

"Skizzer," she said, kneeling beside it and pulling the knife from its neck. "Calls 'em that 'cause they hisses when they runs. They eats snakes, but they'll go after children what ain't careful."

Meric dropped down next to her. The skizzer's body was covered with short black fur, but its head was hairless, corpse-pale, the skin wrinkled as if it had been immersed too long in water. Its face was squinty-eyed, flat-nosed, with a disproportionately large jaw that hinged open to expose a nasty set of teeth.

"They's the dragon's critters," said Jarcke. "Used to live in his bunghole." She pressed one of its paws, and claws curved like hooks slid forth. "They'd hang around the lip and drop on other critters what wandered in. And if nothin' wandered in. . . ." She pried out the tongue with her knife—its surface was studded with jagged points like the blade of a rasp. "Then they'd lick Griaule clean for their supper."

Back in Teocinte, the dragon had seemed to Meric a simple thing, a big lizard with a tick of life left inside, the residue of a dim sensibility; but he was beginning to suspect that this tick of life was more complex than any he had encountered.

"My gram used to say," Jarcke went on, "that the old dragons could fling themselves up to the sun in a blink and travel back to their own world, and when they come back, they'd bring the skizzers and all the rest with 'em. They was immortal, she said. Only the young ones came here 'cause later on they grew too big to fly on Earth." She made a sour face. "Don't know as I believe it."

"Then you're a fool," said Meric.

Jarcke glanced up at him, her hand twitching toward her belt.

"How can you live here and *not* believe it!" he said, surprised to hear himself so fervently defending a myth. "God! This . . ." He broke off, noticing the flicker of a smile on her face.

She clucked her tongue, apparently satisfied by something. "Come on," she said. "I want to be at the eye before sunset."

The peaks of Griaule's folded wings, completely overgrown by grass and shrubs and dwarfish trees, formed two spiny hills that cast a shadow over Hangtown and the narrow lake around which it sprawled. Jarcke said the lake was a stream flowing off the hill behind the dragon, and that it drained away through the membranes of his wing and down onto his shoulder. It was beautiful beneath the wing, she told him. Ferns and waterfalls. But it was reckoned an evil place. From a distance the town looked picturesque—rustic cabins, smoking chimneys. As they approached, however, the cabins resolved into dilapidated shanties with missing boards and broken windows; suds and garbage and offal floated in the shallows of the lake. Aside from a few men idling on the stoops, who squinted at Meric and nodded glumly at Jarcke, no one was about. The grass-blades stirred in the breeze, spiders scuttled under the shanties, and there was an air of torpor and dissolution.

Jarcke seemed embarrassed by the town. She made no attempt at introductions, stopping only long enough to fetch another coil of rope from one of the shanties, and as they walked between the wings, down through the neck spines—a forest of greenish gold spikes burnished by the lowering sun—she explained how the townsfolk grubbed a livelihood from Griaule. Herbs gathered on his back were valued as medicine and charms, as were the peels of dead skin; the artifacts left by previous Hangtown generations were of some worth to various collectors.

"Then there's scale hunters," she said with disgust. "Henry Sichi from Port Chantay'll pay good money for pieces of scale, and though it's bad luck to do it, some'll have a go at chippin' off the loose 'uns." She walked a few paces in silence. "But there's others who've got better reasons for livin' here."

The frontal spike above Griaule's eyes was whorled at the base like a narwhal's horn and curved back toward the wings. Jarcke attached the ropes to eyebolts drilled into the spike, tied one about her waist, the other about Meric's; she cautioned him to wait, and rappelled off the side. In a moment she called for him to come down. Once again he grew dizzy as he descended; he glimpsed a clawed foot far below, mossy fangs jutting from an impossibly long jaw; and then he began to spin and bash against the scales. Jarcke gathered him in and helped him sit on the lip of the socket.

"Damn!" she said, stamping her foot.

A three-foot-long section of the adjoining scale shifted slowly away. Peering close, Meric saw that while in texture and hue it was indistinguishable from the scale, there was a hairline division between it and the surface. Jarcke, her face twisted in disgust, continued to harry the thing until it moved out of reach.

"Call 'em flakes," she said when he asked what it was. "Some kind of insect. Got a long tube that they pokes down between the scales and sucks blood. See there?" She pointed off to where a flock of birds was wheeling close to Griaule's side; a chip of pale gold broke loose and went tumbling down to the valley. "Birds pry 'em off, let 'em bust open, and eats the innards." She hunkered down beside him and after a moment asked, "You really think you can do it?"

"What? You mean kill the dragon?"

She nodded.

"Certainly," he said, and then added, lying, "I've spent years devising the method."

"If all the paint's goin' to be atop his head, how're you goin' to get it to where the paintin's done?"

"That's no problem. We'll pipe it to wherever it's needed."

She nodded again. "You're a clever fellow," she said; and when Meric, pleased, made as if to thank her for the compliment, she cut in and said, "Don't mean nothin' by it. Bein' clever ain't an accomplishment. It's just somethin' you come by, like bein' tall." She turned away, ending the conversation.

Meric was weary of being awestruck, but even so he could not help marveling at the eye. By his estimate it was seventy feet long and fifty feet high, and it was shuttered by an opaque membrane that was unusually clear of algae and lichen, glistening, with vague glints of color visible behind it. As the westering sun reddened and sank between two distant hills, the membrane began to quiver and then split open down the center. With the ponderous slowness of a theater curtain opening, the halves slid apart to reveal the glowing humor. Terrified by the idea that Griaule could see him, Meric sprang to his feet, but Jarcke restrained him.

"Stay still and watch," she said.

He had no choice—the eye was mesmerizing. The pupil was slit and featureless black, but the humor . . . he had never seen such fiery blues and crimsons and golds. What had looked to be vague glints, odd refractions of the sunset, he now realized were photic reactions of some sort. Fairy rings of light developed deep within the eye, expanded into spoked shapes, flooded the humor, and faded—only to be replaced by another and another. He felt the pressure of Griaule's vision, his ancient mind, pouring through him, and as if in response to this pressure, memories bubbled up in his thoughts. Particularly sharp ones. The way a bowlful of brush water had looked after freezing over during a winter's night—a delicate, fractured flower of murky yellow. An archipelago of orange peels that his girl had left strewn across the floor of the studio. Sketching atop Jokenam Hill one sunrise, the snowcapped roofs of Regensburg below pitched at all angles like broken paving stones, and silver shafts of the sun striking down through a leaden overcast. It was as if these things were being drawn forth for his inspection. Then they were washed away by what also seemed a memory, though at the same time it was wholly unfamiliar. Essentially it was a landscape of light, and he was plunging through it, up and up. Prisms and lattices of iridescent fire bloomed around him, and everything was a roaring fall into brightness, and finally he was clear into its white furnace heart, his own heart swelling with the joy of his strength and dominion.

It was dusk before Meric realized the eye had closed. His mouth hung open, his eyes ached from straining to see, and his tongue was glued to his palate. Jarcke sat motionless, buried in shadow.

"Th . . ." He had to swallow to clear his throat of mucus. "This is the reason you live here, isn't it?"

"Part of the reason," she said. "I can see things comin' way up here. Things to watch out for, things to study on."

She stood and walked to the lip of the socket and spat off the edge; the valley stretched out gray and unreal behind her, the folds of the hills barely visible in the gathering dusk.

"I seen you comin'," she said.

A week later, after much exploration, much talk, they went down into Teocinte. The town was a shambles—shattered windows, slogans painted on the walls, glass and torn banners and spoiled food littering the streets—as if there had been both a celebration and a battle. Which there had. The city fathers met with Meric in the town hall and informed him that his plan had been approved. They presented him a chest containing five hundred ounces of silver and said that the entire resources of the community were at his disposal. They offered a wagon and a team to transport him and the chest to Regensburg and asked if any of the preliminary work could be begun during his absence.

Meric hefted one of the silver bars. In its cold gleam he saw the object of his desire—two, perhaps three years of freedom, of doing the work he wanted and not having to accept commissions. But all that had been confused. He glanced at Jarcke; she was staring out the window, leaving it to him. He set the bar back in the chest and shut the lid.

"You'll have to send someone else," he said. And then, as the city fathers looked at each other askance, he laughed and laughed at how easily he had discarded all his dreams and expectations.

It had been eleven years since I had been to the valley, twelve since work had begun on the painting, and I was appalled by the changes that had taken place. Many of the hills were scraped brown and treeless, and there was a general dearth of wildlife. Griaule, of course, was most changed. Scaffolding hung from his back; artisans, suspended by webworks of ropes, crawled over his side; and all the scales to be worked had either been painted or primed. The tower rising to his eye was swarmed by laborers, and at night the calciners and vats atop his head belched flame into the sky, making it seem there was a mill town in the heavens. At his feet was a brawling shantytown populated by prostitutes, workers, gamblers, ne'er-do-wells of every sort, and soldiers: the burdensome cost of the project had encouraged the city fathers of Teocinte to form a regular militia, which regularly plundered the adjoining states and had posted occupation forces to some areas. Herds of frightened animals milled in the slaughtering pens, waiting to be rendered into oils and pigments. Wagons filled with ores and vegetable products rattled in the streets. I myself had brought a cargo of madder roots from which a rose tint would be derived.

It was not easy to arrange a meeting with Cattanay. While he did none of the actual painting, he was always busy in his office consulting with engineers and artisans, or involved in some other part of the logistical process. When at last I did meet him, I found he had changed as drastically as Griaule. His hair had gone gray, deep lines scored his features, and his right shoulder had a peculiar bulge at its midpoint—the product of a fall. He was amused by the fact that I wanted to buy the painting, to collect the scales after Griaule's death, and I do not believe he took me at all seriously. But the woman Jarcke, his constant companion, informed him that I was a responsible businessman, that I had already bought the bones, the teeth, even the dirt beneath Griaule's belly (this I eventually sold as having magical properties).

"Well," said Cattanay, "I suppose someone has to own them."

He led me outside, and we stood looking at the painting.

"You'll keep them together?" he asked.

I said, "Yes."

"If you'll put that in writing," he said, *"then they're yours."*

Having expected to haggle long and hard over the price, I was flabbergasted; but I was even more flabbergasted by what he said next.

"Do you think it's any good?" he asked.

Cattanay did not consider the painting to be the work of his imagination; he felt he was simply illuminating the shapes that appeared on Griaule's side and was convinced that once the paint was applied, new shapes were produced beneath it, causing him to make constant changes. He saw himself as an artisan more than a creative artist. But to put his question into perspective, people were beginning to flock from all over the world and marvel at the painting. Some claimed they saw intimations of the future in its gleaming surface; others underwent transfiguring experiences; still others—artists themselves—attempted to capture something of the work on canvas, hopeful of establishing reputations merely by being competent copyists of Cattanay's art. The painting was nonrepresentational in character, essentially a wash of pale gold spread across the dragon's side; but buried beneath the laminated surface were a myriad tints of iridescent color that, as the sun passed through the heavens and the light bloomed and faded, solidified into innumerable forms and figures that seemed to flow back and forth. I will not try to categorize these forms, because there was no end to them; they were as varied as the conditions under which they were viewed. But I will say that on the morning I met with Cattanay, I—who was the soul of the practical man, without a visionary bone in my body—felt as though I were being whirled away into the painting, up through geometries of light, latticeworks of rainbow color that built the way the edges of a cloud build, past orbs, spirals, wheels of flame. . . .*

—FROM *THIS BUSINESS OF GRIAULE*
BY HENRI SIOCHI

II

There had been several women in Meric's life since he arrived in the valley; most had been attracted by his growing fame and his association with the mystery of the dragon, and most had left him for the same reasons, feeling daunted and unappreciated. But Lise was different in two respects. First, because she loved Meric truly and well; and second, because she was married—albeit unhappily—to a man named Pardiel, the foreman of the calciner crew. She did not love him as she did Meric, yet she respected him and felt obliged to consider carefully before ending the relationship. Meric had never known such an introspective soul. She was twelve years younger than he, tall and lovely, with sun-streaked hair and brown eyes that went dark and seemed to turn inward whenever she was pensive. She was in the habit of analyzing everything that affected her, drawing back from her emotions and inspecting them as if they were a clutch of strange insects she had discovered crawling on her skirt. Though her penchant for self-examination kept her from him, Meric viewed it as a kind of baffling virtue. He had the classic malady and could find no fault with her. For almost a year they were as happy as could be expected; they talked long hours and walked together, and on those occasions when Pardiel worked double shifts and was forced to bed down by his furnaces, they spent the nights making love in the cavernous spaces beneath the dragon's wing.

It was still reckoned an evil place. Something far worse than skizzers or flakes was rumored to live there, and the ravages of this creature were blamed for every disappearance, even that of the most malcontented laborer. But Meric did not give credence to the rumors. He half believed Griaule had chosen him to be his executioner and that the dragon would never let him be harmed; and besides, it was the only place where they could be assured of privacy.

A crude stair led under the wing, handholds and steps hacked from the scales—doubtless the work of scale hunters. It was a treacherous passage, six hundred feet above the valley floor; but Lise and Meric were secured by ropes, and over the months, driven by the urgency of passion, they adapted to it. Their favorite spot lay fifty feet in (Lise would go no farther; she was afraid even if he was not), near a waterfall that trickled over the leathery folds, causing them to glisten with a mineral brilliance. It was eerily beautiful, a haunted gallery. Peels of dead skin hung down from the shadows like torn veils of ectoplasm; ferns sprouted from the vanes, which were thicker than cathedral columns; swallows curved through the black air. Sometimes, lying with her hidden by a tuck of the wing, Meric would think the beating of their hearts was what really animated the place, that the instant they left, the water ceased flowing and the swallows vanished. He had an unshakable faith in the transforming power of their affections, and one morning as they dressed, preparing to return to Hangtown, he asked her to leave with him.

"To another part of the valley?" She laughed sadly. "What good would that do? Pardiel would follow us."

"No," he said. "To another country. Anywhere far from here."

"We can't," she said, kicking at the wing. "Not until Griaule dies. Have you forgotten?"

"We haven't tried."

"Others have."

"But we'd be strong enough. I know it!"

"You're a romantic," she said gloomily, and stared out over the slope of Griaule's back at the valley. Sunrise had washed the hills to crimson, and even the tips of the wings were glowing a dull red.

"Of course I'm a romantic!" He stood, angry. "What the hell's wrong with that?"

She sighed with exasperation. "You wouldn't leave your work," she said. "And if we did leave, what work would you do? Would . . ."

"Why must everything be a problem in advance!" he shouted. "I'll tattoo elephants! I'll paint murals on the chests of giants, I'll illuminate whales! Who else is better qualified?"

She smiled, and his anger evaporated.

"I didn't mean it that way," she said. "I just wondered if you could be satisfied with anything else."

She reached out her hand to be pulled up, and he drew her into an embrace. As he held her, inhaling the scent of vanilla water from her hair, he saw a diminutive figure silhouetted against the backdrop of the valley. It did not seem real—a black homunculus—and even when it began to come forward, growing larger and larger, it looked less a man than a magical keyhole opening in a crimson-set hillside. But Meric knew from the man's rolling walk and the hulking set of his shoulders that it was Pardiel; he was carrying a long-handled hook, one of those used by artisans to maneuver along the scales.

Meric tensed, and Lise looked back to see what had alarmed him. "Oh, my God!" she said, moving out of the embrace.

Pardiel stopped a dozen feet away. He said nothing. His face was in shadow, and the hook swung lazily from his hand. Lise took a step toward him, then stepped back and stood in front of Meric as if to shield him. Seeing this, Pardiel let out an inarticulate yell and charged, slashing with the hook. Meric pushed Lise aside and ducked. He caught a brimstone whiff of the calciners as Pardiel rushed past and went sprawling, tripped by some irregularity in the scale. Deathly afraid, knowing he was no match for the foreman, Meric seized Lise's hand and ran deeper under the wing. He hoped Pardiel would be too frightened to follow, leery of the creature that was rumored to live there; but he was not. He came after them at a measured pace, tapping the hook against his leg.

Higher on Griaule's back, the wing was dimpled downward by hundreds of bulges, and this created a maze of small chambers and tunnels so low that they had to crouch to pass along them. The sound of their breathing and the scrape of their feet were amplified by the enclosed spaces, and Meric could no longer hear Pardiel. He had never been this deep before. He had thought it would be pitch-dark; but the lichen and algae adhering to the wing were luminescent and patterned every surface, even the scales beneath them, with whorls of blue and green fire that shed a sickly radiance. It was as if they were giants crawling through a universe whose starry matter had not yet congealed into galaxies and nebulas. In the wan light, Lise's face—turned back to him now and again—was teary and frantic; and then, as she straightened, passing into still another chamber, she drew in breath with a shriek.

At first Meric thought Pardiel had somehow managed to get ahead of them; but on entering he saw that the cause of her fright was a man propped in a sitting position against the far wall. He looked mummified. Wisps of brittle hair poked up from his scalp, the shapes of his bones were visible through his skin, and his eyes were empty holes. Between his legs was a scatter of dust where his genitals had been. Meric pushed Lise toward the next tunnel, but she resisted and pointed at the man.

"His eyes," she said, horror-struck.

Though the eyes were mostly a negative black, Meric now realized they were shot through by opalescent flickers. He felt compelled to kneel beside the man—it was a sudden, motiveless urge that gripped him, bent him to its will, and released him a second later. As he rested his hand on the scale, he brushed a massive ring that was lying beneath the shrunken fingers. Its stone was black, shot through by flickers identical to those within the eyes, and incised with the letter S. He found his gaze was deflected away from both the stone and the eyes, as if they contained charges repellent to the senses. He touched the man's withered arm; the flesh was rock-hard, petrified. But alive. From that brief touch he gained an impression of the man's life, of gazing for centuries at the same patch of unearthly fire, of a mind gone beyond mere madness into a perverse rapture, a meditation upon some foul principle. He snatched back his hand in revulsion.

There was a noise behind them, and Meric jumped up, pushing Lise into the next tunnel. "Go right," he whispered. "We'll circle back toward the stair." But Pardiel was too close to confuse with such tactics, and their flight became a wild chase, scrambling, falling, catching glimpses of Pardiel's smoke-stained face, until finally—as Meric came to a large chamber—he felt the hook bite into his thigh. He went down, clutching at the wound, pulling the hook loose. The next moment Pardiel was atop him; Lise appeared over his shoulder, but he knocked her away and locked his fingers in Meric's hair and smashed his head against the scale. Lise screamed, and white lights fired through Meric's skull. Again his head was smashed down. And again. Dimly, he saw Lise struggling with Pardiel, saw her shoved away, saw the hook raised high and the foreman's mouth distorted by a grimace. Then the grimace vanished. His jaw dropped open, and he reached behind him as if to scratch his shoulder blade. A line of dark blood eeled from his mouth and he collapsed, smothering Meric beneath his chest. Meric heard voices. He tried to dislodge the body, and the effects drained the last of his strength. He whirled down through a blackness that seemed as negative and inexhaustible as the petrified man's eyes.

Someone had propped his head on their lap and was bathing his brow with a damp cloth. He assumed it was Lise, but when he asked what had happened, it was Jarcke who answered, saying, "Had to kill him." His head throbbed, his leg throbbed even worse, and his eyes would not focus. The peels of dead skin hanging overhead appeared to be writhing. He realized they were out near the edge of the wing.

"Where's Lise?"

"Don't worry," said Jarcke. "You'll see her again." She made it sound like an indictment.

"Where is she?"

"Sent her back to Hangtown. Won't do you two bein' seen hand in hand the same day Pardiel's missin'."

"She wouldn't have left. . . ." He blinked, trying to see her face; the lines around her mouth were etched deep and reminded him of the patterns of lichen on the dragon's scale. "What did you do?"

"Convinced her it was best," said Jarcke. "Don't you know she's just foolin' with you?"

"I've got to talk to her." He was full of remorse, and it was unthinkable that Lise should be bearing her grief alone; but when he struggled to rise, pain lanced through his leg.

"You wouldn't get ten feet," she said. "Soon as your head's clear, I'll help you with the stairs."

He closed his eyes, resolving to find Lise the instant he got back to Hangtown—together they would decide what to do. The scale beneath him was cool, and that coolness was transmitted to his skin, his flesh, as if he were merging with it, becoming one of its ridges.

"What was the wizard's name?" he asked after a while, recalling the petrified man, the ring and its incised letter. "The one who tried to kill Griaule. . . ."

"Don't know as I ever heard it," said Jarcke. "But I reckon it's him back there."

"You saw him?"

"I was chasin' a scale hunter once what stole some rope, and I found him instead. Pretty miserable sort, whoever he is."

Her fingers trailed over his shoulder—a gentle, treasuring touch. He did not understand what it signaled, being too concerned with Lise, with the terrifying potentials of all that had happened; but years later, after things had passed beyond remedy, he cursed himself for not having understood.

At length Jarcke helped him to his feet, and they climbed up to Hangtown, to bitter realizations and regrets, leaving Pardiel to the birds or the weather or worse.

It seems it is considered irreligious for a woman in love to hesitate or examine the situation, to do anything other than blindly follow the impulse of her emotions. I felt the brunt of such an attitude—people judged it my fault for not having acted quickly and decisively one way or another. Perhaps I was overcautious. I do not claim to be

*free of blame, only innocent of sacrilege. I believe I might
have eventually left Pardiel—there was not enough in the
relationship to sustain happiness for either of us. But I
had good reason for cautious examination. My husband
was not an evil man, and there were matters of loyalty
between us.*

*I could not face Meric after Pardiel's death, and I
moved to another part of the valley. He tried to see me on
many occasions, but I always refused. Though I was
greatly tempted, my guilt was greater. Four years later,
after Jarcke died—crushed by a runaway wagon—one of
her associates wrote and told me Jarcke had been in love
with Meric, that it had been she who had informed
Pardiel of the affair, and that she may well have staged
the murder. The letter acted somewhat to expiate my
guilt, and I weighed the possibility of seeing Meric again.
But too much time had passed, and we had both assumed
other lives. I decided against it. Six years later, when
Griaule's influence had weakened sufficiently to allow
emigration, I moved to Port Chantay. I did not hear from
Meric for almost twenty years after that, and then one day
I received a letter, which I will reproduce in part:*

*". . . My old friend from Regensburg, Louis Dar-
dano, has been living here for the past few years,
engaged in writing my biography. The narrative has a
breezy feel, like a tale being told in a tavern, which—if
you recall my telling you how this all began—is quite
appropriate. But on reading it, I am amazed my life has
had such a simple shape. One task, one passion. God,
Lise! Seventy years old, and I still dream of you. And I
still think of what happened that morning under the wing.
Strange, that it has taken me all this time to realize it was
not Jarcke, not you or I who was culpable, but Griaule.
How obvious it seems now. I was leaving, and he needed
me to complete the expression on his side, his dream of
flying, of escape, to grant him the death of his desire. I am
certain you will think I have leaped to this assumption,
but I remind you that it has been a leap of forty years'
duration. I know Griaule, know his monstrous subtlety. I*

can see it at work in every action that has taken place in the valley since my arrival. I was a fool not to understand that his powers were at the heart of our sad conclusion.

"The army now runs everything here, as no doubt you are aware. It is rumored they are planning a winter campaign against Regensburg. Can you believe it! Their fathers were ignorant, but this generation is brutally stupid. Otherwise, the work goes well and things are as usual with me. My shoulder aches, children stare at me on the street, and it is whispered I am mad. . . ."

—FROM *UNDER GRIAULE'S WING*
BY LISE CLAVERIE

III

Acne-scarred, lean, arrogant, Major Hauk was a very young major with a limp. When Meric had entered, the major had been practicing his signature—it was a thing of elegant loops and flourishes, obviously intended to have a place in posterity. As he strode back and forth during their conversation, he paused frequently to admire himself in the window glass, settling the hang of his red jacket or running his fingers along the crease of his white trousers. It was the new style of uniform, the first Meric had seen at close range, and he noted with amusement the dragons embossed on the epaulets. He wondered if Griaule was capable of such an irony, if his influence was sufficiently discreet to have planted the idea for this comic-opera apparel in the brain of some general's wife.

". . . not a question of manpower," the major was saying, "but of. . . ." He broke off, and after a moment cleared his throat.

Meric, who had been studying the blotches on the backs of his hands, glanced up; the cane that had been resting against his knee slipped and clattered to the floor.

"A question of matériel," said the major firmly. "The price of antimony, for example . . ."

"Hardly use it anymore," said Meric. "I'm almost done with the mineral reds."

A look of impatience crossed the major's face. "Very well," he said; he stooped to his desk and shuffled through some papers. "Ah! Here's a bill for a shipment of cuttlefish from which you derive. . . ." He shuffled more papers.

"Syrian brown," said Meric gruffly. "I'm done with that, too. Golds and violets are all I need anymore. A little blue and rose." He wished the man would stop badgering him; he wanted to be at the eye before sunset.

As the major continued his accounting, Meric's gaze wandered out the window. The shantytown surrounding Griaule had swelled into a city and now sprawled across the hills. Most of the buildings were permanent, wood and stone, and the cant of the roofs, the smoke from the factories around the perimeter, put him in mind of Regensburg. All the natural beauty of the land had been drained into the painting. Blackish gray rain clouds were muscling up from the east, but the afternoon sun shone clear and shed a heavy gold radiance on Griaule's side. It looked as if the sunlight were an extension of the gleaming resins, as if the thickness of the paint were becoming infinite. He let the major's voice recede to a buzz and followed the scatter and dazzle of the images; and then, with a start, he realized the major was sounding him out about stopping the work.

The idea panicked him at first. He tried to interrupt, to raise objections; but the major talked through him, and as Meric thought it over, he grew less and less opposed. The painting would never be finished, and he was tired. Perhaps it was time to have done with it, to accept a university post somewhere and enjoy life for a while.

"We've been thinking about a temporary stoppage," said Major Hauk. "Then if the winter campaign goes well. . . ." He smiled. "If we're not visited by plague and pestilence, we'll assume things are in hand. Of course we'd like your opinion."

Meric felt a surge of anger toward this smug little monster. "In my opinion, you people are idiots," he said. "You wear Griaule's image on your shoulders, weave him on your flags, and yet you don't have the least comprehension of what that means. You think it's just a useful symbol. . . ."

"Excuse me," said the major stiffly.

"The hell I will!" Meric groped for his cane and heaved up to his feet. "You see yourselves as conquerors. Shapers of destiny. But all your rapes and slaughters are Griaule's expressions. *His* will. You're every bit as much his parasites as the skizzers."

The major sat, picked up a pen, and began to write.

"It astounds me," Meric went on, "that you can live next to a miracle, a source of mystery, and treat him as if he were an oddly shaped rock."

The major kept writing.

"What are you doing?" asked Meric.

"My recommendation," said the major without looking up.

"Which is?"

"That we initiate stoppage at once."

They exchanged hostile stares, and Meric turned to leave; but as he took hold of the doorknob, the major spoke again.

"We owe you so much," he said; he wore an expression of mingled pity and respect that further irritated Meric.

"How many men have you killed, Major?" he asked, opening the door.

"I'm not sure. I was in the artillery. We were never able to be sure."

"Well, I'm sure of my tally," said Meric. "It's taken me forty years to amass it. Fifteen hundred and ninety-three men and women. Poisoned, scalded, broken by falls, savaged by animals. Murdered. Why don't we—you and I—just call it even."

Though it was a sultry afternoon, he felt cold as he walked toward the tower—an internal cold that left him light-headed and weak. He tried to think what he would do. The idea of a university post seemed less appealing away from the major's office; he would soon grow weary of worshipful students and in-depth dissections of his work by jealous academics. A man hailed him as he turned into the market.

Meric waved but did not stop, and heard another man say, "*That's* Cattanay?" (That ragged old ruin?)

The colors of the market were too bright, the smells of charcoal cookery too cloying, the crowds too thick, and he made for the side streets, hobbling past one-room stucco houses and tiny stores where they sold cooking oil by the ounce and cut cigars in half if you could not afford a whole one. Garbage, tornadoes of dust and flies, drunks with bloody mouths. Somebody had tied wires around a pariah dog—a bitch with slack teats; the wires had sliced into her flesh, and she lay panting in an alley mouth, gaunt ribs flecked with pink lather, gazing into nowhere. She, thought Meric, and not Griaule, should be the symbol of their flag.

As he rode the hoist up the side of the tower, he fell into his old habit of jotting down notes for the next day. *What's that cord of wood doing on level five? Slow leak of chrome yellow from pipes on level twelve.* Only when he saw a man dismantling some scaffolding did he recall Major Hauk's recommendation and understand that the order must already have been given. The loss of his work struck home to him then, and he leaned against the railing, his chest constricted and his eyes brimming. He straightened, ashamed of himself. The sun hung in a haze of iron-colored light low above the western hills, looking red and bloated and vile as a vulture's ruff. That polluted sky was his creation as much as was the painting, and it would be good to leave it behind. Once away from the valley, from all the influences of the place, he would be able to consider the future.

A young girl was sitting on the twentieth level just beneath the eye. Years before, the ritual of viewing the eye had grown to cultish proportions; there had been group chanting and praying and discussions of the experience. But these were more practical times, and no doubt the young men and women who had congregated here were now manning administrative desks somewhere in the burgeoning empire. They were the ones about whom Dardano should write; they, and all the eccentric characters who had played roles in this slow pageant. The gypsy woman who had danced every night by the eye, hoping to charm Griaule into killing her faithless lover—she had gone away satisfied. The man who had tried to extract one of the fangs—nobody knew what had become of him. The scale hunters, the artisans. A history of Hangtown would be a volume in itself.

The walk had left Meric weak and breathless; he sat down clumsily beside the girl, who smiled. He could not remember her name, but she came often to the eye. Small and dark, with an inner reserve that reminded him of Lise. He laughed inwardly—most women reminded him of Lise in some way.

"Are you all right?" she asked, her brow wrinkled with concern.

"Oh, yes," he said; he felt a need for conversation to take his mind off things, but he could think of nothing more to say. She was so young! All freshness and gleam and nerves.

"This will be my last time," she said. "At least for a while. I'll miss it." And then, before he could ask why, she added, "I'm getting married tomorrow, and we're moving away."

He offered congratulations and asked her who was the lucky fellow.

"Just a boy." She tossed her hair, as if to dismiss the boy's importance; she gazed up at the shuttered membrane. "What's it like for you when the eye opens?" she asked.

"Like everyone else," he said. "I remember . . . memories of my life. Other lives, too." He did not tell her about Griaule's memory of flight; he had never told anyone except Lise about that.

"All those bits of souls trapped in there," she said, gesturing at the eye. "What do they mean to him? Why does he show them to us?"

"I imagine he has his purposes, but I can't explain them."

"Once I remembered being with you," said the girl, peeking at him shyly through a dark curl. "We were under the wing."

He glanced at her sharply. "Tell me."

"We were . . . together," she said, blushing. "Intimate, you know. I was very afraid of the place, of the sounds and shadows. But I loved you so much, it didn't matter. We made love all night, and I was surprised because I thought that kind of passion was just in stories, something people had invented to make up for how ordinary it really was. And in the morning even that dreadful place had become beautiful, with the wing tips glowing red and the waterfall echoing. . . ." She lowered her eyes. "Ever since I had that memory, I've been a little in love with you."

"Lise," he said, feeling helpless before her.

"Was that her name?"

He nodded and put a hand to his brow, trying to pinch back the emotions that flooded him.

"I'm sorry." Her lips grazed his cheek, and just that slight touch seemed to weaken him further. "I wanted to tell you how she felt in case she hadn't told you herself. She was very troubled by something, and I wasn't sure she had."

She shifted away from him, made uncomfortable by the intensity of his reaction, and they sat without speaking. Meric became lost in watching how the gun glazed the scales to reddish gold, how the light was channeled along the ridges in molten streams that paled as the day wound down. He was startled when the girl jumped to her feet and backed toward the hoist.

"He's dead," she said wonderingly.

Meric looked at her, uncomprehending.

"See?" She pointed at the sun, which showed a crimson sliver above the hill. "He's dead," she repeated, and the expression on her face flowed between fear and exultation.

The idea of Griaule's death was too large for Meric's mind to encompass, and he turned to the eye to find a counterproof—no glints of color flickered beneath the membrane. He heard the hoist creak as the girl headed down, but he continued to wait. Perhaps only the dragon's vision had failed. No. It was likely not a coincidence that work had been officially terminated today. Stunned, he sat staring at the lifeless membrane until the sun sank below the hills; then he stood and went over to the hoist. Before he could throw the switch, the cables thrummed—somebody heading up. Of course. The girl would have spread the news, and all the Major Hauks and their underlings would be hurrying to test Griaule's reflexes. He did not want to be there when they arrived, to watch them pose with their trophy like successful fishermen.

It was hard work climbing up to the frontoparietal plate. The ladder swayed, the wind buffeted him, and by the time he clambered onto the plate he was giddy, his chest full of twinges. He hobbled forward and leaned against the rust-caked side of a boiling vat. Shadowy in the twilight, the great furnaces and vats towered around him, and it seemed this system of fiery devices reeking of cooked flesh and minerals was the actual machinery of Griaule's thought materialized above his skull. Energyless, abandoned. They had been replaced by more efficient equipment down below, and it had been—what was it?—almost five years since they were last used. Cobwebs veiled a pyramid of firewood; the stairs leading to the rims of the vats were crumbling. The plate itself was scarred and coated with sludge.

"Cattanay!"

Someone shouted from below, and the top of the ladder trembled. God, they were coming after him! Bubbling over with congratulations and plans for testimonial dinners, memorial plaques, specially struck medals. They would have him draped in bunting and bronzed and covered with pigeon shit before they were done. All these years he had been among them, both their slave and their master, yet he had never felt at home. Leaning heavily on his cane, he made his way past the frontal spike—blackened by years of oily smoke—and down between the wings to Hangtown. It was a ghost town, now. Weeds overgrowing the collapsed shanties; the lake a stinking pit, drained after some children had drowned in the summer of '91. Where Jarcke's home had stood was a huge pile of animal bones, taking a pale shine from the half-light. Wind keened through the tattered shrubs.

"Meric!" "Cattanay."

The voices were closer.

Well, there was one place where they would not follow. The leaves of the thickets were speckled with mold and brittle, flaking away as he brushed them. He hesitated at the top of the scale hunters' stair. He had no rope. Though he had done the climb unaided many times, it had been quite a few years. The gusts of wind, the shouts, the sweep of the valley and the lights scattered across it like diamonds on gray velvet—it all seemed a single inconstant medium. He heard the brush crunch behind him, more voices. To hell with it! Gritting his teeth against a twinge of pain in his shoulder, hooking his cane over his belt, he inched onto the stair and locked his fingers in the handholds. The wind whipped his clothes and threatened to pry him loose and send him pinwheeling off. Once he slipped; once he froze, unable to move backward or forward. But at last he reached the bottom and edged upslope until he found a spot flat enough to stand.

The mystery of the place suddenly bore in upon him, and he was afraid. He half turned to the stair, thinking he would go back to Hangtown and accept the hurly-burly. But a moment later he realized how foolish a thought that was. Waves of weakness poured through him, his heart hammered, and white dazzles flared in his vision. His chest felt heavy as iron. Rattled, he went a few steps forward, the cane pocking the silence. It was too dark to see more than outlines, but up ahead was the fold of wing where he and Lise had sheltered. He walked toward it, intent on revisiting it; then he remembered the girl beneath the eye and understood that he had already said that goodbye. And it *was* goodbye—that he understood vividly. He kept walking. Blackness looked to be welling from the wing joint, from the entrances to the maze of luminous tunnels where they had stumbled onto the petrified man. Had it really been the old wizard, doomed by magical justice to molder and live on and on? It made sense. At least it accorded with what happened to wizards who slew their dragons.

"Griaule?" he whispered to the darkness, and cocked his head, half-expecting an answer. The sound of his voice pointed up the immensity of the great gallery under the wing, the emptiness, and he recalled how vital a habitat it had once been. Flakes shifting over the surface, skizzers, peculiar insects fuming in the thickets, the glum populace of Hangtown, waterfalls. He had never been able to picture Griaule fully alive—that kind of vitality was beyond the powers of the imagination. Yet he wondered if by some miracle the dragon were alive now, flying up through his golden night to the sun's core. Or had that merely been a dream, a bit of tissue glittering deep in the cold tons of his brain? He laughed. Ask the stars for their first names, and you'd be more likely to receive a reply.

He decided not to walk any farther—it was really no decision. Pain was spreading through his shoulder, so intense he imagined it must be glowing inside. Carefully, carefully, he lowered himself and lay propped on an elbow, hanging on to the cane. Good, magical wood. Cut from a hawthorn atop Griaule's haunch. A man had once offered him a small fortune for it. Who would claim it now? Probably old Henry Sichi would snatch it for his museum, stick it in a glass case next to his boots. What a joke! He decided to lit flat on his stomach, resting his chin on an arm—the stony coolness beneath acted to muffle the pain. Amusing, how the range of one's decision dwindled. You decided to paint a dragon, to send hundreds of men searching for malachite and cochineal beetles, to love a woman, to heighten an undertone here and there, and finally to position your body a certain way. He seemed to have reached the end of the process. What next? He tried to regulate his breathing, to ease the pressure on his chest. Then, as something rustled out near the wing joint, he turned on his side. He thought he detected movement, a gleaming blackness flowing toward him . . . or else it was only the haphazard firing of his nerves playing tricks with his vision. More surprised than afraid, wanting to see, he peered into the darkness and felt his heart beating erratically against the dragon's scale.

It's foolish to draw simple conclusions from complex events, but I suppose there must be both moral and truth to this life, these events. I'll leave that to the gadflies. The historians, the social scientists, the expert apologists for reality. All I know is that he had a fight with his girlfriend over money and walked out. He sent her a letter saying he had gone south and would be back in a few months with more money than she could ever spend. I had no idea what he'd done. The whole thing about Griaule had just been a bunch of us sitting around the Red Bear, drinking up my pay—I'd sold an article—and somebody said, "Wouldn't it be great if Dardano didn't have to write articles, if we didn't have to paint pictures that color-coordinated with people's furniture or slave at getting the gooey smiles of little nieces and nephews just right?" All sorts of improbable moneymaking schemes were put forward. Robberies, kidnappings. Then the idea of swindling the city fathers of Teocinte came up, and the entire plan was fleshed out in minutes. Scribbled on napkins, scrawled on sketchpads. A group effort. I keep trying to remember if anyone got a glassy look in their eye, if I felt a cold tendril of Griaule's thought stirring my brains. But I can't. It was a half-hour's sensation, nothing more. A drunken whimsy, art-school metaphor. Shortly thereafter, we ran out of money and staggered into the streets. It was snowing—big wet flakes that melted down our collars. God, we were drunk! Laughing, balancing on the icy railing of the University Bridge. Making faces at the bundled-up burghers and their fat ladies who huffed and puffed past, spouting steam and never giving us a glance, and none of us—not even the burghers—knowing that we were living our happy ending in advance. . . .

—FROM *THE MAN WHO PAINTED
THE DRAGON GRIAULE*
BY LOUIS DARDANO

Further Reading

Novels
Rouge Dragon, Avram Davidson
The Dragon and the George, Gordon R. Dickson
The Furthest Shore, Ursula K. Le Guin
The Wizard of Earthsea, Ursula K. Le Guin
Dragonflight, Anne McCaffery
The Hobbit, J.R.R. Tolkien
The Dragon Masters, Jack Vance

Anthologies
Dragon Tales, edited by Isaac Asimov, Martin H. Greenberg, & Charles Waugh
Dragons of Darkness, edited by Orson Scott Card
Dragons of Light, edited by Orson Scott Card
DragonFantastic, edited by Martin H. Greenberg
Dragons and Dreams, edited by Jane Yolen, Martin H. Greenberg, & Charles Waugh

Reference Books
The Book of the Dragon, Judy Allen & Jeanne Griffiths
The Encyclopedia of Monsters, Daniel Cohen
Topsell's Histories of Beasts, edited by Nelson Hall
Dragons and Dragon Lore, Ernest Ingersoll
The Lungfish, the Dodo, and the Unicorn, Willy Ley
Men and Snakes, Desmond Morris & Rowana Morris
The Dragons of Eden, Carl Sagan
Arthur C. Clarke's Mysterious World, Simon Welfare & John Fairley
The Bestiary: A Book of Beasts, T.H. White

Short Fiction
"The Last Dragon Master," A.A. Attanasio, *Beastmarks*
"A Hiss of Dragon," Gregory Benford & Marc Laidlaw, Carr's *Best SF of the Year #8*
"One Winter in Eden," Michael Bishop, *Dragons of Light*

"The Better Mousetrap," L. Sprague de Camp & Fletcher Pratt, *Tales from Gavagan's Bar*
"The Emperor's Fan," L. Sprague de Camp, *The Best of L. Sprague de Camp*
"The Gadarine Dig," Philip C. Jennings, *IAsfm*, December 1990
"The Rule of Names," Ursula K. Le Guin, *The Wind's Twelve Quarters*
"The Dragon That Lives in the Sea," Elizabeth A. Lynn, *The Woman Who Loved the Moon*
"The Ice Dragon," George R.R. Martin, *Dragons of Light*
"The Harrowing of the Dragon of Hoarsbreath," Patricia McKillip, *Elsewhere II*
"Awaken Dragon," Gene O'Neill, *F&SF*, May 1990
"The Passing of the Dragons," Keith Roberts, *The Passing of the Dragons*
"The Father of Stones," Lucius Shepard, *IAsfm*, September 1989
"The Glassblower's Dragon," Lucius Shepard, *F&SF*, April 1987
"The Scalehunter's Beautiful Daughter," Lucius Shepard, *IAsfm*, September 1988
"The Fallen Country," Somtow Sucharitkul, *Elsewhere II*
"The Dragon Line," Michael Swanwick, *Terry's Universe*
"Last Dragon," Steve Rasnic Tem, *Amazing*, September 1987
"Gaudi's Dragon," Ian Watson, *IAsfm*, October 1990
"Old Noon's Tale," Cherry Wilder, *Strange Plasma 3*
"Chinese Puzzle," John Wyndham, *Phoenix Feathers*
"Cockfight," Jane Yolen, *Dragons of Light*
"Dragonfield," Jane Yolen, *Dragonfield & Other Stories*
"The Dragon's Boy," Jane Yolen, *F&SF*, September 1987
"The George Business," Roger Zelazny, *Unicorn Variations*

Reference Articles
"An Abundance of Dragons," Avram Davidson, *IAsfm*, July 6, 1981

FANTASY FROM ACE—FANCIFUL AND FANTASTIC!

___HERE BE DEMONS Esther Friesner 0-441-32797-4/$3.50
The archdemon Atamar and his team of junior demons are banished from Hell—unless they can learn how to corrupt more mortal souls.

___CASTLE PERILOUS John DeChancie 0-441-09418-X/$4.50
An unemployed philosophy major finds himself living in a castle worlds away from home . . . and behind each of its 144,000 doors is a new world to explore!

___JHEREG Steven Brust 0-441-38554-0/$4.50
Vlad Taltos, brave adventurer, chose the route of assassin to advance in the world. And making this progress even quicker are a smattering of witchcraft and a young reptilian jhereg who offers loyal protection and undying friendship.

___STORMWARDEN Janny Wurts 0-441-78757-6/$3.50
Anskiere, wizard of wind and water, joined powers with Ivain, master of fire and earth, to bind forever the Mharg-demons. Yet, Ivain betrayed Anskiere, and the winds still speak of Anskiere's powerful oath of revenge.

___QUOZL Alan Dean Foster 0-441-69454-3/$4.95
From the New York Times bestselling author of Glory Lane comes a hilarious new out-of-this-world adventure. The Quozl knew they'd love Earth . . . but it never occurred to them that anyone lived there!

For Visa, MasterCard and American Express ($15 minimum) orders call: 1-800-631-8571

FOR MAIL ORDERS: CHECK BOOK(S). FILL OUT COUPON. SEND TO: BERKLEY PUBLISHING GROUP 390 Murray Hill Pkwy., Dept. B East Rutherford, NJ 07073	POSTAGE AND HANDLING: $1.75 for one book, 75¢ for each additional. Do not exceed $5.50.
NAME_____	BOOK TOTAL $ _____
ADDRESS_____	POSTAGE & HANDLING $ _____
CITY_____	APPLICABLE SALES TAX $ _____ (CA, NJ, NY, PA)
STATE_____ ZIP_____	TOTAL AMOUNT DUE $ _____
PLEASE ALLOW 6 WEEKS FOR DELIVERY. PRICES ARE SUBJECT TO CHANGE WITHOUT NOTICE.	PAYABLE IN US FUNDS. (No cash orders accepted.)

EXTRAORDINARY ADVENTURES

by New York Times bestselling author

PIERS ANTHONY

_Virtual Mode   0-441-86503-8/$5.99

Enter a realm where it is possible to travel between this world and another world full of wonder. When Colene finds a strange man lying on the side of the road, he speaks of this magical place. Colene suspects Darius is crazy...but she's prepared to follow him to an infinite world of dragons, monsters and impossible dreams.

The Apprentice Adept Series—Welcome to the astonishing parallel worlds of Phaze and Proton. Where magic and science maintain an uneasy truce. And where Mach, a robot from Proton, and his alternate self, magical Bane from Phaze, hold the power to link the two worlds—or destroy them completely.

_OUT OF PHAZE	_PHAZE DOUBT
0-441-64465-1/$4.99	0-441-66263-3/$5.50
_ROBOT ADEPT	_UNICORN POINT
0-441-73118-X/$5.50	0-441-84563-0/$5.50

Bio of an Ogre—Piers Anthony's remarkable autobiography! A rich, compelling journey into the mind of a brilliant storyteller. "Fascinating!"—Locus

_BIO OF AN OGRE   0-441-06225-3/$4.50

For Visa, MasterCard and American Express orders ($15 minimum) call: 1-800-631-8571

FOR MAIL ORDERS: CHECK BOOK(S). FILL OUT COUPON. SEND TO:

BERKLEY PUBLISHING GROUP
390 Murray Hill Pkwy., Dept. B
East Rutherford, NJ 07073

NAME _____

ADDRESS _____

CITY _____

STATE _____ ZIP _____

POSTAGE AND HANDLING:
$1.75 for one book, 75¢ for each additional. Do not exceed $5.50.

BOOK TOTAL $ _____

POSTAGE & HANDLING $ _____

APPLICABLE SALES TAX $ _____
(CA, NJ, NY, PA)

TOTAL AMOUNT DUE $ _____

PAYABLE IN US FUNDS.
(No cash orders accepted.)

PLEASE ALLOW 6 WEEKS FOR DELIVERY.
PRICES ARE SUBJECT TO CHANGE WITHOUT NOTICE.